Hardcover

Hardcover

BY WAYNE WARGA

ARBOR HOUSE | New York

Manufactured in the United States of America

10 9 8 7 6 5 4 3 2 1

Library of Congress Cataloging in Publication Data

Warga, Wayne.
  Hardcover.

  I. Title.
PS3573.A755H3   1985   813'.54   85-7460

ISBN: 0-87795-749-5

The individual characters who appear in this book are wholly fic-
tional. No character bears any resemblance to any person, alive or
dead, whom I have ever known. Any apparent resemblance of a
character to any person alive or dead is purely coincidental.

This book is for

JAKE

. . . and for Jim

Hardcover

1

HE SAW THE books and reached out instinctively, as one does to old friends. For a long time they had been his, and then, three, maybe four, years ago—he couldn't remember when exactly, but he did remember why—he had sold them.

He took them off the shelf one at a time and looked at their dust jackets, seeing again the familiar creases and tears. He was certain these were the same books; he would have known them anywhere. *Cannery Row* and *Sweet Thursday* were his favorite John Steinbeck books and these two—first editions in good condition issued in 1945 and 1954 respectively—had been his for a number of years. He had bought them from a used-book dealer for next to nothing, protected their deteriorating dust jackets with clear plastic covers, probably the same covers that were still on them, and read both books again. He had taken them with him, more for a comfort than commerce, when he opened his own bookstore.

Jeffrey Dean loved books, had always loved them, and

1

now they were his business as well. He was a man given to few passions, but those few he allowed to possess him completely. He was tall and trim, his hair dark and curly, his moustache and sideburns touched with gray. The most prominent feature on his face was his nose—not quite hawklike, but large, making his brown eyes seem even more inquisitive than they naturally were. His was an essentially serious nature, but his wit was quick and his smile genuine, a mixture of reserve and friendliness. As do most thoughtful men who have turned forty—Jeffrey was forty-two—he had about him a slight melancholy brought on by the first strong sense of his own mortality.

The Los Angeles Antiquarian Book Fair spread over three big meeting rooms, booth after booth crammed with every sort of arcana imaginable, the aisles busy with people whose one shared obsession was collecting. They collected everything: illustrated sixteenth-century medical texts, color-plate bird books of the 1850s, ancient botanical prints, children's books, rare books on California history, modern first editions—a loose term for a loose time period running from roughly the turn of the century up to the newest popular author being collected. Jeffrey dealt in modern first editions and detective fiction, and as did most dealers, he also collected them. It was a small professional conflict he had learned to live with and it did not bother him at all, because his philosophy was to keep a book and enjoy it for as long as possible and then, when someone else wanted it, to sell it. He had a few put away he would never part with, and others with which he parted reluctantly. *Cannery Row* and *Sweet Thursday* had begun as the former and then, of necessity, become the latter.

His instinct, which seldom misled him, told him these

were the very books he had once owned. Still, he wanted to be sure, and so he placed *Cannery Row* cover-down in the palm of his left hand and flipped open the back cover and looked at the upper right-hand corner of the page to see if his code was still there. Each dealer had his own code, usually numbers assigned to the corresponding letters of a favorite author's name, which told the dealer—and not the customer—how much he had paid for the book originally. There had been pencil markings on the last page of *Cannery Row*, now erased, and so Jeffrey could not positively identify the book as once having been his. There was no new code in its place. He was about to flip open the back cover of *Sweet Thursday* when the salesman interrupted him.

"May I help you?" The accent was British. Jeffrey looked up and saw he was standing in the booth occupied by Serendip Books of London. He was mildly surprised, because American first editions did not often turn up in London, Steinbeck would qualify as a particularly infrequent traveler, and, besides, the English were notoriously chauvinistic when it came to American authors.

"No thanks, just looking." The salesman's dark suit formed a sharp contrast to Jeffrey's casual button-down shirt, corduroys, and loafers, and his British manner had the desired effect of making him seem a bit superior.

Jeffrey, who was not easily intimidated, looked directly at the salesman, nodded, and flipped open the back cover of *Sweet Thursday*. There it was, exactly as he had written it: "HN/D." His code was based on the name Hemingway, which had no repeating letters. *H* represented the numeral one and on up to *Y* as nine, to which he had added an *X* as zero. The final letter was for his last name. He had paid $15 for the book. He flipped to the inside of

the front cover to look at the current price. It was $900,
easily double what the book was worth. Jeffrey's puzzled
look must have been obvious, because the salesman
quickly justified the figure.

"Fine inscriptions," the man said.

"Inscriptions?"

"Both books are inscribed by the author," the salesman
said, sounding insufferably condescending.

"I know what *inscribed* means," Jeffrey replied coolly.
He turned to the title page of *Sweet Thursday* and saw,
written in ink, "To Edward, with many thanks, John
Steinbeck." It was undated. He picked up *Cannery Row*
and saw that it was inscribed "For Mary Louise Owen,
with many thanks for a fine dinner." It, too, was undated.
He looked for the price: $1,500.

As well as he could remember, the signatures looked exactly like Steinbeck's. He was not at all expert at hand-
writing—it was an obscure specialty with but few
dependable experts—but he was familiar with Steinbeck's
signature. These looked real.

Except for one thing. Steinbeck had already been dead
several years when Jeffrey had sold these exact books, sold
them uninscribed and unsigned. The inscriptions—and
Steinbeck's signatures—were forged. His surprise turned
swiftly to anger, because of the defilement of two books he
had treasured. Forgery—especially the forgery of literary
manuscripts, inscriptions, and signatures—was a form of
sacrilege he found intolerable. Had he paused to objec-
tively examine his anger, the matter of money might have
turned out a contributing factor as well. He felt guilty for
ever selling them in the first place, all the more so because
his own constant need for money had forced him to sell
them. He knew the prices on the books were high, and he

also knew they would probably be sold—if not here, then somewhere else. He decided to keep that from happening.

"I can give you a special price for the two of them," the salesman said. "Twenty-two hundred, say, for both."

"No thanks." Jeffrey paused, then looked up again to the sign over the booth. "Are you the owner of Serendip Books?"

"No, I am the manager," the man said, extending his hand. "Smithson, Thomas Smithson."

"Jeffrey Dean. I'm a local dealer."

"Then I can give you a professional discount as well. These are fine Steinbecks."

"Could I ask how you acquired them?"

"From a private party."

The question remained on Jeffrey's face.

"Who prefers to remain anonymous," the salesman added.

"I'll bet."

"I beg your pardon?"

"Thank you anyway," Jeffrey said. He turned and started down the aisle. His anger fragmented his concentration, made it impossible to sort through his alternatives. Forgeries were not uncommon among rare books and book dealers, yet to anyone with integrity in this particular profession—and there were mostly honest people involved—forgery was an offense to history and tended to provoke quick reactions. Jeffrey stopped and observed the people wandering up and down the aisles of the fair, watched them browse and talk, some with their wrapped purchases in their hands, others still looking hopeful. Jeffrey had found a form of refuge in the world of bibliophiles and bookdealers, had found a new beginning for himself, and he felt protective of his world. It took several minutes to make his decision, but when he did, he acted on it immediately.

First he went back to the Serendip Books booth, where the salesman, Smithson, saw him, thought he'd come to buy the books, and so welcomed him with a conspiratorial grin. He was so confident he even walked away from another customer, pulling his shirt cuffs in anticipation. Jeffrey calmly took the books down from the shelf, one at a time.

"Come to have another look?"

"Yes, yes I did. I don't often see forgeries as good as these."

"I beg your pardon?" The grin vanished and the look of surprise that took its place seemed genuine enough to Jeffrey.

"Forgeries. They're fakes."

"There must be some mistake, Mr.—Mr.—"

"Jeffrey Dean. I'm sure there must be."

"They were owned by a man of impeccable—"

"Could be. But sometime in the last four or five years, somebody forged those inscriptions and the signatures. I owned both of these books for ten years. For some crazy reason my code is still marked inside *Sweet Thursday*. They didn't even think to erase it. Several years after Steinbeck's death, I sold them to a client. They weren't inscribed or signed then, and dead men don't write."

"I'm aware of that, Mr. Dean," he was looking down at Jeffrey through thick lenses, trying hard to hang on to his fading sense of superiority. "Surely you must have mistaken these books."

"No, no mistake. None at all."

Smithson began to take on the look of a man who is slowly being relieved of his credibility and is helpless to stop the process. He tried for the initiative.

"To whom did you sell the books? That is, if these are the books."

"I'm not certain. I don't want to say without first checking my records. I think I remember who, but I don't want to say until I've made sure. But these are the books. Absolutely."

"This is a serious accusation."

"You bet."

"I'll have to consult my owner."

"Do that. I'll be around if he has any questions."

"I would appreciate your not saying anything about this until we've made our decision."

"I'm sorry, I can't do that. I'm going to inform the fair chairman."

"Now see here—" Smithson sputtered helplessly.

"I'm sorry, Mr. Smithson, but these are forgeries and should be removed from sale. The chairman should be told."

The chairman was a rotund, balding, nervous man, unaccustomed even to the small celebrity that comes with being chairman of a book fair—a gentle occupation if ever there was one—and he turned pale when Jeffrey told him about the Steinbeck books.

"Oh, dear," he said, and scurried off to consult his fellow officials. It was the custom in matters such as these that the chairman be informed and that he, in turn, consult with the Fair Committee and perhaps an expert on the disputed books before asking that they be removed from sale. It was a request that was seldom refused.

There was one other person Jeffrey wanted to tell, and he found her exactly where he knew she would be, holding court in her booth. She was something of an institution among bookdealers. Lena Sabin and her husband had fled Russia, come to New York penniless, and within a few

years established themselves among the country's leading
dealers. Her husband was long dead, but Lena carried on.
She was old, artful, regal, a tiny generator of energy and
an incorrigible gossip. Though he had met her on at least
a dozen previous occasions, had twice sat beside her at
dinner parties, she nevertheless pretended not to recognize
him. He had long ago caught on, as had everyone else.
Still her ploy always permitted her to seize control of the
situation.

"Jeffrey, my dear, you don't say!" she exulted, her den-
tures clacking merrily. She was off her high stool and
leading Jeffrey across the aisle in an instant. He was just
six feet tall, but next to Lena Sabin he looked a giant, a
Brobdingnagian being led by the queen of the Lillipu-
tians. She marched him straightaway to another New
York dealer, Oliver Barrett, a scholarly man who was
widely respected as an expert on both Steinbeck and
Hemingway. Barrett, a rumpled, pipe-smoking man, listened attentively, then accompanied Jeffrey to the Serendip bookstall. Lena Sabin, true to her nature, scurried off
to spread the news, exactly as Jeffrey expected. She would
make sure everybody knew, and in the process impede—
maybe even halt—the sale of the books.

This time the salesman was not alone. Standing beside
him was a short, bearded Arab man, elegantly dressed in a
three-piece pinstripe suit. His eyes were hooded, and his
gaze made Jeffrey think first of Peter Lorre and then, as he
looked closer, of some malevolent reptile. The man reeked
of Canoe cologne and he was nervously shooting his shirt
cuffs, pulling thin white edges out from under his coat.
Smithson introduced him as Narib Zaki, the owner of
Serendip Books. The introductions were, at best, perfunctory.

"Why is it that I should take this man's word?" Zaki demanded in excellent though thickly accented English. "Who is he to say these are forgeries?"

Before anybody could answer, the rotund chairman of the book fair arrived. He had, it turned out, been looking for Barrett to give an expert opinion. Beads of sweat were forming on his forehead and when he spoke, it was as quietly as possible so as not to attract a crowd.

"Now, now, gentlemen. If you will show me the books, please, Mr. Zaki."

"The books are for sale. Do you wish to buy them? Or do you intend to make more trouble?"

"I would like Mr. Barrett to look at the inscriptions. He may be able to confirm their authenticity."

"Very well," Zaki said, and then, not quite snapping his fingers, but almost, "Smithson! The books."

Smithson, obviously accustomed to barked orders, handed the two books to Barrett, who immediately began to study the inscription in *Cannery Row*. After several minutes he put it down and began to scrutinize the writing in *Sweet Thursday*. The others stood in a semicircle, watching him, saying nothing. Jeffrey's posture was assured, his hands in his pockets. Zaki stood beside him, his hands clasped behind his back, his look defiant. The chairman would have liked to pace, but there wasn't room in the small booth and so he shifted his weight from one foot to the other. Smithson stood obediently behind Zaki. Barrett withdrew a magnifying glass from his jacket pocket and proceeded with the examination.

"I will not accept this man's decision if I do not wish to," Zaki told the small gathering. "I know nothing of his reputation—or of the reputation of the man"—he nodded at Jeffrey—"who started this—this vicious rumor."

Jeffrey, who considered it neither vicious nor a rumor, but would honestly admit to starting it, was wondering how it was the forger did not think to remove Jeffrey's code from the back of *Sweet Thursday*. What an easy way to get caught, though he was certain he would know the books without the code. These above all. He was reasonably certain whom he had sold the books to, but he wouldn't say without first checking. He wondered where Zaki had gotten them, whether he had been the forger, and he wondered, too, how the books had gotten to London in the first place.

"Mr. Dean is well known to us," the fair chairman practically whispered, "and though he is not an exhibiting member, he is certainly one whose word we would accept."

"I agree with that," Barrett said, placing the books one on top of the other. "But I'm not sure—absolutely sure—about these inscriptions. Whoever forged them did a very good job."

"Are you saying they are forged?" Zaki demanded. He was either a very good actor or genuinely shocked.

"No, no, I'm not. I'm saying, based on what Mr. Dean here has said, that it is very likely they are forged. I accept his word for it until such time as you can have some expert check the inscriptions scientifically."

Zaki, barely containing his anger, turned on the fair chairman. "Are you saying we should withdraw these books from sale? Well?"

"Under the circumstances I think that would be the best thing," the chairman said.

Zaki grabbed the books and shoved them onto a shelf under the curtained counter in the back of his booth. Without so much as a nod to the others, he turned and stalked out of the booth and down the aisle of the exhibit hall, striding swiftly away on the maroon and gold carpeting that, to Jeffrey, made him look like a small insect crawling across the marbled endpapers of an old book. A bookworm, maybe, and typically destructive.

Smithson began meticulously tidying books, his back toward the others. The fair chairman hurried away, rushing to put trouble behind him. No doubt, Jeffrey thought, for the bar. Jeffrey and Barrett started off down the aisle in opposite directions, Barrett back to his booth and Jeffrey to look for books. He found a dealer with a shelf of Graham Greene books. Jeffrey bought two: *A Sort of Life,* which he considered one of the finest modern literary autobiographies; and *England Made Me,* a book that contained a favorite character of Jeffrey's, Ferdinand Minty, the shabby remittance man and one of Greene's most pathetic and comic characters.

Thoughts of thirst or even hunger, for he had missed lunch, were soon gone. That was the thing about this peculiar little world: It seemed at times to take hold of him, to capture him as though the musty smell of books were a drug. With his two Graham Greenes under his arm, he proceeded on his way. He bought a signed, early Ross Macdonald novel for a client, and for himself a first edition of John Fowles's *Daniel Martin,* a book he had always intended to read but had never gotten around to. The bulk of a Fowles novel was one thing; that the author was demanding of his readers was quite another. Jeffrey was a devout admirer who was usually one or two books behind Fowles, never hurrying to catch up and always struck by—and sometimes stuck in—the depth of the work.

His intention was to buy books that he could resell at a higher price, and he was quite good at it. He also had

weaknesses and would sometimes buy books simply to
have them, aware that the price he paid was a bit too
high. It was, in all, a peculiar profession and it attracted
some very peculiar people. For every dealer selling a
$10,000 book with another, more expensive, to back it up,
there were two hundred dealers out there spending their
weekends scouring garage sales hoping to find the books to
make their next month's rent. A very few had elegant
stores, a few more just plain stores, while the great majority operated primarily by mail, issuing periodic catalogs
and some exhibiting their wares only at the several exhibits held each year in either New York, Boston, Chicago,
Los Angeles, or San Francisco.

Jeffrey's position in the spectrum of dealers was well up
from the middle. He had his own small store, a mail-order
business that fluctuated depending on the quality and frequency of the catalogs he issued, and it all made a reasonable profit. He no longer spent his weekends at garage
sales, though he seldom let a likely one get by; it is not in
the nature of a bookdealer to pass by a pile of books no
matter where. The world is full of unrecovered treasures,
and just as full of people searching for them, and only a
few well informed enough to know their pot of gold when
they see it.

Jeffrey's specialties—modern first editions and detective
fiction—were choices made because they formed the read-
ings of a lifetime and because, as he had acquired books
over the years—long before he even considered becoming
a dealer—he had refused to part with those he especially
liked. Since his teens, books had been the only clutter in
his life, possessions given free rein in what was otherwise
an orderly, somewhat spartan existence. When he had finally gone into business, he had an instant inventory. The

two Steinbecks had been among them, kept out of view for sentiment's sake for several years until economic necessity prevailed.

Along with his inventory, he also had an instinct. In part because of his long experience as a journalist, he was quick to spot trends and to use them to his advantage. When bound galleys became the big thing, Jeffrey's contacts in the book world provided them for him. For a while the soft-bound books, which publishers sent to critics before the final book was ready, were even more popular—and expensive—than first editions. That soon passed, though galleys still were in demand among hardcore collectors and their prices continued to be steep.

He knew which authors were hot, which were not. Tom Robbins's first novel, *Another Roadside Attraction,* had been an instant success with collectors and was selling for as much as $350 within a few years of publication. Jeffrey had predicted Robbins would fall from favor quickly and he had been right. That $350 first book now sold for $75, and there was only slight demand for the Robbins books that followed.

Hemingway, Fitzgerald, Faulkner, and Steinbeck were the most popular twentieth-century writers among collectors. Each fell into disfavor from time to time, but it was always slight and seldom for long. Steinbeck had faded from critical favor briefly, but was now a force again. Among living authors, Kurt Vonnegut was on the rise and, among collectors of detective fiction, Ross Thomas.

Among the British writers, Graham Greene had cooled a bit, not because of a decline in his popularity but because it was so difficult to find his earlier books. John le Carré fetched reasonable prices for his recent books, while his first, a minor thriller titled *Call for the Dead,* had recently sold for $1,600.

Jeffrey liked attending fairs not just for the books but also for the people they attracted. A customer stopped Jeffrey in the aisle. He was a man with a nervous tic and a consuming passion for W. Somerset Maugham that wouldn't rest until he owned every Maugham book written—no easy feat, for Maugham was the most prolific author of his generation. Jeffrey had a poor copy of *Ashenden,* and nothing else, and so the man walked away without so much as a thank-you, a suitor spurned. The notion made Jeffrey smile.

He paused several minutes later to watch an English professor from UCLA who was known and not liked at all among bookdealers because of his custom of playing one dealer off against another and then taking forever to pay his bills. The good professor was also known to pull a shady deal once in a while and the dealers' informal warning system managed to stay just ahead of him most of the time. The professor had turned up at Jeffrey's one day with a couple of books to offer, and then—to Jeffrey's surprise and pleasure—offered him a small selection of Victorian pornography. Jeffrey had looked over the stereoptic photographs of heavy women with pendulous breasts and hairy armpits going at it with skinny, naked men, nearly all of whom wore drooping socks. Jeffrey declined the collection politely and later learned they were cleverly reproduced photocopies of the originals, no doubt done in the professor's own darkroom.

He proceeded on through the fair until he found himself back in the aisle occupied by Serendip Books and Lena Sabin. He could see Smithson helping a customer. Narib Zaki was nowhere to be seen. Lena Sabin, however,

waved a summons and invited Jeffrey to join her for dinner, an invitation Jeffrey interpreted as a reward for his
providing the one good piece of gossip so far in the fair.
He begged off, pleading another commitment, and
thanked her.

Had Lena Sabin learned of his other commitment, she
would have regally banished him from her carefully culti-
vated kingdom. There was half a chicken and a bottle of
dry white wine in his refrigerator and that was what he
wanted. Lena Sabin would relish the forgeries, hold forth
at dinner about all the others she had seen over the years.
Jeffrey had already heard most of the stories and did not
care to hear them again. The forged Steinbeck books sad-
dened him, filled him with a small and private mourning
and made him wish he could do something about them.
But there was nothing to do. They were ruined, fine books
that hereafter would be looked upon as imperfect curiosi-
ties, fine objects defiled. Who, he wondered, would do
such a thing? And why?

There was the occasional collector who forged on the
side, but they were few and largely known among dealers,
Jeffrey included. There was a man in New York whose
specialty was forging inscriptions of collected living authors—John Updike and Gore Vidal were two of his best
signatures—on remaindered copies of their first editions at
prices low enough to attract the unwary. He was a sad,
dishonest man eking out a small living at his crime, his list
of customers diminishing steadily as word of his forgeries
spread.

Every dealer in modern first editions—and probably a
number of other specialized dealers—would have heard of
the Steinbeck forgeries by the next morning. Lena would
make sure of that, which was why he had gone to her in

the first place. It was unlikely they would be sold. At least for now. Jeffrey figured he had heard the last of them, believed that justice, however small and insignificant it might seem in the larger scheme of things, had prevailed. There was satisfaction in that at least.

ii

A DOOR SEPARATED his work from the rest of his life, a door that was seldom closed and almost never locked. Jeffrey Dean Books occupied a capacious room on the second floor of what was once a disused, decrepit building and was now midway through the metamorphosis into chic. The building was in the shape of a horseshoe with a large brick-and-cement patio in the center, two big shade trees, and, at the open end of the horseshoe, a second building, which had become a popular restaurant with indoor and outdoor dining.

Jeffrey's store looked down into a big pepper tree, under which tables filled each lunch and dinner hour. A flight of stairs, the walls of which he had hung with posters of movies made from famous mystery books, led to his store and, beyond the door on the wall opposite the entrance, to his apartment. When he had first rented the space, the area of Ventura Boulevard in Sherman Oaks in which it was located was largely vacant and the landlord, happy to have a reliable tenant, had agreed to lease him a small suite of offices adjoining his store, which Jeffrey rebuilt into an apartment. In those days there were few customers for the first-floor stores, fewer still for the second floor, and so the agreement was mutually beneficial. Even now with the building filling up, second-floor tenants were still hard to come by, so Jeffrey was just six months into a new five-year lease, a feeling of permanence he liked.

Ventura Boulevard—Romaine Gary had once described it to Jeffrey as one of the most fascinating streets in the world—wove languidly along the base of the Santa Monica Mountains separating the San Fernando Valley from the Los Angeles basin, and it had been only a matter of time until the urban sprawl of the city spread into the valley. When it did, Ventura Boulevard began to change. Its genuine eccentricity gave way in some places to cold highrises, in others to studied, self-conscious fashion and style. Disused and low-rent storefronts became boutiques or intimate little restaurants, ranging from the inevitable French to exotic Thai. At one time the boulevard boasted fourteen Thai restaurants to choose among—something Jeffrey considered a bit of Hobson's choice since Thai food, while good, wasn't quite varied enough for so many places. Specialty stores abounded on the street: One dealt only in Coca-Cola memorabilia, another in handmade dollhouses, one in comic books, and another in baseball cards. Within one long block not far from Jeffrey's, there were popular bookstores dealing exclusively in science fiction and feminist literature. A store called Scene of the Crime specialized in mystery and detective books.

Jeffrey was one of two antiquarian bookdealers along the boulevard, and the only one dealing in modern literature. As the renaissance of the boulevard took place, Jeffrey's drop-in business increased and he began to keep regular office hours several afternoons each week. In addition to books, Jeffrey also sold film scripts, a growing interest among collectors and one Jeffrey found increasingly lucrative since the area was filled with film writers and practically all the major studios were nearby.

The store itself consisted of the one big room and a large closet, which was used for wrapping and mailing books. Purchases by mail comprised a good two-thirds of his business, sometimes more, depending on the popularity of the catalogs he issued six to eight times a year. In the room itself, Jeffrey had built shelving for all the walls, stained it dark brown, then finished it to a high gleam. The shelves were nearly full, the books stacked carefully together, most of them in protective covers. Two sections of the shelving were enclosed by glass and could be locked. In these were signed and inscribed first editions and other valuable books. Toward the center of the room, facing the big window, was a large, antique desk, the surface of which was cluttered but orderly. It was from here Jeffrey operated his business.

Through the door was Jeffrey's apartment. Working evenings and weekends for months, he remodeled it himself, learning as he went along, undoing his mistakes and reworking his ideas until he had them right. It was a challenge he accepted in part out of necessity and in part out of curiosity. The kitchen was small and compact, the bedroom and living-dining areas open and light. Where the shop seemed old, the apartment was purposefully modern, with white walls, light wood floors, and contemporary furniture, stylish but comfortable.

The result—store and apartment together—was a carefully constructed haven, a refuge both physically and psychologically. It was a place Jeffrey liked to be in, his self-created environment. He was a man with few illusions about the world he lived in. It was not so much that he was cynical, for indeed he was not. It was more that he considered himself prepared—for what, he was never sure. He himself would say he was doubtful and questioning, attitudes left over from the years he had worked as a journalist. He had seen firsthand and at length things most people see in short, tolerable takes on the television news at night.

Television, he believed, had a peculiar habit of making the intolerable acceptable by making it short and quick and following it with a fast cut to a new story or a commercial before the impact of what was being shown produced the reaction the television executives feared the most: being turned off. Life just wasn't like that. He had seen a civil war in the Dominican Republic; the tail end of the revolution—and much of its consequences—in Cuba; the civil-rights movement in the American South; and the beginning of the serious political unrest in Central America. What was transpiring in El Salvador and Nicaragua did not surprise him in the least. He had, he once said, become a reluctant expert on banana republics, reluctant only because his despair for their people grew in direct ratio to the extent of his knowledge.

He had written a great deal about writers, which improved his book collection immeasurably because he invited each subject to inscribe a book and each happily complied. He would often bring not just the author's new book for an inscription but also one of the writer's earliest books. The writers were invariably flattered and Jeffrey's passion satisfied.

The work had been glamorous and exciting, but in fact

for each adventure, each place of employment, there had been a bad ending. *Life* magazine had died. A news magazine promoted him and ordered him to come to New York as an editor, a promotion he resisted until it was subtly suggested he look elsewhere for work. His years with a newspaper had been the best; the stories and the work went well, until a change of middle management, an editor devoid of character and loyalty, and his own restless search for change brought him down. He had been fired, and the loss of self-worth had made him angry and bitter. He could have kept writing. The offers for free-lance work were plentiful enough, but he refused nearly all of them, accepting the occasional assignment that interested him and paid well enough. But it was over, and the restless search for change that had helped bring it to an end had led him finally to his present work, and to his emerging sense of satisfaction.

There had been a significant ending in his personal life as well, a peculiar ending because it persisted still as a large part of his life. He had married in his late twenties, a union that at first withstood the rigors of his constant travel and work, but finally began to disintegrate. No sooner had this process begun than a son was born. The ending persisted not because of the child. Jeffrey adored him and saw him almost daily, the one unqualified close relationship in his life. It persisted because his ex-wife remained very much a part of his life. She had never remarried; had instead gone back to school, gotten her master's degree in library science, a good job at UCLA, and emerged an infinitely more interesting woman than she had been when they married. She had stood by loyally when the newspaper days ended, even refusing his child-support checks. She had been responsible for the initial

success of his business as well. Through her work at
UCLA, she would occasionally hear of private libraries
being sold, and she would involve Jeffrey. Because of her
he had purchased four good collections that he had
quickly resold at a considerable profit.

She could also be a gigantic pain in the ass. She would
volunteer to check over the proofs of one of Jeffrey's catalogs or make some other helpful offer and then, somehow,
begin telling him how to run his business. She could be as
irritating as she was helpful. Every so often Jeffrey would
convince himself she stayed as close as she did not because
of their son but because she still wanted him. He would no
sooner begin thinking this than she would plunge into one
of her periodic love affairs and painfully explode his theory. Men, Jeffrey included, were a complicated, treacherous territory for her, one full of unresolved angers, unful-
filled expectations, and ongoing desires. The only male
she accepted without reservations was her son.

Lydia Thompson—she had resumed her maiden name
shortly after the divorce, for that was part of her process of
liberation—remained a presence, for better or worse,
usually both.

Their one area of constant agreement was their son.
Michael was a bright, independent child, loved by both of
his parents and, just ten, sophisticated beyond his years.
In the community in which he lived, divorce was closer to
the rule than marriage and so he showed no particular
stress about his parents' divorce. They, in turn, took care
to guide him and provide him with a united front whenever he followed a child's natural instinct and began to
play one parent against the other.

Jeffrey had few close friends and a large number of acquaintances, a mixture of book people, journalists, and

writers. He was not an easy man to know, far too complicated a person for easy access, but most who knew him
became, and remained, friends. As for those who did not,
he had long ago stopped worrying, had stopped asking
himself why, though like most decent people he continued
to care.

He had reached a point in his life where he did many
things alone. For the most part he was alone in his work
and in his store. He ran from his apartment to a nearby
park, around the park several times and back, four times a
week, and this, too, he did alone. He had an occasional
love affair, but nothing lasting. He had neither the confi-
dence nor the dedication necessary, a condition that sad-
dened him somewhat but which he also believed would
eventually change. When he wanted sex, it was usually
available. He was good-looking enough, and available
women were plentiful. They were usually divorced, eager,
and not in the least offended by a casual sexual encounter.

He had, in a sense, taken one step back out of life,
stepped out of line to watch the world pass by. He often
told himself he was just catching his breath, but it was
more than that. He was a survivor and he had the emotional and psychic wounds to prove it. His books, his store,
his apartment, and most of all his son were a balm. Even
Lydia, depending on the state of siege of the moment, was
a comfort. Sometimes it seemed to him his grasp on the
future was tenuous, and at times like this he fought the
gnawing ache of uncertainty with a determined bravado,
one he believed transparent and easily pierced, but one
that others found effective enough.

Some people dislike eating alone. Jeffrey often looked
forward to it. After the fair he returned to his apartment,
opened his wine, and stepped through the door into his

store. Each book was cataloged on a three-by-five card, and the cards were stored alphabetically by author in the top right-hand drawer of his desk. Lydia had set up the system and it gave him instant access to his inventory, complete with description and price, without having to leave the telephone to go looking for a book. When a book was sold, the card was removed, the purchaser's name and the date written on it, and once again filed alphabetically by author in another file—a file stored under the wrapping table in the big closet, seldom used and usually updated only once or twice a year.

Jeffrey squatted, reached under the table, pulled out the old cards, and began thumbing through the S's. When he came to Steinbeck, he slowed down; and when he came to *Cannery Row*, he stopped. The book had been purchased five years before—not long after Jeffrey had started in business—by Victor Dreyfus. So had *Sweet Thursday*. That was who he thought had bought them.

Victor Dreyfus was a man who seemed forever destined to work in the wrong museum, a curator with portfolio for sale. He was a scholar—Jeffrey was under the impression Victor's area of expertise was postimpressionist art—a man who had wandered from job to job all of his life until, some six years ago, he had been hired as a part-time consultant to Metropolitan Oil Corporation, more specifically to polish up the oil company's tarnished image within the community. Dreyfus had engineered a number of art exhibits in the lobby of Metropolitan's downtown highrise headquarters, exhibits noted both for their richness and their lack of controversy. The same might well be said of Dreyfus, for it was well known among gallery owners and bookdealers that he also made purchases for the private collection of Alfred Craventon, the chief executive and founder of Metropolitan, a man as respected by conservatives as he was feared by the liberals of the Los Angeles political scene. In Jeffrey's political scheme, Craventon was slightly to the right of Attila the Hun, but a customer was a customer. Craventon had certain cravings: good modern art; modern first editions; and most of all, money. He was the sort of man who could parlay public do-gooding into private gain, all the while making it appear he was doing it for the benefit of mankind. Craventon got richer and richer.

There was a trickle-down theory involved, a trickle that was closer to an occasional drip, in that some of Craventon's riches found their way into the coffers of various art dealers and bookdealers around town. Through the good offices of Victor Dreyfus, that is, and Dreyfus often expected something in return. Not a kickback exactly— though Jeffrey suspected a few dealers did pass some cash back under the table—but Dreyfus would accept a discount on his own personal purchases. A good-size discount.

Jeffrey liked the old man, admired his cleverness at keeping up the good front. He had managed for God knows how many years—Jeffrey calculated he was well into his sixties—to make a living as an aesthete. Not much was known about him, and most of the information circulated Jeffrey looked upon as rumor. Dreyfus was tall, thin, and always dressed more for New York or London than Los Angeles. He was somewhat epicene, and one rumor had it that he was homosexual, but it was Jeffrey's privately held opinion that Dreyfus's interest in the finer things did not include sex. He imagined Dreyfus always in a pinstripe suit, examining the world through his Ben Franklin glasses, making purchases both wise and careful.

His purchases of *Cannery Row* and *Sweet Thursday*—for $75 and $50 respectively—had not been discounted, which meant they had been bought for the private library of Alfred Craventon.

Jeffrey picked up his wine glass and went back into the kitchen to finish mixing a small salad to go with his cold chicken. His curiosity had been provoked, and the questioning journalist began to natter at the edge of his self-imposed caution. The curiosity persisted. He decided to call Victor Dreyfus in the morning. He would first offer him the signed Ross Macdonald he had bought at the book fair, and then ask what had become of the Steinbeck books.

iii

"Jeffrey! So good to hear from you!" Victor Dreyfus would have made a perfect protocol officer. He had the mixture of bonhomie and formality down pat; it completely obscured his insincerity.

Jeffrey offered him the early inscribed Ross Macdonald, *The Drowning Pool*, and waited briefly for Dreyfus to ask the price. He didn't.

"I'll have to check, Jeffrey. Mr. Craventon likes to okay all purchases over two hundred dollars himself. I'll recommend it to him."

"While you're at it, Victor, would you check to see if the *Cannery Row* and *Sweet Thursday* I sold you five years ago are still in the collection—or if they've been sold?"

"No, not sold. I'm quite certain"—Dreyfus now sounded conspiratorial—"because I do almost all his selling for him and I haven't sold those two. Are the other books ready yet?"

Damn. He had forgotten all about them. Wrapped and

27

ready to mail were four books, two Kurt Vonneguts for
Craventon and two signed Noel Coward plays for
Dreyfus. Jeffrey hated trips to the post office and hadn't
been for a week. He knew Dreyfus was eager to get his
Coward plays. He had a quick notion how to work it
around to his advantage.

"Victor, I'm so sorry. They're still here. I'll tell you
what. You call Mr. Craventon and tell him about the
Macdonald. If he wants it, get back to me and I'll drop all
the books by your house this afternoon."

"I'll be at Mr. Craventon's house working this afternoon." Dreyfus sounded disappointed.

"I'll drive over there." Jeffrey tried not to sound too
eager. He had never seen Craventon's collection and he
wanted to check out the Steinbecks in person. That, at
any rate, was the excuse beneath an emerging impulse.
Jeffrey didn't quite trust Dreyfus, and that, by implication, made him curious about Craventon.

"I'll call you back within the hour, Jeffrey. And I'm
going to recommend the Macdonald strongly to Mr. Craventon."

"Good. Talk to you later." Jeffrey knew he had a deal
because Dreyfus hadn't even bothered to ask the price of
the Macdonald. It was $350. High, but worth it. The in-
scription was long and personal, written by an author famous for his reserve.

At two o'clock that afternoon, Jeffrey drove up the long
driveway, past the lawns and gardens where two Japanese
gardeners, bandannas tied around their sweaty foreheads,
were working. A butler escorted him into the library of
Alfred Craventon's grand Tudor-style home in San Marino, a house that struck Jeffrey as being right out of a
good Ross Macdonald novel, probably the very one he

had in his hand. It looked old in a city where buildings
and people struggled to look young.

Victor Dreyfus was seated at a massive desk, two open
card files before him, pecking away at a small portable
typewriter, listing new books and increasing an already
substantial collection. Polished mahogany shelves lined
every wall of the big room, interrupted by three big
leaded-glass windows and a ceiling-high marble fireplace.
There were two ladders on slides mounted at the top of
the shelves on either side of the room, exclamation marks
at the end of impressive rows of books. There were several
glass cases in the room as well, not the sort one sees in
stores but the kind with carved walnut tables on top of
which sat green-felt-lined glass cases, small cages for big
treasures. In the one nearest Jeffrey was a handwritten
manuscript by Conan Doyle, one of the few that had remained in private hands and not been bought by a rich
library. Wing chairs, floor lamps, and small tables were
scattered throughout the room, places to sit and, Jeffrey
hoped, read. The room had a looked-at but not used quality about it. The musty smell of books perfumed the air,
the same smell as in Jeffrey's office and one that gave him
pleasure on every encounter.

"Wow," he muttered as Dreyfus, slipping immediately
into his greeter's role, took a few stately steps across the
dark red Oriental carpet toward his visitor.

"Jeffrey, so good of you to come. Let me order you a
drink." Dreyfus was eyeing the packages, so Jeffrey
handed them to him. The Macdonald was separate, having been wrapped later, and Dreyfus opened it first, inspected the jacket, and then read the inscription.

"Nice. Very nice," he said as Jeffrey nodded in agreement. The big packages came next. Jeffrey watched as

Dreyfus gave the two Vonnegut books, *Slapstick* and *Welcome to the Monkey House,* only cursory inspection and then focused his pleasure on the two Noel Coward plays, which were for his own collection. "Lovely. Lovely," Dreyfus said as he caressed them. "He had such great style, such wit. Now about that drink, what will you have?"

"Nothing, thanks," Jeffrey replied. He was looking around the room, trying to take it all in. The ingestion of such incredible excess was not easy.

"Make yourself at home," Dreyfus said expansively. Jeffrey walked slowly around the room, looking at the books, too overwhelmed by their number and quality to concentrate on any particular one.

"Oh, yes. I'd forgot. There. Second shelf from the top." Dreyfus pointed to the center of a case just above a large window. He slid the ladder, which rolled along its track without a sound, to Jeffrey. "You look for the books and I'll check my card file."

Jeffrey climbed the ladder, found the Steinbecks, and began reading their titles.

"They're not there." The unfamiliar voice startled Jeffrey, who turned slightly, almost losing his balance. He saw looking up at him a corpulent man, his silver hair cropped close, his sport coat and slacks so conservative they seemed on first impression to be a suit. He wore thick, concave eyeglasses that made his eyes seem even larger than they were. His jowls were flabby, his frown sealed from years in place, and his manner tangibly superior. Alfred Craventon, captain of industry. And he knew his library well.

"I'm afraid they were stolen some time ago. It wasn't until you asked that I remembered. I thank you for reminding me, Mr.—Mr.—"

"Dean," Dreyfus interrupted. "Jeffrey Dean Books."

"How do you do," Craventon said, making it a statement.

Jeffrey stepped off the ladder and shook the man's hand. It was strong and firm. "Good to meet you," Jeffrey said. "This is a most impressive collection in a most impressive room." He thought he sounded a bit too overcome by it all and wished he'd said it differently. Still, it *was* impressive.

"Thank you. I'm pleased you like it. It is, however, minus two Steinbecks I admired very much."

"Aha! The cards are still in the file," Dreyfus announced, waving two three-by-five cards in the air. "I'll report it to the insurance company."

Jeffrey said nothing, and so Craventon moved to fill the silence. "We entertain here rather a lot and sometimes things are stolen. Not often, but it does happen. *Mislaid* is the term my wife prefers, but the unfortunate truth is that people steal things."

"Mr. Craventon has many requests from charitable organizations to use his house for parties," Dreyfus explained. "Sometimes charity groups are not entirely composed of charitable people."

Craventon stepped to the desk, and as he did, Dreyfus picked up the Macdonald and handed it to him. Craventon looked at the jacket, turned the book around to inspect its spine, and then opened it to Macdonald's inscription.

"I don't remember *The Drowning Pool*, specifically, though I think I've read all of his early books," Craventon said. "After a while the stories sort of mix together in my memory. It's how he writes, how he sees this place, that I remember."

"I sometimes feel the same about Chandler," Jeffrey responded. "Only with Chandler it's easier to remember the plots because he didn't write anywhere near as many books as Macdonald has."

"How many is it for Chandler?"

"Seven," Jeffrey answered quickly. He wondered if he was being tested.

"I've got all but one," Craventon said.

"All but two," Dreyfus corrected him.

"I would have sworn I was missing only *The Long Goodbye.*"

"Yes, and"—Dreyfus flipped officiously through the cards in the file box on the big desk—"and *The Big Sleep.*"

A look clouded Craventon's face and Jeffrey couldn't tell if it was worry, puzzlement, or suspicion. Whatever it was, he covered himself quickly and when Craventon looked up he was smiling slightly.

"Two missing Steinbecks and I'm short two Chandlers. Ah, well. I would appreciate, Mr. Dean, if you would find the two books to replace the two stolen. And also if you'd get the two Chandlers for me. I imagine it won't be *that* difficult to find similar firsts of *Sweet Thursday* and *Cannery Row*, now will it?"

"No, not very difficult at all. The Chandlers, however—"

"Very scarce, I know," Craventon said before Jeffrey could finish his sentence. "Well, a collection such as this ought to have a complete set. At least."

"I'm sure if they can be found, Jeffrey will find them," Dreyfus said. There was an edge to his voice, and Jeffrey wondered if it was because Dreyfus didn't like his patron issuing his commissions directly.

"I'll do my best."

"I'm sure. Would you like a drink, Mr. Dean?"

"Victor already offered, thanks," Jeffrey said diplomatically. "Some other time, perhaps. I've got to be going."

He said nothing about the forged inscriptions in the stolen books, and while he was driving back to his apartment, he wondered if it was because of suspicion or instinct. Instinct, he finally decided, for it was not in his nature to volunteer information unless it was to be in exchange for even more useful information, a habit honed to a fine capability when he was a journalist. And as for suspicions, he didn't really have any. Craventon, who struck him as a clever and calculating man who took much pleasure from his books and paintings but was probably incapable of cherishing them, didn't have to forge a damn thing. He had the money to buy whatever he wanted. Dreyfus, whom he thought probably not above the occasional shady maneuver, also struck him as the sort who could not tolerate the thought of ink on his immaculate fingers, someone whose aesthetic sensibilities would be deeply offended by the idea of forgery.

It did seem odd that anybody would steal those two books, all the more so because whoever did it had to be a risk-loving fool. What other sort of person would want to climb up a ladder and rise above the heads of a crowd to steal two books? How conspicuous could you get? It was very odd. By the time Jeffrey got to his office he had pushed his theoretical thief to the back of his mind.

There were four messages on his answering machine. Two were to order books from his most recent catalog, and there was one each from Lydia and Michael. Lydia was calling to warn Jeffrey that Michael wanted to go on a

father-son Cub Scout overnight camping trip, wanted it
very much. Michael's call was to ask if the two of them the
uncertainty in his son's voice and felt for sure he had better make the trip. His idea of camping out was a good
hotel and room service, and Michael knew it. No matter,
Michael wanted it. He called to tell him so and got
Lydia's answering machine, waited for the beep, and, instead of saying yes, asked Michael to call him in the
morning. He wanted to tell him himself and share his excitement. He hung up thinking of the answering machine
as an aid to modern divorce; he and Lydia had communi-
cated with one another three times in the last week without speaking once.

The next day promised to be a busy one. Saturdays always were, and this Saturday he wanted to go back to the
book fair for one last check, so he was up early and out
running by seven o'clock. As was his custom, he took a
longer run on Saturday than he did the other three times
he ran each week. He was not quite a compulsive runner,
but he did recognize the benefits of exercise, both physio-
logical and psychological, and so he stayed at it with a
dogged determination. On Saturdays he drove west to the
Sepulveda Basin, a big dam created by the Army Corps of
Engineers, most of which was now a golf course crossed
by running paths and intersected by the Los Angeles
River. It was country in the middle of the city, with
cornfields, large open spaces, lush wooded areas, and,
for the adventurous, one six-mile path that cut across
the edge of the dam itself. That was Jeffrey's Saturday
challenge.

He ran past an army reserve unit barracks, through a
eucalyptus grove, then up the small incline across the

railroad tracks and out onto the edge of the dam. He continued across its edge, his feet beating out a steady rhythm on the gravel surface, his heart feeling the pull of the steady incline. To his left, mostly obscured by a dense growth of foliage, was the San Diego Freeway. To his right, down the sharp, rocky incline of the dam's edge, was a large open field, neatly plowed, and a small park area with trees and tables. Ahead of him were the Santa Monica Mountains, still clear and sparkling in the early sunlight. Highrises dotted Ventura Boulevard in the distance, some of them bouncing the sun off their mirrored facades. Jeffrey had the sensation of running in the city but, somehow, above it, as if the slight elevation of the dam separated him from the land around, made him all-seeing for the fifteen minutes it took to cross the dam.

He was not quite halfway across when he heard a sharp crack, then felt a shaft of air burn by him at a high velocity. It shattered his concentration and caused him to look to his feet, toward the freeway, from where it seemed the sound had come. He was looking, trying to decipher the sound—it was both familiar and also so long submerged in his memory that it took several seconds before it came to him—when there was another crack, another shaft of air shooting by him. Then he knew.

He spun around and saw a man standing a hundred yards or so behind him, just off the edge of the freeway on the incline up to the dam. He was sighting down a telescopic sight on a rifle, a rifle aimed directly at Jeffrey.

He turned right and raced down the steep incline, shored by big white rocks of the dam, panicked and fell heavily on the rocks. When he scrambled upright, he saw blood streaming from the scrapes on his knees and as he looked behind him he realized he could still be seen, and

so he stooped and began to run again. The only cover, a
clump of shrubs and trees at the edge of the park, was several hundred yards away.

He felt terror, and the terror gave him speed, sent massive amounts of adrenaline pumping through his system.
He heard the crack of the rifle again. This time he did not
feel the shaft of air shoot by him, and for one split second
during which it seemed to him everything was happening
in slow, strangely altered time, he waited for a bullet to hit
him. It did not happen. Finally, he reached the trees.

He was soaked with sweat, and from his knees on down
his legs the sweat was mixed with blood from the fall on
the gravel. His ribs were sore from the fall and he winced
in pain as he bent from the waist, his arms folding across
his stomach, trying to catch his breath and at the same
time not vomit. Finally, the little food that was in him
came up and when he was finished his breathing had
slowed and his thoughts began to clear.

He could not see who had fired the shots. Just a man
with a rifle, too far behind him to be defined any more
than that. A man. Jeffrey couldn't even estimate his
height or guess at his coloring. He thought he was wearing
blue, but he wasn't even sure of that. He peered out of the
bushes and did not see him. If he was still looking for Jeffrey, he would have to come to the edge of the dam in
order to look for him, and then he would be visible. Still,
Jeffrey waited.

He knew the area fairly well, well enough anyway to
figure out a way to get back to the parking lot by the golf
club without running along any of the streets that tra-
versed the area. He would have to figure out how to
scramble across the river, but he knew it wouldn't be too
hard to find a shallow spot. He knew the first mile or so of

the run back was in wide-open field, making him an easy target. But he knew, too, every step away from the edge of the dam made him a smaller target.

If the man wanted to come after him, he either had to get back onto the freeway and drive to the closest off ramp, then come back to the surface street, or he had to get back across the railroad tracks at the start of the dam's edge, get to his car on a nearby street, turn around and start back.

Time. Jeffrey guessed that if he started running that instant he would cross the one street between himself and relative safety before the man could get there. Without a second's hesitation, Jeffrey broke into a run, the fastest he had ever run. Ten minutes later he was at the street, a broad avenue with a planted center divider surrounded by open spaces, and there was no car in sight. Even better, there were several other runners and so he slowed his pace and fell in behind them. When he came to the approach to the bridge over the river—another place where he would make a very big target—he turned in alongside the river, staying on a dirt path used by the farmers who rented the fields from the government. By now he had run about seven miles at speeds well beyond his usual ability and he was rapidly tiring. When he found a small rapid across the river, a rapid of cement boulders and beer cans, he scrambled into the tall willows along the river's edge and sat down to rest.

None of it made any sense whatsoever. Why would anybody want to kill him? Was it some insane freeway killer, one of those psychopaths he had read about in the papers? Or by what possible stretch of the imagination—and Jeffrey's, which was a rich one, could not make the long stretch—could this have anything to do with the forged

Steinbeck books? God, no, it had to be much more than
that. But what? That Arab—what was his name?—who
owned Serendip Books. Narib Zaki. Jeffrey chastised himself for being prejudiced against Arabs, something he
looked upon as the new American disease. People don't
kill over forged books. No, Jeffrey thought, rubbing his
painful calves, not even Arabs.

The blood on his knees had dried and his legs were
filthy with blood and dirt, so he bent to the river and
splashed the contaminated water on his legs, wincing as it
stung the cuts on his knees. Then he stepped across the
rapids, barely wetting his shoes, climbed the small incline,
and started along the dirt path on the opposite side of the
river, a path that followed the edge of the golf course back
to the parking lot where he had left his car. The path was
well populated with runners, and the course was full of
golfers, so at least for now he felt somewhat safe.

He set out at a slow jog, aware for the first time of the
pain in his legs, especially his knees. Pain, he remembered
reading somewhere, is a luxury reserved for the living.
Everywhere he looked he could see people, enough of
them to give him an illusion of safety. There were even
people in the parking lot, people in cars on the freeway,
and people walking along Ventura Boulevard when he
drove into the parking lot beside his office.

In little more than an hour, he had shaved, showered,
and cleaned his cuts. As he dressed, he saw the bruises
begin to form along his rib cage. He limped painfully into
the kitchen to turn on his coffee maker, his body barely
working and his mind in total confusion. He hoped the
coffee would both refresh and reorder his thinking a bit.
He decided three times to go to the police and three times
he changed his mind. What proof did he have of what had

happened? What sense could be made out of any of it? He shook his head and then limped through the door into his store, intending to check his answering machine for messages. The phone rang just as he got to it.

"Jeffrey Dean Books."

"Hi, dad."

"Hi, honey."

"Well?" One thing about Michael, he went straight to the point.

"Well, what, Mike?"

"Oh, dad. You know. The camping trip. Please." There was much teasing between them, but this time Michael wasn't sure if he was being teased or not and he wanted to go so badly he was willing to beg.

"I've got a big date that night. Something I really wanted to do."

"Oh, dad. C'mon."

"Well, there goes my night on the town."

"Really? You mean it?"

While they were talking, Jeffrey straightened up his desk, almost an unconscious habit he had when talking on the phone. He checked the pad on which the books ordered by phone were listed, and added the four books Craventon asked him to get. As he wrote down *Cannery Row* and *Sweet Thursday,* he remembered the index cards he had pulled out of his sold file and stuck in his desk drawer, so he pulled open the drawer to take them out and put them back under the table in the wrapping room.

"Of course, Mike. I'd love to go."

"Oh, wow! Wow!" Michael's outbursts of enthusiasm were infrequent but intense, and Jeffrey smiled.

"Do me a favor. Borrow a sleeping bag from one of your friends. And an air mattress. Your dad is getting old."

He felt for the cards where he had left them. He didn't find them. He pulled open the drawer and stared at it in disbelief. The contents of the drawer had been completely searched and no attempt had been made to put things back as they were.

He pulled open the other desk drawers. All but one had been searched. He looked again, even rummaged through his wastebasket. Gone. Two cards describing two books, including the prices paid for them and the name of the person, Victor Dreyfus, who had bought them. Jeffrey remembered exactly what was on each one of them. They proved nothing, except that two books had been sold to one man for another man's collection. They didn't even prove that, really, to anybody except Jeffrey. They were gone. But one thing was becoming abundantly clear. The man with the rifle wasn't some psychopath taking a random shot. He was shooting at Jeffrey for a reason.

A hard knot of dread began to grow in his stomach, a feeling of foreboding and fear. He sensed there was a connection somehow between the books and the sniper, and he knew for certain that they—whoever they were—knew much more than he did. He had accidentally stumbled onto something when he had picked up those two Steinbeck books in the Serendip booth, and whatever it was, whatever it meant, he knew only that his involvement was just beginning. He was in that bizarre, nearly intolerable, always interminable warp of time between the first shot and the impact. He wondered what would happen next.

iV

HE WAS SITTING at his desk, putting things back where they belonged, trying to sort through the confusion all around him and debating whether or not to go back to the book fair. There were several more books he wanted to get, a couple of dealers whose shelves he had not explored as thoroughly as he intended. It hurt like hell to walk. He was trying to ignore his aching body when he saw a man walk across the courtyard and disappear under the pepper tree, but his presence meant nothing until Jeffrey heard his footsteps on the stairs leading up to his store.

"Who's there?"

"David Ketchum, Jeff. A voice from the past, you might say."

"Jesus Christ." Jeffrey was stunned and peculiarly disoriented. It couldn't be. He unlocked the door and opened it. There, standing before him, was David, his pockmarked face and thick red curly hair seemingly untouched by the years—it must have been ten or twelve at least—

since Jeffrey had last seen him. Ketchum's smile was as big and as hammy as his outstretched hand, and as the two men shook hands, Jeffrey began to feel both relief and dread.

"How about some of that coffee I smell?"

"Sure, David. Anything you'd like. Up to a point." Jeffrey couldn't quite believe all this was happening, couldn't adjust to the idea that the past was being replayed and that it was now part of the present as well.

"How long has it been, Jeff?"

"I suspect I'm about to find out it hasn't been long enough."

"Ah, Jeff. Ever suspicious."

Ketchum followed as Jeffrey led the way into his kitchen, and as they crossed the room Jeffrey couldn't help noticing that the face wasn't all that was unchanged about David. He still wore suits slightly out of fashion; ties far too narrow; and, no matter what color his suit or his shoes, white sweat socks. Wherever he was, Ketchum stood out in a crowd, the sort of man who always got a second look.

"Suspicious with reason," Jeffrey said, pouring the coffee.

Ketchum shrugged and smiled.

"Besides," Jeffrey added, nodding in the direction of his store, "I'm in a new business and it's one I don't think will be any use to you."

"You never know."

"I don't think so. Just books. Not much travel, certainly none to the sort of places that interest you."

"The places weren't important. It was the people."

Jeffrey supposed that was so, but in his mind it was people in particular places: the Dominican Republic,

Cuba, El Salvador, Honduras. Places where he had been and places where he had, from time to time, encountered David Ketchum. No, *encountered* wasn't the right word. Places where David Ketchum had turned up and then sought out Jeffrey or several other journalists. Sought them out with the care and cleverness of a man who knew exactly what he wanted and exactly how to get it. For all his sartorial oafishness, David Ketchum was a subtle and smooth man, one whose method of getting what he wanted was as unobtrusive as his clothing was not.

They'd first met in 1965. Lyndon Baines Johnson had sent the marines ashore in the Dominican Republic, followed almost immediately by an assault wave of journalists. When Jeffrey arrived, the utilities had been on strike for two days; garbage and human feces—there wasn't an abundance of indoor plumbing in the poorer sections— formed a rank contrast with the physical beauty of the country. He was still at the airport when he heard shooting, and the sound of gunfire became a constant almost immediately. One day it would be obvious that the small war in the Dominican Republic was the beginning of the political upheavals that would strike nearly every small Central American country, bringing them a unity in revolution they never had in anything else except for their poverty. At the time, though, it was just another routine overthrow of a military dictatorship, one that was suddenly deemed more serious than usual when the revolutionaries—a ragtag collection of liberals, leftists, Marxists, and Communists—appeared for several days to be well organized. The reinstatement of order, which meant the reinstatement of still another military dictatorship promising elections, took several weeks. In those weeks the fighting was constant and bloody. The U.S. Marines at-

tempted to appear as peace-preserving when in fact they
were on hand purely and simply to protect American interests. Protecting American interests in the Dominican
Republic meant preventing the creation of another Communist satellite in the Caribbean. That, in turn, meant
controlling the country.

Both sides spoke to the journalists but did not speak to
one another except with bullets, and while the Dominican
military was quite willing to talk with the American ad-
visers, the rebels were noticeably less so. The community
of journalists, running from government offices to rebel
outposts, became a key communicating factor, in terms of
both getting the story out of the country and carrying information from one side in the dispute to the other.

In the latter case, most journalists were inadvertent
collaborators, though a number of them routinely provided valuable information to the American government
representatives on a less than casual basis. In those pre-
Watergate days, journalists often cooperated with the government. Patriotism wasn't dead. Not yet, anyway. Patriotism for pay was not unheard of either, but it was fairly
rare. After all, the government usually got its information
in exchange for future favors and information, favors and
information dutifully rendered. It was the American way,
exchanging one bit of information for another, a neat little microcosm of the capitalist function. You tip me off,
I'll tip you off. The problem was that, in terms of real
power, the government was getting far more than it was
giving. The gathering of the information was a delicate
and important matter, which is where David Ketchum
came in.

During the more intense periods of fighting in the Dominican Republic, the government forces and the U.S.
Marines, acting in concert, required foreign journalists to

observe an 8:00 P.M. curfew. Local journalists were allowed to roam at will—neither the U.S. Marines nor their fellow countrymen cared whether or not they were shot. Most foreign journalists stayed at the Nacional Hotel and spent their evenings drinking, gambling, or reading. Jeffrey did a lot of reading, and he also did a good bit of gambling. The casino at the hotel operated on the European pleasure principle, and so blackjack was called "vingt-et-un," giving a hard-edged card game the sound of class.

Jeffrey was just breaking even one night when he became aware that the red-haired man with the pockmarked face at his table was consistently winning. A conversation ensued, nothing of any weighty consequence and certainly nothing to do with what would one day become something quite different, well beyond ordinary conversation. They exchanged names, occupations—Jeffrey said he was with Time, Inc.; David said he was a government economist assigned to the U.S. Embassy—and that was that.

A couple of nights later they had drinks, and the night after that they had dinner in the hotel dining room. David had an ingratiating charm and Jeffrey enjoyed his company. He was not a pack journalist, did not stay close to the others, preferring instead to work pretty much on his own. When the others went to dinner or to gamble or to a press conference en masse, Jeffrey as often as not was out on his own. His stories tended to be more informed, his contacts more reliable, and, unlike the others, he was reasonably fluent in Spanish.

David Ketchum knew all of this, of course, and by the time the dinner ended that night, Jeffrey had a good idea what Ketchum was up to as well. Ketchum never came out and said he was feeding information to the CIA or

that he was an agent of any sort—the actual admission
was never made—but there was a tacit understanding
about his work. He was looking for information, information of the sort someone like Jeffrey just might be able to
provide, and in exchange he would grant certain favors,
arrange access to certain people and information the
others would not be privy to.

Jeffrey's hesitation before he agreed was brief. He felt a
slight discomfort, a small moral reservation, but he also
knew what was expected of him. What was expected was
that he get the best story first, and to that end he could do
anything he felt necessary even if that included cooperat-
ing with the CIA. In time these relationships would be
terminated, their previous existence even denied, but at
the time of the war in the Dominican Republic and for
some years thereafter, the collaboration continued to the
benefit of both parties involved.

Jeffrey's independence, his knowledge of the language,
enabled him to have contacts beyond those most journalists possessed, particularly when it came to dealing with
the distrustful rebel forces. From time to time they used
Jeffrey, for reasons that were never purposefully stated, to
leak information, to convey conditions. Never anything of
major importance, just small pieces of a gigantic jigsaw
puzzle any number of people were trying to fit together,
pieces delivered in the context of an interview, dutifully
reported to Ketchum and then written in story form and
Telexed to the New York offices of Time, Inc.

Jeffrey and David struck up a friendship of sorts during
their weeks in the Dominican Republic, one based on mutual professional needs and personal compatibility, one
that pretty much expired after a few weeks when Jeffrey
left the small half-island republic.

David came back into Jeffrey's life two more times. The first was less than a year after they originally met, when Jeffrey and the *Life* photographer accompanying him were about to leave on what was then an unprecedented assignment: a weeklong visit to Cuba, something rarely granted American journalists. Jeffrey was in Mexico City waiting for the weekly Air Cubana flight to Havana, his visa and credentials cleared with the Cuban consulate, sitting in the bar at the Del Paseo Hotel having a drink when David Ketchum walked in and pulled up the stool beside him.

What he wanted this time was somewhat more complicated, a bit dangerous, and well out of the line of Jeffrey's usual services. Ketchum laid out his plan carefully and precisely.

There were some papers and also some undeveloped film—all of it highly secret, extremely sensitive material. Ketchum proposed Jeffrey bring all of this material out in the big sturdy red cardboard envelopes *Life* magazine used for shipping undeveloped film. The envelopes, with their "Danger—Do Not Open" and "Caution, Undeveloped Film" stickers on them were both official and conspicuous, and for this trip, labels in Spanish were also on the envelopes, which were actually the size of small briefcases.

"What's on the film?" Jeffrey asked.

"Photographs of military installations, of a new training facility near Santiago, of the harbor defenses in Havana. Stuff like that."

"And the papers?"

"If we're lucky, they're the plans for exporting the revolution."

"Wow!"

"You can see why it is so important to us," Ketchum told him, lowering his voice as the bartender moved toward them to refill their drinks. "The problem is getting the stuff out of Cuba. We have no diplomatic relations, so there are no couriers. Refugees can't really be trusted and they are all searched at least three times. The Spanish government does occasional favors for us, but we can't risk asking them to do this. All hell could break loose."

Jeffrey nodded. Ketchum paused before continuing. "You're the perfect way. You're a guest of the government, and the customs people will know that. You're traveling with a photographer, so of course there will be unexposed film. The chances of your getting caught are minimal."

"And if I am?"

"We'll get you out. Don't worry."

"How will I get the film?"

"You will be contacted in your room at the hotel, probably in the middle of the night. It will be a woman, dressed as a maid, and when she sees you're in the room, she'll say, in English, 'Oh, I am so sorry. I am Marta, your cleaning woman. I was told you called for me.' You will say, 'Let's do it.' If she's our woman, she'll give you the package. If she's not, she will think you want sex and will react accordingly."

Jeffrey smiled. It all sounded so simple, right out of a spy novel. Yet here it was, and here he was a part of it. It excited him, appealed to his basically adventurous nature, and for a moment he saw himself as a romantic figure, in a trench coat, in black and white, Bogart at the end of *Casablanca*. Then, in the next second, a moral qualm settled on him. It was an ambiguous feeling, but distinct nonetheless. Castro was being extremely bellicose these days, there was a genuine fear of his spreading terrorism throughout much of Central America, yet it somehow seemed to Jeffrey that in the confrontation between the United States and Cuba, an elephant had come to kill a gnat, and though it had not succeeded yet, it was obvious to anyone it eventually would. Cuba, he suspected, would one day be relegated to the status of a naughty child and some sort of accommodation, some means of coexistence would be found.

Still. There was some risk involved, some danger. Jeffrey turned from staring at his beer, his eyes and forehead showing his reservations, and looked straight at Ketchum.

"It's important, Jeff, and it will not be hard to do. I know it isn't the usual sort of thing you've done in the past, but you've become very valuable. My superiors have told me I can make you an offer, bargain with you up to ten thousand dollars. What I will tell them is that we bargained, I lost, and you get ten thousand when you bring the material out next week."

"We'll talk about that when the time comes," Jeffrey told him. He knew others had been paid and in the past he had not. There had never been an offer of cash and Jeffrey preferred instead the reciprocal exchange of information and favors. That, to him, was what it was about anyway. Doing a favor for his government and receiving a favor in return kept it clean, if not entirely ethical. The ethical debate was still off in the future somewhere. Right now it was a form of practical patriotism, a term that suited both Jeffrey and the times perfectly. It was also smart journalism.

The week in Cuba was fascinating. Jeffrey was intrigued with the country and its people, and though he was doubtful about the government, he knew he had a damn good story. The country was clean, the people energetic and friendly, and their poor economy everywhere evident. It had been a bad year for the sugar crops, yet the Russian ships in the harbor were proof enough that the aid continued to pour in. The American embargo, far from harming the country, merely caused the most peculiar shortages. Ceilings. Those with square white panels, the kind shot through with tiny holes, were everywhere in official buildings, and everywhere squares were missing. Toilets. Any toilet manufactured in America—and it seemed that in Cuba most of them had been—tended to be without a seat. It appeared they didn't last as long as they should and there were no replacements. Cars. Most of the cars were American but now sprouted cannibalized parts. Jeffrey saw a Ford with a Chevrolet hood fitted on and what he was certain was a Chrysler rear bumper. Making do.

Yet the essential Cuban exuberance endured. Smiles were quick and ready, and Jeffrey noticed that the citizens' teeth appeared to be particularly healthy. He found out there was free dental care for everyone. The Cuban middle class, or rather what was left of it, bumped elbows and bottoms with the Cuban elite on the big dance floor at the Tropicana, a prerevolutionary nightclub that still flourished, its floor show more lavish than ever. Decadence lives, Jeffrey thought.

A few hours before he was to leave Cuba, he was back in his room at the Habana Libre Hotel—formerly the Havana Hilton and now without most of its modern comforts but still perilously hanging on to its garish decor. He was going over his notes and packing when the maid he had been expecting every night opened his door and walked in unannounced. She gave her short speech and Jeffrey said,

"Let's do it." She was a heavy woman, but looked strong and accustomed to hard work, and she ackowledged his response with the hint of a small smile. She turned and walked into the hall, then came back into the room with a stack of fresh towels for his bathroom. When she was inside, she pulled two manila envelopes from between the towels.

"This one—the film," she said in thickly accented English. "The other—the plans, wrapped in round tubes to look like film."

"Good," Jeffrey said, taking them. She turned and left before he could question her, left without even a display of manners so typical of the Cuban people. He put the film canisters into a *Life* envelope, then sealed it shut with the heavy tape he always carried. He picked up the small tubes with the plans in them, suppressed his instinct to unwrap them and look at them, and placed them in another envelope, which he also taped shut. The rolls of film shot by the *Life* photographer, which *Life* editors considered the responsibility of the reporter and not the photographer, were all stacked in neat rows on the desk in his room. He scooped them up and dumped them on his bed and began placing them in envelopes. Finally, because he knew they would be confiscated by American customs, he placed a box of freshly made Cuban cigars—he had actually watched them being rolled in an ancient cigar factory—in one of the envelopes.

The two envelopes for Ketchum he marked on the back with a felt-tip pen, marks that looked accidental enough but would enable him to tell the two from the others, making delivery to Ketchum easy and—just in case—letting him know which two to dispose of in a hurry if it became necessary and if he had the time.

Back in Mexico City, sitting on the same barstool he

had occupied a little over a week before, Jeffrey encountered Ketchum, who walked in immediately after him and took his same place, too.

"Well?"

Jeffrey handed him the two big red envelopes.

"I left them in the envelopes in case you have trouble getting them back into the U.S."

"I won't. The embassy will ship them from here. Diplomatic pouch. No problems, then?"

"None. Went just as you said it should go. I felt deceitful, which is something I hadn't felt doing these things before, but I sure didn't feel like a spy."

"You weren't. Not really. More like a courier. And to help get rid of the other feelings, this should help." He reached into his coat pocket and pulled out a cashier's check. It was for $10,000 and had been drawn on a bank in Miami.

"No thanks. I'm not for hire," Jeffrey said, handing the check back to Ketchum.

"Oh, for Christ's sake. Take it. Nobody will miss it and it'll come in handy. Enjoy, enjoy," Ketchum said expansively, tucking the check into Jeffrey's hand.

"No. I'll take another sort of payment. I'll have an interview with the head of the CIA explaining the Cuban operation."

"Be serious. You know that can't be done. Hell, I don't even know the guy myself."

"You're part of the operation and you don't know your boss?"

"I'm not part of any operation. Take the check and forget about it. Nobody will know."

"I'll know. Look, Dave, it's been good doing business with you, but this time it was a little bit too—"

"That's why the check," Ketchum interrupted. "Gives you a reason."

"Whatever reasons I have for doing it are my own. I will set the terms of payment and they will be the usual. I'll ask for favors from time to time and you'll deliver."

"Can't on this one, buddy. That's what I'm trying to tell you."

"Why?"

"Nobody knows about this. Very special job you did. Favors usually need explaining beforehand. We can't explain this one. Can't tell anybody anything. Can't have anyone even try to get close. That's why it's cash on the barrelhead."

"No money. I don't work that way." Jeffrey wanted to say it made him feel dirty, tainted somehow, though he did not deceive himself about what he had done this time or the times before. He was not the sort of man to practice self-deceit, certainly not about something like this.

"You won't be alone, if that's what's worrying you. Several of your colleagues at *Time* are paid for their services. There are others at other magazines and newspapers, too."

"I've heard. Thanks anyway, Dave. It's not for me."

"This some great moral stand or something?"

"No, just a small one. Mine. And not really very important in the scheme of things. I know that. But it's how I want it."

A month later, when Jeffrey was back in Los Angeles, his bank statement arrived and he saw that $10,000 had been deposited into his checking account. He went directly to the bank and had a cashier's check for $10,000 made out to the Central Intelligence Agency, and mailed it to David Ketchum c/o the CIA, Langley, Va.

It was well over a year before Jeffrey encountered David
Ketchum again, this time in Panama during one of the
political protests about ownership of the Canal, a seed of
protest Jeffrey's editors believed about to sprout. As protests went, this one was not much. Within three days Jeffrey retreated to the pool at the Hilton. He was lying on
his back in the sun, the sweat matting the hair on his
chest, when he looked up and saw David Ketchum, so
pale he was conspicuous even in his swimsuit, stroll by.

Jeffrey called out to him, propped himself up on his
elbow, and extended his hand in greeting. Ketchum's response was typically robust, and the two sat knee-to-knee
on adjoining lounges talking. Their conversation consisted
solely of pleasantries, as if substance was to be avoided, as
indeed it was. Jeffrey said nothing of the check he had sent
Ketchum. Ketchum said nothing about Cuba, nor, in
fact, about anything else he was doing or had done in the
intervening year. There was something uneasy about their
talk that Jeffrey sensed immediately, something Ketchum
seemed to be purposefully ignoring.

It was not until Ketchum asked Jeffrey what book he
was reading, gesturing at the tattered paperback beside
the lounge, that a sense of ease entered their conversation.
Both men were readers and had on previous occasions
suggested books to one another. Talk about books provided refuge from the obvious, though Jeffrey knew better
than to ask Ketchum why he was in Panama and had his
response ready if Ketchum asked for any help. In less than
ten minutes, just as the conversation was beginning to ex-
pire from the weight of the unspoken, Ketchum stood up
and excused himself, saying he was late for an appoint-
ment.

Jeffrey did not see him again, and in the years to come

seldom thought of him. He tucked David Ketchum into a corner of his past and expected he would remain there forever, a memory summoned for the occasional anecdote about another time, another life.

V

"NICE PLACE," Ketchum said, looking at Jeffrey's apartment and bookstore.

"Nice life," Jeffrey added.

"Are you sure those Steinbeck inscriptions are forgeries?"

How in hell does he know about that? Jeffrey knew better than to ask. "Absolutely."

"What do you know about Narib Zaki?"

"I'd never heard of him until yesterday."

"Serendip Books?"

"The same. You interested in the rare-book business now?"

"Yes, it seems I am."

Jeffrey sensed David was about to impart some choice bit of information and so he said nothing.

"You've become a target, Jeff."

"I'm aware of that." Painfully aware, he thought. His legs and his rib cage protested his every move.

"Oh?"

"Go on." Jeffrey's strongest instinct told him to say no more than necessary because he just might seal off his own escape route. If there was one.

"The forgeries." Ketchum seemed to be thinking aloud, verbalizing key words and then thinking the sentences and the facts to himself. "Zaki is one of Qaddafi's men. That much we know. He's kind of a front man, probably no less fanatic but obviously more acceptable. Serendip is sort of his base of operations. His front. He funnels money in and out, pays Qaddafi's people in London, helps out a good bit with the PLO, too. That sort of thing. Now he's started coming to the U.S. Ostensibly on book business, but probably not."

"Probably?"

"We haven't found out anything. Yet. That's where you come in."

"We'll see."

Ketchum pretended not to hear him. "Who did you sell the books to?"

Jeffrey told him. Victor Dreyfus, Alfred Craventon, all of it. He even included his own visit to Craventon's library.

"Do you think they're telling it right?"

"That somebody stole the books? Probably. Craventon's collection is big and he entertains a lot. There are people who think nothing of picking up a book and walking out with it."

"Where does Craventon get his money?"

Jeffrey sketched in Craventon's beginnings as well as he knew: Metropolitan Oil, its great success, Craventon's philanthropy.

"You've done something that has somebody scared,"

Ketchum said when he was finished. Yeah, Jeffrey thought. Me. Ketchum continued: "I think something to do with the forgeries. What we've got to find out is if there are more of them and whether or not Zaki is using them to make money for Qaddafi."

"We?" Jeffrey moved from the kitchen stool to the counter for more coffee, bumped his leg on the counter, and winced from the pain.

"Why are you limping? I had a man at the book fair yesterday and he didn't say anything about you limping."

"You were watching me?"

"Zaki. Then you came along, too."

"Some son of a bitch took shots at me while I was running this morning."

Ketchum shook his head and let out a low whistle. "You don't have 'em scared, you've got 'em angry. Jeffrey, my boy, I think you're on to something."

"I'd like to be well out of it."

"No way. Obviously. But you won't be working without a net."

"Look." Jeffrey's tone made his determination abundantly clear. "I don't like this sort of thing. I don't want any part of it."

"When someone shoots at you, I'd say you're a part of it. Like it or not."

"Get me out of it. I seem to remember you owe me a favor or two."

"How? I don't know who's after you any more than you do. I wish I could, Jeff, but I can't."

Jeffrey stood, grimaced, and walked uneasily into the small kitchen. He unplugged the coffee maker and took out the grounds, dumped them, and proceeded to wash

the pot. Coffee time was over, he seemed to be saying, and
so is this conversation. Ketchum had no intention of stopping.

"We'll keep you under surveillance. Don't worry about
that. If something starts to go wrong, we'll move right in."

Jeffrey said nothing. He knew he was expected to
express appreciation, but he had no such feelings. Why is
it, he wondered, that victims are always expected to be so
grateful?

"Did you get a look at the guy who took the shots at
you?"

"No, not really. He was too far away and I was in a big
hurry to get the hell out of there."

"I think the thing to do next," Ketchum said, "is to go
back to Zaki at the book fair. Let him know you think he
knew all along he was peddling forgeries."

"I think I'll just keep a very low profile."

"Too late now. Smoke him out. If it's him after you,
we'll find out soon."

"Selling forged books to raise money for Qaddafi is not
going to make a hell of a lot of money."

"I agree. But that's what you and I think. We don't
know what they think, let alone what they're doing."

"What about . . ." Jeffrey stopped. "Hell, I forgot his
name. The man who works for Zaki."

"Thomas Smithson."

"Him. What about him?"

"He was working at the store when Zaki bought it three
years ago. Cambridge-educated, a scholar of sorts. Homosexual. Probably isn't involved in this at all, but we're
watching him just in case."

"You don't miss much, do you?"

"Can't afford to miss anything."

Ketchum looked up suddenly. "I've got a better idea. Don't have the conversation with Zaki about the forgeries. Go up to him and be very self-righteous. Tell him you'll buy the books because you want to have some special tests made on them. You want to find out who did the forgeries."

"And?"

"That ought to really get him after you. If it is Zaki and his Libyan friends."

"He'll refuse."

"That doesn't matter. We'll get the books some other way."

"Why the books?"

"We can run some pretty sophisticated tests on them. I have access to facilities and documents you wouldn't believe."

"I probably wouldn't."

Ketchum smiled. "Well, we're together again. I never thought I'd see the day."

Jeffrey's manner could be ingratiating and charming if he wanted it so, and it was what made it possible for him to say things that might otherwise be interpreted as either rude or thoughtless. He was also a quick man to make an accommodation. He knew he was in this, knew he couldn't get out right now, and realized he had no choice but to rely on Ketchum. And so, with an eloquent shrug of his shoulders, Jeffrey responded to Ketchum's forced bonhomie.

"I had counted on not seeing you again."

Ketchum laughed. "I'll disappear in no time at all."

"But not too soon, I hope."

"Now. A couple of things." Ketchum reached into his suit, pulled his wallet from his breast pocket, and deftly extracted a card, which he handed to Jeffrey. The only thing on it was a phone number.

"If you need me, call. They'll get on to me immediately. Also, if Zaki agrees to sell you the books, buy them. You'll be reimbursed for whatever you spend."

"How about the wear and tear on my body?" Jeffrey said as he walked gingerly from his apartment into the bookstore.

"Medical expenses included. Not to worry."

"Who me? Worry? Jesus."

Ketchum delivered his best, most reassuring smile, looked around the office, and then stepped to the glass-encased shelves. They were unlocked. Jeffrey could remember unlocking them an hour or so before, but he could not remember what for. He couldn't tell for sure if it was because he was so frightened from the shots or if he was more distracted than frightened now. Nothing, not even his own perception of his emotional state, was making a whole lot of sense.

"Why are these in a glass case?"

"They're inscribed, signed, or otherwise particularly valuable."

"I see." Ketchum cocked his head slightly, the better to read the titles on the spines of the books. "Wow," he said as he read through them, "it's like a museum."

"Museums and libraries are pretty good customers usually. At least they were until the budget cuts hit them."

"Ah, well," Ketchum sighed, obviously acting. "When this is over, you'll have enough to buy a couple more glass cases and the books to fill them."

Jeffrey said nothing, and stood looking directly at Ketchum.

"Only this time, don't send the money back."

"I always wondered if you got it."

"I got it."

So. What little doubt Jeffrey had about Ketchum's direct employer was now resolved.

"You will always have a choice, of course," Ketchum, now very businesslike, told him. "And if you choose, you can send the check back. You'd be a fool if you did. But you have no choice about whether or not to be involved this time. That much should be very clear by now. So take the goddamn money this time. Look on it as a sort of incentive for something you have to do whether you want to do it or not."

Jeffrey nodded. Ketchum was right, of course, and this time Jeffrey felt no moral taint, no twang of patriotism, no professional compromise. It did not seem odd at all that time had changed his feelings toward such things.

"Good. I'll check with you later tonight to see how it went with Zaki." Ketchum turned and started out the door of the shop. He stopped, turned back, and looked directly at Jeffrey, then lowered his gaze a bit, a habit of his when he was lying. "With a little bit of luck, we can do this with a minimum of fuss. Zaki's got a plane ticket back to London the day after tomorrow."

VÎ

He started down the long aisle toward Serendip Books, moving carefully, aware now that if he moved steadily he hurt less. He saw her first in a brief peripheral glance, and quickly turned to look at her, so quickly he winced from the movement. She was standing in Lena Sabin's booth, holding a book out to a customer, yet looking directly at Jeffrey.

She had shoulder-length thick black hair pulled back from her face and held in place by two gold clips. Her clear, light skin contrasted sharply with her dark hair. Jeffrey wanted to touch her. Her eyes were dark, too. She caught Jeffrey's glance, smiled at him, then turned back to her customer. She was wearing a tailored black wool jacket and a pleated wool plaid skirt, and a delicate gold necklace shone on the silk of her white blouse. Very feminine, Jeffrey thought. Very ... *pretty* wasn't the right word; she was what one might describe as attractive. Not one of those thin, angular women so much in fashion, but rather one with just a hint of heaviness about her. Rather like one of the old photographs of Victorian women he remembered seeing in one of the fair booths. She looked old-fashioned and he liked that. He guessed her to be in her early thirties.

"Look at the books and not at my niece," Lena Sabin ordered, startling Jeffrey. She had sneaked up behind him just as he was about to step into the booth, and had accurately read his mind. The young woman heard her aunt's remark and smiled, not the least embarrassed.

"Better still, look at her. She's not married and she has a master's degree." This remark, though it still didn't embarrass her, brought on a look of mock chagrin.

"A master's in what?" Jeffrey smiled.

"English," she said. "I teach."

"This is Jeffrey Dean, dear." Lena plunged right in. "And, Jeffrey, this is my niece, Rachel. You two ought to get along just fine."

"Why?" Rachel asked.

"Because I said so."

"All right then. Jeffrey Dean and I will go have a drink and find out if you're right."

She just looked old-fashioned. Jeffrey had the distinct impression he was being picked up.

"I accept," he said quickly, and then he moved for the initiative, "providing you pay, of course. Times are changing, after all."

"Some things change for the better and some for the worse," she said, pulling her purse out from behind the counter at the back of the booth. "But if women's equality means getting stuck with the check now and then, so be it."

"Where I come from, the man always pays," Lena protested.

"I'll bet he does," Jeffrey said pointedly.

Rachel laughed; Lena frowned.

As they left, he looked down the aisle and could see Zaki was not at the Serendip booth. Only Smithson was there, towering over a customer. He looked up and frowned at Jeffrey as they walked by. Jeffrey stopped.

"Do you expect Mr. Zaki this afternoon?"

"Yes. In about half an hour." Smithson's response was terse, his tension obvious.

"Would you tell him that I think I can help him and I'd like to have a word with him?"

"Yes. Of course."

"That's the place with the forged Steinbecks, isn't it?" Rachel asked as they walked away.

"That's it."

"I think my aunt has told everybody she's seen about them."

"I figured."

"She is very good at what I call 'dispensing information.' "

"So I've heard."

"Oh, there are secrets. Things you won't ever get out of her. But she does love a good bit of gossip."

"Don't we all?"

She ordered soda water with lime, he a Heineken beer. She insisted on paying and so he let her, then led the way to a small table in the open bar area. The bar was crowded and they were right near the entrance, could see people arriving and departing, most of the latter with their purchases in sealed brown bags. The perfect spot to wait for Zaki; he'd see him the minute he walked in.

"You work with your aunt?"

"Yes, but only part-time. I've learned a lot, I must say."

"I forgot. You said you taught."

"Yes. At Cal State Long Beach. Freshman English."

Here, he thought, here. Because she was with Lena, he had assumed she lived in New York, too. Jeffrey was feeling small jolts, little "zats" as his son called them, tiny shocks of curiosity striking him steadily. He had become so expert at casual encounters, he had almost forgotten how good something special felt.

"You're her West Coast representative then."

"That's me. Actually I do quite a lot more than I expected to be doing. And you are a dealer, I gather from my aunt's talk."

"Jeffrey Dean Books, Jeffrey Dean, Proprietor."

"Good thing you like your name."

"It fits." She looked puzzled, so he explained. "I have a friend whose last name when I first met him was Davidovich. He was a barber. Now he owns his own place, very fashionable, and has his name on all of the products he sells. Only now his name is Davids. You know why he changed it?"

"To sound American?"

"Nope. He couldn't get the name Davidovich on a bottle of shampoo. It just didn't fit anywhere. Not enough room. That's what I mean by fitting. Jeffrey Dean fits."

"Nice WASP name. Safe." She smiled at him.

He nodded, smiled, and took a good slug of beer. She wasn't going to be easy. "I didn't hear your last name."

"Sabin. My father is Lena's brother-in-law. Early Jewish."

"Ah, a JAP!"

"Hardly. They never buy drinks for strangers."

"Not even WASP strangers?"

"Especially not WASP strangers."

He wanted to change the direction of the conversation, in part because he always felt on thin ice with WASP-JAP jokes and also because he didn't think teasing was the best way to hold her interest. "How long have you been working with your aunt?"

"Just over a year. I spent the summer before last in New York learning about the business—a short apprenticeship—and it is something I really like. But I don't know about moving back to New York."

"Back?"

"I grew up there and now my family wants me to come back and begin to take over her business. She's really getting on and I don't know how much longer she can keep going."

"You're the logical choice?"

"You might say the only choice. My brother is a lawyer and he and his family are living here now. We're a small family."

Every new relationship has its awkward moments, pieces of time to fill—sometimes well, sometimes impulsively, sometimes not at all. There are minutes of animated conversation, punctuated by small desperate silences in which each searches for something to say. Outwardly Jeffrey appeared poised and in control, but in point of fact he was sweating slightly, his palms moist from anxiety, and at the same time he was besieged by the pleasant sensations Rachel caused in him. Such conflicting feelings were to be expected in a man who looked upon himself as one of the walking uncommitted being suddenly invited to step back into territories he had abandoned long ago.

He wondered if he looked right enough for her and glanced down to see if he was dressed well enough. He always took care to look his best, and he liked good clothes. He was wearing loafers, neatly pressed jeans, a button-down white shirt, and a Harris Tweed gray herringbone sport coat. I'll pass, he thought, plunging his hand into his coat pocket for a Kleenex to wipe the sweat from his palms.

She sat perfectly still, willing herself to appear relaxed and attentive. She feared her teasing him, her inviting him for a drink, might have been the wrong beginning. She wasn't even sure she wanted any beginning at all—except—except that she had been telling herself for weeks that when the first interesting-looking man came along she was going to get his attention. She was always telling herself things like that, concocting imaginary campaigns to change the course of her life.

She was thoroughly a woman of her time, and for every taste of independence and freedom, she received an equal measure of fear and tugging tradition. She was hopelessly caught in the tide of her times, and so her liberation—it was a word she loathed, though she was a vigorous be-liever in equal rights—was a decidedly mixed blessing. As did many other smart, educated, and attractive women, she wanted the best of both worlds, and if the inevitable conflicts sometimes weakened her resolve, she could deal with that, too. She had been first the aggressor with this interesting man, and now—such a calculated move made her cheeks redden slightly from embarrassment—now it was time to back off a bit. She knew from past experiences that many men, when confronted with what they per-ceived to be an aggressive woman, fled.

They were in the midst of a brief silence. Jeffrey looked up and spotted Zaki striding into the fair, a presence that snapped him abruptly back to the encounter still to come. He tensed slightly and she noticed immediately.

"I've got to go," he said. She had been too aggressive; he was about to flee. She was searching for some appropriate tactic when he looked at her and grinned. "The fair ends tonight," he said. She nodded. "At six-thirty." She nodded again. "I propose stopping by and helping you and your aunt pack up your books. Then I propose taking you to Chinatown for dinner. Lena, too, if she would like to come."

"I'm sure she'd appreciate the help with the books, but I happen to know she is having dinner with an old friend of hers who also happens to be an old customer."

"Of course." He waited for her response, thought he could see a glint of amusement brighten her dark eyes, and so when she remained silent he plunged in. "And you? No old friend for you tonight?"

"No, a new one." The eyes were laughing again.

He wasn't at all certain he was that new friend. He matched her tease with an easy charm. "Present company excepted?"

"Present company included."

"I'll see you in about an hour then and we'll start packing."

Zaki's greeting fell somewhere between calculated disdain and studied indifference. Jeffrey had thought how he wanted the conversation to work and had decided to first try an appeal that he hoped would strike Zaki as well short of logical but candidly emotional.

"I am sorry for all the trouble about the books," Jeffrey began as Zaki nodded. The Arab had not even extended his hand in greeting. Jeffrey spoke formally, an attitude he sometimes struck when speaking with foreigners or to people from whom he wanted a favor, and Zaki was both. "I am also sorry for the inconvenience this has caused you.

I hope you will understand that those two books meant a good deal to me."

"To me as well." Zaki was a small man, but his manner was that of someone accustomed to having his own way, and there was a threat oddly implicit in his remark.

"I would like to make amends for what has happened. I will buy both books. I would still like to have them again, even in their"—he hoped Zaki saw him search for the proper word—"altered condition."

"I'm afraid that won't be possible."

"I'm willing to pay the amount you were asking for them."

"Whatever for? You insist yourself that they are forgeries."

Jeffrey could look easily over Zaki's head, and see up the aisle from where he was standing. He saw Rachel return to her aunt's booth, and saw Lena point toward him. The old lady wasn't missing a thing. His appeal to Zaki was going nowhere, so he moved on to his next plan.

"Yes, and I'm certain when they've been tested you'll agree. It's just that—"

"Tested?"

"Yes. I have a customer who is starting a collection of forgeries. He came to me because I have some expertise in that area. Also, he is planning a scholarly study and wishes to have the books tested, to learn, if he can, how the forgery was done, and when it was done."

"And by whom it was done, I suppose."

Jeffrey became aware that Smithson had moved closer to them, no doubt the better to eavesdrop, and so he lowered his voice. "Yes, possibly that, too, though I doubt it. You need rather a lot of evidence, not all of it scientific, to prove a forgery."

"And even then, the proof doesn't mean much." Zaki's tone placed quotation marks around the word *proof,* made it questionable and unreliable.

"Proof isn't necessarily what he wants. It's the phenomenon he's interested in."

"Is it a phenomenon?"

"That's not the right word. If forgery is a phenomenon, just now I'm unaware of it. My client is interested in collecting and studying forgery."

"He has no doubt read Charles Hamilton's book of famous forgeries?"

"Yes. Of course." Jeffrey knew the book and had used it as a reference several times.

"And Graham Payne's book on document detection?"

That one he didn't know, but he did know he was being tested. He decided to be evasive. "I'm sure he has."

"He may even find out the inscriptions are authentic."

"That would be a great surprise." He wondered if he sounded hopeful.

"I find it odd that the same man who had the fair chairman ask me to remove the books from sale by saying they are forgeries is now trying to buy them himself."

"Yes. Ironic, certainly."

"Mr. Dean," Zaki said coldly, "you have caused me considerable trouble and I want no more of it. The books are no longer for sale. Not to you, not to anybody."

"I'll pay well."

"The answer is no."

"Please reconsider." Jeffrey stated his plea without sounding the least bit pleading. He had gone far enough.

"I wonder, Mr. Dean, if you realize what this is all about."

"Two books. *Cannery Row* and *Sweet Thursday.* I believe

they are forgeries. In fact, I'm sure of it. I'm offering to buy them from you." There was more, of course, much more, but he was wishing it were all just as he was saying it.

"I see."

"If I were in your place, I'd be delighted by the offer."

"Well, you are not in my place. The books are not for sale. Good day, Mr. Dean."

Jeffrey had been dismissed, he had failed, and it was up to him to exit gracefully. He nodded courteously and turned to leave. As he stepped out of the booth, Zaki's thickly accented English trailed behind him.

"It just may be that one day you will be glad you did not own the books, Mr. Dean."

Jeffrey said nothing and continued on his way.

"Oh, and, Mr. Dean, one thing, if you please." Zaki's courtesy was as heavy as it was artificial.

Jeffrey turned. "Yes?"

"You would do well to know there is no such thing as a book on document detection by Graham Payne."

"Well, who knows, Mr. Zaki?" Jeffrey said, a smile beginning to spread across his face. "With people like you around, there may soon be."

vii

THERE ARE NO blatant colors in good Chinese food, but there are sharp and distinctive tastes, and nearly all of them appealed to Jeffrey, and Rachel, too, which pleased him.

"Step on my foot and my mouth opens," she said as she plunged into the dishes, chopsticks flying. Jeffrey was intrigued by her odd combination of humor and what he perceived to be her vulnerability. He felt she could hold people at a distance or bring them close to her with her quickness, and he wondered which it would be for him.

They ate and talked amid the happy clatter of mostly Oriental and a few occidental customers at the Plum Tree Inn, a restaurant in the middle of Chinatown. Their conversation was a pleasant rush of shared information. She told him she had read a lot ever since she was a child, had studied American and English literature at Columbia, then had abandoned her doctoral studies and moved to California to teach.

"Why here?" he interrupted her.

"Why not?" she lied. She had come to be with the man she was going to marry, or rather the man her family expected her to marry. She had soon realized it was a mistake and ended the relationship. And she had stuck resolutely to her guns and remained in California, despite her parents' protests. There had been other men since, but she had come to think of herself as congenitally wary. Along with many other women of her generation, she had set herself an independent course and she was determined to follow it. From time to time, interesting and appealing men appeared in her life, but usually not for very long. She wondered if the good-looking man sitting across from her would understand, Maybe, maybe not. She didn't understand why, but she felt different with him. And she was attracted to him.

"What are students like these days?"

"Well." She laughed. "Since you ask, they're pretty horrible." She launched into her standard lecture about the deteriorating quality of students starting college each year. In addition to freshman English, she also taught single-unit courses on Emily Dickinson, Ernest Hemingway, and William Faulkner.

Jeffrey nodded approvingly at her mention of Dickinson and Hemingway and indicated his indifference toward Faulkner.

"You don't like Faulkner? The greatest American innovator? A winner of the Nobel Prize?"

"I always say he's an acquired taste, and one I just haven't acquired," Jeffrey said. "In fact, I have tried any number of times and I think he's overpraised and overvalued, and his books bore me."

"Are you speaking as a reader or a bookdealer?"

"Failed reader. As for people who collect his work and push up the prices, that's fine with me."

"Spoken like a true wheeler-dealer."

"If I were really a wheeler-dealer, I wouldn't be in this business."

"Don't be too sure." She smiled.

"You know something I don't know?"

"I've got some ideas."

"Tell me." He was genuinely interested.

"You? You're the competition!"

Not for tonight, he hoped. They were lingering over the last of the wine, prolonging the evening, and he was explaining to her the current interest in film scripts—something she hadn't heard about at her safe remove from the film business—when she happened to ask how he had known the Steinbeck books were forged. He told her the story, gave her details when she asked, and took care not to embellish anything. When he got near the end of it, the subsequent events involving the books—the shooting at him, the visit from Ketchum—intruded into the evening, threatened to dispel his mood.

"Why did you go back there today?" she asked when he was done.

"Back where?" He was scrambling to think of an answer.

"To Serendip Books. To Zaki."

"Oh, that. To apologize for the trouble. I got the impression Zaki thought I was accusing him of knowing they were forgeries. I just wanted to clear it up."

"Do you think it might have been him?"

"Who knows?" But, yes, he was beginning to think Zaki had known. He fell silent and kept his speculation—and all of what had happened since he discovered the forgeries—to himself.

"You had a special feeling for those books, didn't you?"

"Yes. I'd had them a long time and in a way they got me started in this business."

"How's that?"

"I actually read *Cannery Row* and *Sweet Thursday* during some time I spent in Monterey—on Cannery Row, in fact—a long time ago. I bought them in a used-book store in Monterey without really understanding about first editions. And, of course, at the time Steinbeck wasn't being collected much. I paid next to nothing for them. I kept the books from then on as souvenirs of a time and of a particular discovery. Then, over the years, I learned about first editions, began to collect them as I traveled around, and finally my avocation became my vocation."

"You mean when you left journalism?"

"Right. And I needed the money. They had become valuable."

"Jeffrey Dean Books, Jeffrey Dean, Proprietor." She was smiling at him now. "It seems odd that they'd end up in England. Who bought them?"

"A local collector, a very wealthy man named Alfred Craventon. Or, rather, they were bought for Craventon by a man named Victor Dreyfus."

"Oh, yes. Dreyfus was by this morning. Bought a couple of books. Henry Millers, I think. My aunt knows him. Craventon. The name is familiar."

"He owns Metropolitan Oil, is a big civic booster."

"I've seen his name in the papers," she said. "And Dreyfus buys for him?"

"Yes."

Silence. Their waitress, a pretty young girl who had served Jeffrey many times before, cleared the table. When she was done, she brought them fresh tea, an invitation—rare in Chinese restaurants—to linger after dinner.

"Married?" Rachel asked.

"What?" He was surprised.

"Are you married?"

"No. Not anymore." He wondered if she had thought all along she was going out with a married man.

"Ah, divorced. No doubt with two point three kids."

"No, just one. Two point three, I gather, being the national average?"

"Right."

"Well, you can't be divorced as long as I have been and have two point three."

"There are a lot of married men out there pretending not to be married."

"There are?"

"There are. So I just ask straight out. Saves trouble that way."

"Oh. I'm no big moralist or anything like that," he said, leaning across the table, "but I agree with you. You did make one assumption about me I object to."

"Oh?" She looked genuinely puzzled.

"The national average of two point three children?"

"Yes?" She stepped obediently into his trap.

"What makes you think for one minute that I fit into the average of anything?"

"Oh, I see." She laughed. "Not your average ego, either. Right?"

"Right. You're catching on fast."

"Now I have to tell you that much as I loathe leaving your far-above-average company, I promised my aunt I'd get back to the hotel at a decent hour because I've got to get up and drive her to the airport very early in the morning. I have noticed that the older people get, the earlier they want to get to the airport.

"Here," Rachel said, reaching into her purse and extracting a piece of paper and a pen. She wrote her phone number and address on it and handed it to him.

"I thought you'd never offer." He grinned.

"It isn't an offer, it's an invitation to dinner next Tuesday night."

"I take that to be an offer."

"You accept my invitation?"

"Yes, with pleasure. Red wine or white?"

"Red. Very dry, please. And now you may drive me back to the hotel, where I will spend the last of three nights listening to my aunt talk in her sleep and get up ten times to go to the bathroom."

"Funny," he said. "That's just what I do, too."

"At least you won't be bothering me." Her smile was neatly enigmatic.

When he drove up to the entrance of the hotel, he stopped the car, intending to reach over and kiss her goodnight. Instead, she impulsively leaned across the seat and gave him a gentle kiss on the cheek. When he turned his lips to hers, she put a finger across them, smiled, and said goodnight. A trace of her perfume, light and forthright, lingered long after she had gone.

He pulled the mail out of his mailbox, bounded up the stairs two at a time despite his sore legs, unlocked and opened his office door, tossed the mail on his desk as he walked through to his apartment and, in a practiced motion, grabbed a brandy snifter off the old oak table that served as his bar, while with the other hand he snapped up a bottle of Cognac, put the cork firmly between his teeth, pulled it, then poured the Cognac. He put down the bottle; shoved the cork back in with a determined *thwack*, a sound that made him smile; took a sip of the Cognac; and finally, in an uninhibited explosion of pleasure, belched.

The Cognac was a ritual reserved as an ending for particularly pleasurable evenings, and this certainly had been one. He had not been able to forget the events he had been forced to involve himself in, but he had succeeded in putting them aside for a few hours—and then there was Rachel. She had accomplished what no other woman had been able to do for some time now. She had provoked both his interest and his curiosity, stirred in him near-forgotten feelings. The Cognac and the thoughts of Rachel warmed him from inside, enveloped him in a pleasant reverie.

It was late. He was still sore, and yet he felt alert and wide awake, so he flipped on his stereo, tuned it to the jazz station, and, snifter in hand, wandered back into his office. He turned on his old brass desk lamp and began opening the mail. There was the usual batch of throwaways—Jeffrey claimed that when he started his business, "Occupant" got more mail than he did—several bills, and six orders for books he had in stock.

"Not bad," he muttered, the same comment he made to himself whenever the amount of bills received was exceeded by the amount of orders in any particular mail delivery. It was, to Jeffrey, a small measure of how his business was doing. In truth, it was an unfair and inaccurate measure since he actually did much better, but nevertheless the theory was applied.

The message indicator on his answering machine read 4, so he flipped the dial to playback and, as the squeal of his messages played by backward, he picked up a pencil and pulled up a pad of paper. Pencil poised, he listened to the messages.

The first was from a bookdealer friend in Santa Barbara looking for some James Thurber books, titles that Jeffrey noted down. He knew he had at least one, maybe two, of them. The second was from a customer, a man whose particular passion was for Mark Twain, asking Jeffrey to call him back.

The third was from Lydia—Jeffrey grinned at the notion of still another conversation conducted by answering machine—telling him a good library was going on sale in Santa Barbara. It'd been left to UCLA and she was calling to give him a head start at looking it over. She said she could get him in Tuesday at 5:00 P.M. with a few other dealers UCLA had chosen for an early look. Jeffrey noted down the address and wrote "Tue. 5p" next to it. As he did so, he realized that that was the night he had been invited to Rachel's for dinner. Damn, he'd have to cancel the date. The library sounded simply too good to miss. Maybe she'd like to drive up with him. No, she probably had classes to teach that afternoon. He'd ask anyway. He also made a note to call Lydia in the morning and thank her in person.

The fourth message was from Ketchum. Jeffrey listened to it once, was momentarily confused by it, and so he played it again.

"Jeff, this is Dave. You're at dinner right now and I hope you're having a good Saturday night out. You deserve it. I'm turning in for the night and will be in touch first thing tomorrow. Our friend Zaki has parted with his books, though I don't think he knows that yet. One is going back to Langley for some very careful testing, the other is where you'll find it. Talk to you tomorrow."

Jeffrey looked around his desk and on the few other flat surfaces in the office and could see no book. He walked back into this apartment. It wasn't there either. Then it occurred to him to go back into his office and look in the locked glass case where he kept his best books. He flipped on the overhead light, walked to the case, and looked in it. There, between a Gertrude Stein and another Steinbeck, was *Sweet Thursday*. Jeffrey pulled at the door, but it was locked, and when he bent down to inspect the lock, he could see no sign of forced entry. Ketchum and his people were pros—that was abundantly clear. He took out his key, unlocked the cabinet, and pulled the book from the shelf. He opened it and read the inscription again: "To Edward, with many thanks, John Steinbeck."

He immediately knew why Ketchum had put the book on his shelf: so Zaki and his people would find it if they came looking. They would be certain Jeffrey had stolen it.

"Shit," he muttered to himself as he locked the cabinet and went for another glass of Cognac. His good mood dissipated like a fog burned away by intense sun, replacing a pleasant haze with the harsh light of reality.

viii

Sunday. One more day and Zaki would be gone, lessening and maybe even ending Jeffrey's involvement in this mess. And how much could go wrong on a Sunday? Not much, he thought. He was sitting on the edge of his bed, looking at the shiny, bright red sores on his knees and shins where he had fallen onto the rocks. He tenderly touched the bruises along his rib cage and winced. He took a long shower, then dressed in Levi's fresh from the laundry, creased and stiff, a red-and-white-checked Brooks Brothers shirt, and brown penny loafers, his California Sunday best. He decided to spend the morning working.

He had fallen behind, and there is nothing so compulsive as a victim of the work ethic in arrears. Each waiting chore seemed to him to fragment itself into a whole series of jobs waiting to be done. He had a long list of orders, all of which had to be wrapped individually, packed in boxes, the boxes wrapped, labeled, and, first thing Monday morning, taken to the post office. Considerable industry was required, and for that, help was on the way in the form of his son, whose youthful interest in acquiring funds was beginning to motivate him to work a bit for them.

Jeffrey began with the orders. For each one he first typed an invoice, keeping one copy for himself, and a mailing label, then placed each order, whether for one, two, or five books, in a pile on the floor of the office.

The stereo was tuned to KUSC-FM, which as usual was rebroadcasting a New York Philharmonic concert from the day before, this one a peculiar mix of Copland, whose music Jeffrey adored, and Stravinsky, whom he admired, though without any of the passion Stravinsky seemed to inspire among music lovers. The orchestra was working its way admirably through the abrupt rhythms of Copland's *Rodeo* when Jeffrey finished the fifteenth, and last, pile of books and heard, in sharp counterpoint to the rhythm of the music, Michael's footsteps running up the stairs, striking each with an energetic staccato.

Jeffrey was up and at the door to kiss and hug his son, to pull his sturdy young body close if only for a second. Every time he did, he dreaded the day his son would be too old or too self-conscious for such displays of affection.

"You help me wrap and there's three dollars *and* a movie this afternoon."

"Five."

"Four."

"Five."

"Okay, five." Jeffrey liked his son's determination to bargain and encouraged it. They bartered for almost everything, and it had become a game between them.

"Five, and I get to choose the movie."

"Now wait a minute."

"You chose last week."

"Your mother lets you choose all the time when the two of you go."

"That's a different arrangement. Five dollars and I choose the movie."

"Okay, but you've also got to come by after school Monday and help me get all this to the post office."

"That isn't fair. You know I'm already coming here to do my homework."

"Right. Gotcha." Jeffrey laughed. "Now start wrapping."

Michael's interest in making money was not unwavering and Jeffrey had to boost him along several times, but within two hours the books were all packed and the packages stacked on the floor and table of the wrapping closet, nearly filling it. Jeffrey and Michael were in the kitchen, eating tuna sandwiches they had made together, poring over the movie listings in the newspaper. It was too soon after the Christmas holidays and not far enough into the new year for there to be many new films playing, and Michael had seen most of the more popular films over the holidays, some of them twice because when he went with one parent and saw a film he particularly liked, it was never a problem to talk his other parent into going with him on another occasion.

"The new Bond?" Jeffrey suggested.

"I've seen it twice already."

"Here. How about this? *The Third Man.*"

"What's that?"

"A classic," Jeffrey said, and Michael frowned slightly. "Very suspenseful." Michael looked more interested. "With a great chase at the end, through the sewers of Vienna."

"Gross."

"You just see them, you don't smell them."

"Yuk."

"At the Sherman."

"Real popcorn," Michael added. The Sherman was a small, prewar theater on Ventura Boulevard, about a mile and a half west of Jeffrey's store, a theater whose floor flooded in heavy rainstorms but whose fare was that of a well-run revival house, and it was a theater Michael and Jeffrey, Jeffrey especially, went to often. Jeffrey, who was by nature given to special small enthusiasms, had made much of the fact that the popcorn was popped on the premises and that the butter on it was real. Michael, for a time, had referred to the theater as "the Real Popcorn Movie."

The theater itself was decorated in what Jeffrey called deteriorating discount art-deco, with chipped gold sconces hiding lights, and badly drawn birds of paradise painted on the walls. Jeffrey and Michael were contentedly chewing on their real popcorn with an extra shot of butter in the middle as the zither theme of *The Third Man* began the film.

"Now I know why you like this movie," Michael whispered.

"Why?"

"It's the only song you know how to play on my guitar."

The boy squirmed a bit as the initial complexities of the plot confused him, while Jeffrey simply and easily succumbed. He considered *The Third Man* one of the best films ever made, a story rich in adventure and romance, appropriately cynical and, finally, just. Its script by Graham Greene and its structure were as close to perfect as any film he had ever seen, and visually it was a stunning mixture of black and white and gray, the odd camera angles distorting the already distorted reality of postwar Vienna.

"Why was penicillin more important then than now?" Michael whispered as the horrors of Harry Lime's black-market dealings were revealed.

"Because it was new and it saved millions of lives. Now there are many other medicines that do the same thing."

Jeffrey figured he had seen the film four, maybe five times before, and each time he found something new in it. What occurred to him now was a further understanding of its cynicism. He thought of it as the despair of Graham Greene's script. *The Third Man* began with a funeral, had as its centerpiece a disinterment, and ended with a funeral. All for the same man. It also explained some of his own cynicism about Ketchum, Zaki, and the whole lot. Where once his patriotism was easily and adroitly tapped by Ketchum, there was now a doubting vacuum. Holly Martins had the right attitude, and Jeffrey watched him with renewed interest.

He noticed Michael scrunch down into his seat and avert his eyes when Martins stepped into a taxi and, before he could state his destination, was taken on a terrifying ride through Vienna, all the while pounding on the glass partition, fearing for his life, only to be unceremoniously dumped into the midst of a literary club for which he had forgotten he was guest speaker. Terror aroused and then rendered harmless means only that more terror is on the way, and Michael sensed it, too.

"Well?" Jeffrey asked his son as they walked out of the theater.

"Good. I recognized the bad guy. He's the fat guy in those wine commercials."

"You know the part where he says nobody thinks in terms of human beings, and that in Italy, in thirty years under the Borgias they produced Michelangelo and Leonardo da Vinci—two of the greatest artists in history?"

"Yeah."

"Well, the Borgias were torturers, murderers, the worst kind of people, but they encouraged great works of art in their honor. That time became known as the Renaissance. Then he goes on to say that in Switzerland, after five hundred years of democracy, all the Swiss managed to do was invent the cuckoo clock?"

"What's it mean?"

"His point was that war, murder, that sort of thing—or so he believed because it justified what he did—produces great art and that peace produces little nothings like cuckoo clocks."

"Oh."

"What's more, when the movie opened, the Germans got very upset."

"Why?"

"Well, it seems they invented the cuckoo clock and not the Swiss."

"Then why didn't they say the Germans invented it?"

"Dramatic license. You know what that is?"

"No."

"Changing facts to fit the story you're telling. Besides, a lot of people do believe the Swiss invented the cuckoo clock, because they are famous for making watches and things like that."

"Now it's the Japanese who make watches."

"There are those who think—and I tend to be one of them," Jeffrey said as they drove back to the store, "that the Germans and Japanese really won the war."

"But they lost. They surrendered."

"Look at it this way. We, the Americans and our allies, defeated them. We were the better fighters and we had the smartest generals. All that rubble in Vienna came from our bombs, too, not just the Germans. And when the war ended, we helped Germany and Japan rebuild. We loaned them money, expertise, everything. We taught them democracy. Now their economies are much stronger and more successful than ours."

"Then why don't they help us now?"

"Times have changed. Now they compete with us, though they are—for the most part—our political allies. We haven't been defeated, not like they were, anyway. There's an expression: 'Won the battle but lost the war.' We won the big battle, World War Two. But it appears we lost the war, the war to have the strongest, the best economy and to be the strongest country in the world."

"Who's the biggest, the strongest?"

"Several. And we are among them, but our economic position has slipped over the years and our prestige has really gone down."

"What's prestige?"

"Clout, Mike. And as you can see, there are a number of kinds of victory. Even in defeat there can be victory."

"Okay, if you say so, dad. Where are we going to eat? I'm hungry."

Jeffrey envied his son's ability to sidestep the complexities of the world around him and to concentrate on his appetite. He regretted little of his youth and was not the sort of man to spend much time looking back. But he did wish he could turn off the present, just for a while, banish it to contemplate some special pleasure. All that was possible now was a few seconds here, a fleeting minute there, and then reality bumped him back. The present, he thought, had all of the grace of a very fat, very rude man trying to butt into a small, orderly line of people waiting to buy tickets to a happy oblivion.

IX

RACHEL WAS UNABLE to make the trip to Santa Barbara with him, a situation that relieved him more than it disappointed him, because he knew Lydia would be there. They had been divorced for six years, and still it seemed to Jeffrey that every encounter not involving Michael was an awkward one. No matter. If it weren't for Lydia, he wouldn't be going up to inspect the library.

She had a selfish reason for getting him in among the first— the child-support checks didn't cover nearly as much as raising a son cost. Both Jeffrey and Lydia acknowledged that the cost had long ago surpassed what he was legally required to pay. Lydia did what she could through the UCLA library to help Jeffrey's business. The private library in Santa Barbara had been left by an eccentric and wealthy woman to the UCLA library along with permission to sell off those books the library did not want. It had been Lydia's assignment to be one of the three librarians from UCLA to select the books for the school and she was to help supervise the sale of the rest. It was also she who had arranged for Jeffrey and a few others to get first crack at them before the other dealers moved in.

Thus, Jeffrey did the polite thing: He asked his ex-wife if she would like a ride to Santa Barbara and to stop for dinner afterward. She declined because the university had asked her to be host to a foreign dealer for the evening, a man who was procuring some special books for UCLA and had expressed interest in the Santa Barbara library.

"Join us for dinner afterward," she suggested.

"Let's see how it goes. I may finish well before the others."

"See you there. By the way, how is the homework coming?"

"Better. He finished in an hour and a half yesterday and it was pretty good work. I guess it's a fair trade."

"How is that?"

"I do the homework fight and you still do the bath fight."

"Right." She laughed. "Fair's fair."

He liked the drive to Santa Barbara once Los Angeles and the crowded freeways were left behind and he came to the green hills near Las Virgnes Road, hills dotted with cattle and the occasional coastal oak tree, the beautiful old trees that had survived drought, fire, and, the worst offender of them all, sprawling suburbia, one of the few indigenous trees to do so.

Not many minutes later he drove down the steep grade into Camarillo, felt the cool sea air, and drove through the lovely eucalyptus grove that, to him, always marked the beginning of the coastal part of the journey though the ocean was still several miles away. Oxnard, Ventura,

Carpinteria sped by, the steep hills on his right, the unlimited horizon of the ocean on his left, a flat vista punctuated by the tall offshore oil derricks scattered up and down the coastline.

After the polo fields, the greens of the shrubs and trees deepened and he entered the outskirts of Montecito. He turned off at Olive Mill Road and continued up into the rolling hills dense with oaks and eucalyptus hiding lavish mansions. He came to Running Springs Road, found his way to number 11, and turned into a winding overgrown driveway at the end of which was a huge expanse of weed-filled lawn ending in a French château–style house, one that had obviously once been grand, but no longer. His car crunched over the gravel in the courtyard and he saw five other cars, one of which was Lydia's.

The front door was open, so he walked into the entry hall, which was empty except for a table, a gilt mirror, and a pile of empty cardboard cartons. From there, off to his right through a pair of glass French doors with elegant brass handles, he could see eight people, all with their backs toward him, inspecting the shelves of books. In the middle of the room, standing at the edge of a vast carved table, a legal-size pad of paper and a pen in her hand, was Lydia. Her long blond hair was tied back in an uneasy compromise between femininity and all-business, which indeed she was. She beckoned him and he went directly to her. She stooped, reached under the table, and pulled out a carton on which—he recognized her hand—was written "SOLD." She flipped it open and Jeffrey could see it contained about twenty-five books, almost all by Ross Macdonald and a few by his wife, Margaret Millar.

"All firsts?"

"Yes."

"How come you didn't mention them to me before?"

"That's just it. I made one last check of the basement just before we opened up the place this afternoon and found these in a carton in a storage room. The old lady apparently liked mysteries, read them but didn't want them on her shelves—and obviously wouldn't part with them either."

"Wow."

"I went through them quickly. All in fine condition, a few nicks and tears in the dust jackets, nothing bad at all. Several of them are signed."

"What should I offer?"

"They're not on the inventory, but I think you ought to play fair for the library at least. Look them over."

Jeffrey started to put the carton on the table and empty the books, thought better of it, and squatted down on the floor. A lot of the early, hard-to-find books were there—*Blue City, Black Money, The Barbarous Coast*—as well as some of the best-known—*The Drowning Pool, The Far Side of the Dollar, The Goodbye Look, The Underground Man.* About half were signed. Jeffrey guessed it was done at a local bookstore by a dutiful Ken Millar, who wrote as Macdonald and was known and admired for his support of the local literary establishment. His wife's books—she had preceded him in print and was considered to be among the best of the practitioners of the genre, along with her husband—were fewer but nevertheless rare enough and in good condition, too: *The Weak-Eyed Bat, Hall of Eyes, Fire Will Freeze,* among the earlier books, and *A Stranger in My Grave, How Like an Angel, The Murder of Miranda,* among her more recent. None of hers were signed.

He grinned as he packed up the carton. "I'll take it. How much?"

"They're down as miscellaneous titles, not displayed, so they aren't particularly valuable. At least not to the library, and we already have a big Macdonald collection."

"So?"

"Two hundred for the lot."

"Jesus, Lydia, you'll get your head chopped off if they find out."

"They won't. It was serendipity. Neither of the other two working through the collection with me would have wanted them, nor would they have known they had a particular value. Sort of a fluke."

"Sold. And thanks. I owe you."

"I'll remember that," she said, smiling evenly.

He would pay, but not with money. Lydia extracted what she considered her due in one way or another, and it was because of moments like this that he let her. For $200 he was buying a carton of books he could resell to collectors and dealers for up to $2,500. He had just made a killing. Lydia knew that as well, but she had no idea how much.

Jeffrey stuffed the books back under the table, stood, and started for the shelves at the far end of the room, intending to begin there and work his way around. As he started off, he noticed one of the people invited by UCLA was Victor Dreyfus, who was going through the books, notepad in hand, with two volumes stuck under his arm. Jeffrey stepped in his direction, tapped him on the shoulder, and greeted him.

"Ah, Jeffrey! I thought I'd see you here. It's a good collection."

"Anything special in it for you?"

"Several things. For me. So far, though, nothing for Mr. Craventon."

"Too bad." Jeffrey smiled. "I'm looking for the two Steinbecks and also for the two Chandlers. I'll probably find some of them within the week."

"Good, good. He'll appreciate that."

"I'll see you before you leave," Jeffrey said, turning to start his own inspection of the books. He had to think a second before he realized why Dreyfus was one of the special few invited: Craventon was a big supporter of the UCLA library, a big wheel in the Friends of the Library, and Dreyfus was his man. Jeffrey also remembered that a big library function, a cocktail party of some sort, was about to take place at Craventon's. No doubt one of those charitable functions where an odd book disappeared from time to time. He had an invitation at home on his desk, had yet to decide whether to go, and now that he thought of it he decided he'd skip the party. Jeffrey was not good at large gatherings, or at least did not consider himself to be so, and thus tended to avoid them. Still, it might be good for business. He wavered a moment, then postponed any decision and headed for the row of shelves that from a distance he could see contained modern fiction.

He was so engrossed in his examination of them that he stepped in front of another dealer, excused himself, and looked back at the shelves before it hit him. When it did, the look on his face was one of such astonishment that even the object of it had to comment.

"My but you look surprised to see me, Mr. Dean," Narib Zaki said politely but with an unmistakable edge.

"I—I—for some reason thought you had gone back to London."

"Oh?"

Because Ketchum said you were leaving Monday, Jeffrey wanted to say, and that was yesterday. He said it would end yesterday, that I'd be through. Jeffrey wanted to let out a long string of obscenities, to clench his fists in frustration, to somehow vent the growing fear inside him. Instead, he got another surprise.

"Jeffrey, this is the man I told you about," Lydia, the librarian as hostess, stepped up to announce. "Jeffrey, I'd like you to meet Narib Zaki." She smiled politely. "Mr. Zaki, this is Jeffrey Dean."

"We've met," Jeffrey said tersely.

"At the book fair," Zaki said, turning on a big smile for his hostess. "It hadn't occurred to me. The two of you are related, yes?"

"We *were* related," she said cheerfully, "and now we're friends."

"I see."

"What is it you're getting for the UCLA library, Mr. Zaki?"

"They've asked me to look out for some of the romantic poets. Shelley in particular."

"Well," Jeffrey said, his tone carefully cynical, "that ought to be interesting to see."

Lydia, who knew Jeffrey was sarcastic only when he was angry, and that anger was difficult to provoke in him, looked undecided for a moment, then quickly redirected Zaki. "Mr. Zaki, there are some good English editions of modern literature over here I'd like to show you," she said, shooting Jeffrey a glance as she took Zaki by the arm and escorted him across the room. As they walked away, Jeffrey could see Lydia, who was five-foot-ten, towering over Zaki, who was smiling at her in such a way that Jeffrey, who thought he was beyond jealousy about Lydia, imagined them in an obscene embrace and turned away in anger, as though putting his back to them would banish the picture from his mind.

"What was *that* all about?" Lydia was back and Jeffrey

could see that Zaki was feigning an interest in the books across the room.

"He was trying to sell a couple of forged Steinbeck inscriptions at the fair. In my old copies of *Cannery Row* and *Sweet Thursday.*"

"Swell. And you had to expose him, right?" Her sarcasm was subtle but unmistakable.

"Right, Lydia. And I'm glad I did. It seems Mr. Zaki is a good bit more than a bookdealer from London. Let's say he's not the sort of person I should think UCLA would want to be affiliated with."

"What do you mean? Dave Grayson asked me to bring him here and said Zaki was going to do some buying for us in London." Dave Grayson was the head UCLA librarian and Lydia's boss, the man charged with running what was generally acknowledged as one of the four or five best university libraries in the United States. He was an adroit, political man who left the academics to their pursuits while he built his empire. He was also Lydia's lover, or so Jeffrey suspected.

"Who sent Zaki to him?"

She was careful to keep her back to Zaki and to speak in a whisper that was close to a hiss. "I don't know. Christ, what is this all about? I don't want you making trouble for him, because it'll just make a mess for me."

"Remember Dave Ketchum? The CIA agent I met in the Dominican Republic? The stuff in Cuba?"

"Good God."

"Right. Well, old Dave reappeared as if by magic to tell me that Zaki is an agent for Colonel Qaddafi and the Libyans."

"Good God," she said again. "What has this got to do with you? Why did Ketchum come to you?"

"I'll explain later. Where is Zaki staying?"

"I don't know. He met me at UCLA this afternoon and I drove him up here."

"Find out, will you? He was at the Ambassador, but I suspect he's probably moved. He was supposed to leave for London yesterday."

"Well, I've known he was coming up here with me for over a week."

"Ketchum got some bad information."

"What then?"

"When you find out, call me. And be very careful. Don't let him know where you live or anything."

"What do I tell Dave Grayson?"

"For now, nothing. Call me tonight when you get home."

She looked up at him with a mixture of curiosity and disbelief. "You amaze me," she told him. "I'm supposed to know all about you. I am part of the past. I was married to you when you knew Ketchum, but I had no idea you"—she didn't know quite what to say, could not begin to articulate her curiosity, did not want to appear too surprised—"were still in touch with them."

"I wasn't. It was all in my long-ago file."

"Oh."

He pulled a checkbook out of the breast pocket of his sport coat and wrote out a check to the UCLA library for $200.

"Is that all you're buying? You haven't even looked through the other books here."

"Those," he said, nodding his head at the carton of Macdonalds and Millars, "more than make my week. And I've got to make a telephone call. Right away."

* * *

He drove down to the small shopping center near the foot of Olive Mill Road and found a pay telephone in the drugstore. He pulled the number Ketchum had given him out of his wallet and made the call. It was answered immediately by a woman who simply said, "Hello," and when he asked for Ketchum, she asked who was calling. She said no more and did not come on the line again, though the call itself went through three more women, each asking the same question, before Ketchum himself came on the line.

"What's up?" Ketchum sounded uneasy.

"Zaki's up. He's here in Santa Barbara. At a book sale with my ex-wife."

"Son of a bitch."

"You said he was leaving Monday and I'd hear from you if he didn't leave."

"He left. My man tailed him into the TWA departure lounge for the nonstop to London Monday afternoon."

"Well, your man didn't see him get on the plane and leave then, did he? And Zaki obviously knows he's being tailed." Jeffrey's head felt light, his pulse quickened, and his hand shook slightly.

"Where are you now?"

Jeffrey told him. There was a pause, and then Ketchum began shooting questions at him.

"Where is Zaki staying?"

"She doesn't know. I asked her to find out."

"Where did she pick him up?"

"At the UCLA library. He drove himself there."

"What kind of car are they in?"

"Volvo. Two-door. Black. 'Seventy-eight, I think."

"License?"

"I don't know."

"Can you go back and get it?"

"Yeah."

"Do. Then call this number back. They'll be waiting for your call. We'll catch up with them on their way into town. The highway patrol can spot them for us and we'll get a tail on Zaki, or we'll get them at UCLA. Sorry to trouble you, old boy, but these things happen. I'll be in touch tomorrow."

It was 10:30 that night before Lydia called, and when she did he was sitting in a chair, drowsing, an open book in his lap and a half-finished glass of wine on the table beside him. Zaki, she said with a small laugh, appeared to lose interest in her as soon as Jeffrey showed up, and as a result the dinner had been more a polite ritual than a social occasion. When she asked, Zaki told her he was staying with friends. She had left him in the visitors' parking lot a little after 9:30.

"Did you see anyone else in the parking lot? Did any other car start up and leave after Zaki?"

"I left ahead of him. Why?"

"They were going to put a tail on him."

"They?"

"Ketchum. His people." Then he told her everything.

X

WHEN HE HAD decided to go to Santa Barbara and broken the date with Rachel they had agreed to meet the next night, Wednesday, at his place. It turned out she had to attend an afternoon conference at UCLA, a gathering of English professors for a lecture she wanted to hear, and she had suggested they meet afterward.

"Red or white?" she had asked, assuming his earlier offer.

"Neither. We're going out and I've got plenty of wine here."

He had looked forward to the evening, all the more so when David Ketchum called late in the afternoon. The call had caused a pleasant anticipation to become something more, an escape, a way to distance himself from a certain unpleasant reality. The reality was that Zaki remained in town and Ketchum wanted Jeffrey to stay available. The tail had picked him up at UCLA and followed him to the Beverly Wilshire Hotel—not quite staying with friends, Jeffrey thought to himself—and was close behind him wherever he went. Ketchum reported Zaki had spent most of his day going to used-book stores along Westwood Boulevard, and nothing much else had happened. Still. The contrast between a seemingly benign bookdealer going about his business and that same person as an agent for Muammar el-Qaddafi—Libya's leader and a fanatic of the worst sort—was a sharp one, almost irreconcilable.

"What next?" Jeffrey had asked Ketchum.

"Be ready. We're working without a net on this one, too. He's up to something, but we don't know what. If I need your help, I'll be in touch."

"I think I've done all that I can do," Jeffrey said. He hoped he had done all he was going to have to do. He had been reluctant from the start and now his desire to get out was getting stronger by the minute.

"You never know," Ketchum said back to him. "And for anything you do now, we'll make some new arrangement. Your original work for us, the things we agreed on, is finished."

"Well, inflation just hit again," Jeffrey told him.

"We'll take care of it if it comes up," Ketchum assured him. "I must say your purity isn't quite what it used to be."

"Nothing's what it used to be. I'm no longer Caesar's wife and I don't even have to be seen to be Caesar's wife—if you get what I mean. Since I have no choice, I'm making the best deal I can."

"I get it," Ketchum went on, suddenly more business-like than usual. "What we've got to get is his connection here. I'll buy his coming to the book fair, but that isn't all or he'd be long gone by now. He's waiting for someone or something."

"Hope you find it."

After the call, Jeffrey filled several more orders, made a couple of telephone calls, then took a quick run up to Sherman Oaks Park and back, just long enough to work up a good sweat. He shaved, showered, and dressed, then changed his mind and dressed again. He was amused at the thought that he was trying to make such a good impression on Rachel. It had been a long time. He finally settled on gray slacks, blue shirt, a red and blue striped tie, and a blue blazer. He was knotting his tie when there was a knock at the door. He looked at his watch. She was early.

"I was nearby and I thought I'd stop in. I've got something to show you." It wasn't Rachel, it was Walter Rigby, a book scout Jeffrey had known since he had gone into business. Rigby was an eccentric who lived alone out in the desert and had turned a lifetime of reading into a business. He spent most of his time on the road going from used-book store to used-book store, from garage sale to Goodwill stores, where, Jeffrey assumed, he also bought his clothes.

"What've you got, Walter?"

"Look." Rigby pulled two books wrapped in newspaper out of the dirty canvas bag slung over his shoulder. Jeffrey unwrapped them and looked them over. One was a first edition of Hemingway's *For Whom the Bell Tolls* with a tattered jacket. Jeffrey checked for the 1940 copyright.

"I'll give you thirty dollars for it," Jeffrey told Rigby. He knew he could resell it immediately for $55.

He was unwrapping the second book when there was another knock at the door. This time it was Rachel. He took her coat and introduced her to Walter Rigby.

"We're doing some business. I'll be just a second. If you'd like, listen in."

Rachel nodded.

The second book was a copy of Tennessee Williams's *The Glass Menagerie,* originally published in 1945. This, too, was a first and was also in slightly tattered condition.

"Would you take fifty dollars?"

"Yeah, sure." Rigby was a man of few words in a business populated with fast talkers. "And here, have a look at this one." This time the book he pulled from his bag was carefully wrapped in plastic.

Jeffrey let out a low whistle when he saw the book. Rachel leaned across the desk to look at it, too. It was a copy of the 1914 first edition of Edgar Rice Burroughs's *Tarzan of the Apes.* Jeffrey opened it and whistled again when he saw the inscription: "To Alma, who by admiring this book honors its author." It was signed and dated in 1917.

"Where'd you get this?" It was not customary to ask book scouts where they found books unless they were particularly valuable. This one was valuable indeed.

"Outside of Oklahoma City, at the auction of a farm some family had lost."

Jeffrey did not ask what Rigby had paid for it. He knew better. He imagined very little. "How much do you want for it, Walter?"

"Three thousand."

"I can't swing it myself right now, but I think I can turn it around real fast. Will you give me a couple minutes?"

"I'll wait here."

Jeffrey motioned to Rachel and she followed him from the store into the apartment.

"Burroughs collectors are avid and then some," he told her. "I know a man who'd kill to have this. It's too much for me to keep and hold out for a high price, but I can broker it right away for a five-hundred-dollar profit."

"That's where you've got it on me. I don't know the collectors out here."

"You will," Jeffrey said as he looked up a number on the Rolodex he had brought with him from his desk. He dialed a number and within less than a minute had resold the book for a $500 profit. The question was in Rachel's look, though she was too polite to ask it.

"A television producer," Jeffrey answered. "Nice guy. He's got two hit series on and now that he has money, he's building one hell of a collection."

Jeffrey wrote a check to Rigby for all three books, thanked him, and showed him to the door. Rachel turned to inspect the books in the locked glass cabinet. Jeffrey took out a key and opened it for her. She bent slightly and began reading titles, and as she did she came close to him and he could smell her perfume again, the same scent that had lingered so pleasantly in his car.

"Nice."

"I'll say."

"I meant your perfume. What is it?"

She stood, turned toward him slightly, and smiled. "An indulgence."

"Never heard of it."

"That's not its name, that's what it is. It's called 'Giorgio.' "

"Nice. Or did I say that already?"

"Twice is nice." She turned back to the books. "Well. This one is obviously the real thing," she said, pulling Steinbeck's *Sweet Thursday* from the shelf. She opened it, read the inscription, then closed it. "Too bad he didn't date it."

"I know." He also knew not to tell her that this was actually one of the forgeries she had asked about a few days before. It was too complicated. It made him seem as though he were much more than he was, and it was against his nature to embellish anything but the humorous. That, and in something like this—which was never what it seemed to be anyway, and could turn ugly without notice—her ignorance would be her safety. Just in case.

"Good copy, though," he said. "They're scarce."

"A lot of Vonnegut, I see."

"Terrific writer. Crazy and humane all at once. One of my personal favorites."

"Mine, too."

"That's a fairly complete collection," he told her. "Missing only a couple of English editions and some of the ephemera."

"Hmm."

"The American firsts are all inscribed."

She pulled one out, a neatly boxed copy of the bound galleys of *Player Piano,* his first novel, opened the box and read the inscription.

"Inscribed to you?" She seemed surprised. He nodded. "All of them?"

"All of them. He's a friend."

"Some friend."

"Yeah."

"That gives you an unfair advantage."

"I know. They're not for sale anyway."

"Nevertheless I'll bet they've attracted a few offers."

"A few."

"My aunt says that dealers should not be collectors, too."

"There are some who see a sort of ethical problem with it. I'm not one of them. For one thing, I'd never compete with a customer for a book. That I think would be unfair."

"Uhhm."

She continued to look at the books, then came across the room and sat on the edge of Jeffrey's desk as he lounged casually in its chair, his feet up on the desk. She glanced down and saw the large, engraved Friends of the UCLA Library invitation and pointed at it. "Going?"

"I doubt it."

"I am."

"Oh?"

"Why not? Sounds nice. Might be good for business."

"I can be persuaded to reconsider. But first dinner."

The process of selecting a restaurant became a complicated one, in part because Jeffrey suggested so many and in part because Rachel was slow to decide and quick to defer to him. Finally they agreed on Casa Verde, an old and popular Mexican restaurant on Beverly Boulevard frequented by actors, politicians, and writers.

Jeffrey opened the sun roof of his maroon Honda Prelude to the cool night breeze and drove up the steep hill to Mulholland and then, with the lights of the city glittering on either side of them, east along Mulholland. He slowed to point out a favorite graffito of his sprayed on a tall cement retaining wall: "Hollywood: Hare Today, Bugs Tomorrow." She read it, thought for a second, and then laughed. "That's how it goes."

"Or as Vonnegut says, 'So It Goes.'"

"So it goes, doc." She laughed again.

It was a clear, late winter night and it seemed to him as though some great, generous deity had dumped treasures of brightly colored jewels across the land and then made electricity to light them. It was a sight he had seen hundreds of times and one that never failed to move him. Its vivid beauty made the pall of smog at other times of the year all the more horrible, because he was a man whose philosophy was always for what could be, not for what was.

He turned onto the steep curves of Benedict Cañon, spinning quickly down the other side of the Santa Monica Mountains. It was a drive he made often but one that he could see made her slightly uncomfortable.

"Am I driving too fast for you?"

"No. I've never gotten used to canyons out here. I used to get carsick when I was a kid and I'm still scared I'll get sick."

"You barf in my car, you clean it up."

"I always hit the person I'm sitting next to," came the quick answer.

Jeffrey slowed slightly. "You really all right?"

"Fine. I find driving canyons easier than being the passenger."

"Me too."

They crossed through the residential area of Beverly Hills, then east on Santa Monica Boulevard to Beverly, and on to the restaurant, which was located in the midst of a series of interior-design and furniture stores, an old, run-down part of town suddenly made chic by the overlay of fashionable businesses. Instant glamor, and in its midst a reborn restaurant that had been fighting for its survival only a few years before.

They waited at the bar, he with a cold Carta Blanca and she with a margarita which, he could see from her wince when she tasted it, was thickly laced with lime and tequila.

"Just another one of your average big drinkers," he teased her.

"You got a torn T-shirt and a TV set to go with that beer?"

They began with guacamole—Jeffrey insisted he could make better, and she declined to dare him or even to challenge him—then ordered cheese enchiladas, chicken tacos, rice, beans, and a chili relleno, which they decided to share.

"Once again, into the breach," she said as dinner was served.

A sea change was occurring between them. The swift tide of sexual interest began to run through their thoughts and their looks at one another. She chatted on, a bit self-consciously, and the more she talked the less he said and the more he simply watched her with deepening interest. In answer to his questions, she described in some detail the lecture she had attended that afternoon, a two-hour session on American expatriate writers in Paris during the 1920s.

"Well," she said, scooping up the last of her enchilada. "You probably think I eat like this all the time."

"I've only seen you eat twice."

"That's what I mean. But it isn't so. Actually, I—well, as you can see, I do like to eat. You do, too. I eat a small breakfast, usually no lunch, and I go to an exercise class nearly every day."

"Me too."

"The meals or the exercise class?"

"I eat lightly during the day. And I run. No class."

Her right index finger was tapping lightly at the end of the knife, a utensil seldom needed in Mexican restaurants but offered nonetheless as a concession to gringo customs. He looked at her, then slid his left hand lightly across the table and took her hand in his.

"As you were saying . . ." he teased.

"Dammit."

"What's the matter?"

"I always do that. Ever since I was a child. Whenever I get the least bit nervous, I talk a lot. I just go on. . . ."

"Do I make you nervous?"

"No, no, not at all. That's not what I mean." She did not say what it was that was making her nervous. It was clear enough.

"When I get nervous," he told her, "I'm just the opposite. I don't say much at all and I tend to pull back and watch."

Afterward, they walked briefly up and down Beverly Boulevard, looking with some interest into the interior-design stores with their windows full of elegant antiques and the latest modern furniture in which it seemed to Jeffrey the Italians had the best.

"Living well is the best revenge," she said, leaning in and touching her body lightly against his.

"Yeah," he said, taking her hand and pulling her closer, "but you've got to wonder if it is really comfortable. I mean, can you imagine sitting in a chair like that?" he said, pointing directly at a hand-carved Chinese chair with its straight back and hard arms and inlay of mother-of-pearl.

"Only on one condition."

"What's that?"

"That I don't have to sit there for more than a minute."

They came to a big window display of a bedroom, all plush and apricot, with throw pillows stacked everywhere and great phallic cacti sticking up out of large round clay pots.

"Which reminds me," he said.

"Of what?" she shot back, barely concealing her grin.

"How about we go back to my place, have a drink, and play a record?"

"How about," she said simply, nodding in agreement.

Going home, he drove out Sunset and at the Beverly Hills Hotel turned back up Benedict Cañon and began negotiating the first turns along the steeply climbing, twisting road. It was, as usual at this time of night on a weekday, virtually empty of traffic and at the first big curve a large deer darted across the road in front of them, causing them both to exclaim in pleasure at the sight of the graceful animal, a hopeful reminder that the constant erosion of the hills by the homes always being built had not chased the natural inhabitants away forever.

As he slowed for the deer, he looked into his rearview mirror and could see a car approaching, but since it was well behind him and it was impossible for anyone to pass on the road, he did not look again for several seconds. When he did, the two headlights had separated somewhat and he realized there were two motorcycles behind him. That, too, was not unusual for it was just after midnight and the midnight drag races—illegal and dangerous— would soon be starting up along Mulholland.

He had once counted the tennis courts he passed going up through the countrylike canyon, and was about to tell her there were twelve at last count when one of the motorcyclists pulled in front of him and then slowed slightly.

At the first of a series of steep curves, one where the horseshoe was narrow, nearly turning back on itself, and the drop off the side of the mountain was steep, he slowed. As he did, the other motorcycle came past, but instead of going on, it stayed exactly at his side and began to edge toward him.

It struck him all at once that something was terribly wrong, and just as it did—he yelled at Rachel to make sure her seat belt was fastened—the motorcycle tried to force him off the side of the hill. He looked down, knew they could not survive the fall, so he slammed his car back into the motorcycle, hitting it with his left front fender and part of his door. The crunch was thick and deadening.

"What—what?" Rachel could not understand what was happening.

"Just hang on. I'm sorry. I never thought they'd do this. . . ."

"They?"

"Hang on!" he yelled as he slammed the Honda against the cycle once again. The lead cycle was starting and stopping, nearly forcing him to rear-end it and distracting him from the machine trying to run him off the road. He knew for certain this was not the sort of cyclists-attack-motorist thing he read of in the papers, and it was not a planned rape or anything like that. It was the books, the people Ketchum was after, and he wondered if he was about to die without knowing exactly who was trying to kill him—and why.

"They? What do you mean *they?"*

"I'll explain." He was about to say "I'm sorry" again when both motorcycles shoved into the small car, sending it off the edge of the highway and onto the rocky edge, dangerously close to the steep drop. Rachel screamed, and her terror gave him an extra shot of adrenaline, enabling him to turn the car back onto the road.

Now the twist in the road moved them fully around, putting the driver's side of the car along the edge of the precipice and Rachel in the passenger seat against the side of the mountain. The two cyclists quickly changed sides and began slamming against Rachel's side of the car. Jeffrey could see several hundred yards down the side of the hill into the backyard of a big house with a pool and a tennis court, and he hoped they landed in the pool and not on the court.

He slammed on the brakes, nearly sending one of the cyclists off the side of the hill. Instead, the driver, who was wearing so much protective gear neither Jeffrey nor Rachel could see his face, twisted in the dry, clay soil, spun dangerously, then put out a heavy boot to right himself and rejoin the chase.

"Speed up. Maybe we can hit him," she yelled, and Jeffrey hit the gas pedal, but the car, with its small engine working up a steep hill, barely moved ahead. Then Jeffrey suddenly remembered a movie he had seen long ago in which the hero began swerving his car as a kind of diversionary action and, doing so, saved the day. Jeffrey swung hard, hitting the lead motorcyclist and, in the process, knocking out the Honda's right headlight. The crunch of the impact and the shatter of glass was met with another crunch from the other cycle.

"Christ, now I can't see!" Jeffrey yelled, twisting the car still again, watching as the road curved sharply once more, again changing the drop from his side of the car to hers. The drop itself increased as they climbed to the top of the hill and Mulholland.

They sped past a starkly modern wood and cement house built on the side of the hill, Jeffrey now on the wrong side of the road, trying to lead the motorcycles into a head-on collision except that he could see no headlights bouncing off the mountains coming at them.

Her scream was sudden, and she also managed to say, "There's another one on my side. Oh, God, oh, God," just as Jeffrey looked up and saw a third motorcycle had joined them, this one riding the narrow dirt shoulder between Jeffrey's battered Honda and the long, rocky drop.

It sped past them, missing them neatly, and began chasing the lead cycle.

Then he saw another—a fourth—motorcycle, this one speeding toward them as they came up from the tight turn and crossed onto the wider stretch of Mulholland. It skidded as it turned and began to try and force its way between the cycle and the Honda.

"Oh, my God," Jeffrey moaned, but as he did his terror began to mix with relief because he suddenly understood the two new cyclists were not trying to run him off the road and were instead coming to his defense.

He raced through a red light at the corner of Beverly Glen and Mulholland, barely missing a car crossing the intersection and sending it hurtling up the lawn divider.

A third cyclist now joined the chase on Jeffrey's and Rachel's side—they assumed the unknown riders were their allies—and for the first time Jeffrey felt the advantage begin to shift toward him. His two tormentors made one more try to send him hurtling off the edge of the mountain and down into the San Fernando Valley, which twinkled and shone in the clear night below them.

He glanced down and saw his speedometer register eighty miles an hour, a speed he would never have thought possible on such a wildly twisting road. He turned left away from the drop and hit the cyclist on his rear tire.

One of the new motorcyclists pulled ahead and tried to force one of the other big bikes off the road. In the roar of five cycles and the high whine of the straining Honda, Jeffrey could not discern the sound of friend or foe, and in the darkness he could not see who was which. He was trying to figure out what to do next when two of the motorcycles suddenly shifted down and roared away from the other three, who did not give chase. Jeffrey was so startled, so relieved, he slowed and started for the side of the road, bouncing wildly over several big rocks, slamming their heads against the roof of the car.

"You all right?" he asked her, but he could see that the color was drained from her face and that she was about to be sick. He started to open his door, but the impact of the motorcycles had sealed it shut. He reached across to open hers, but it was sealed, too. Suddenly a leather-covered arm and hand reached down from the outside, pulled on her door, and it flew open. The man's clothing and his size frightened her, and as he reached in to pull her out, she struck his hand and grabbed for Jeffrey.

"Hey, lady, it's all right. We're the guys who helped chase them away."

She nodded, not quite believing, then unhooked her belt and allowed herself to be helped from the car. Another leather-covered arm and glove began tugging at Jeffrey's door, but it would not give and he was forced to crawl over the shift and across the other seat to get out. When he stood, he felt the rush of blood from his head and suddenly felt nauseated. He looked around and saw Rachel, her hands set defiantly on her hips, her posture an angry, frightened question mark. He took several deep breaths, then bent over, placing his hands on his knees so that the blood would enter his head again.

"Who were your friends?" one of the cyclists asked, removing his helmet to reveal the tousled blond hair and acne of an adolescent.

"I don't know," Jeffrey lied. "They were trying to force us off the side of the hill. Hey, thanks. If you guys hadn't come along . . ."

"We were up here for the midnight races," another of

them said. "We're into sport, not killing." He paused and then added, "Even if our sport is illegal."

"Yeah. I've heard about guys racing up here."

"That's us."

He could see Rachel was listening to everything, tears of anger and fear brimming in her eyes. He pulled her to him gently.

"Help is on the way. It's okay now."

"I don't understand. Who's *they?* What is all of this? My God, they tried to kill us!"

The headlights from the three motorcycles formed a kind of circle, and they stood just outside the edge of it. The three boys stood beside their cycles. They all had their helmets off now and Jeffrey could see they were all young, all wondering what was going on, and every one of them pleased as hell with what they had done.

"Hey, how do I thank you guys?" Jeffrey asked.

"Buy us a six-pack of beer sometime," the blond boy said.

"You're too young to drink."

"He isn't," one of the boys said, pointing to the cyclist in the middle.

"Ah, well, then. Here. Let me give you some beer money as a kind of small thank-you for a very goddamn big favor." He reached into his pocket, pulled out his money clip, and began to peel off some bills.

"Hey, man. No," the blond boy said. "I was just joking."

Jeffrey, who by this time had no perception at all about who was friend or who was foe, looked up, confusion showing on his face.

"We saw them from up here," one of the boys, a dark, good-looking Mexican kid, said. "From along Beverly

Glen where you can look down Benedict. Shit, they were
determined to send you off the side of the hill. So we decided to help."

"Good Samaritans," the oldest boy said to them.

Two more cyclists and three drag racers roared by on
their way across the Mulholland Midnight Racetrack.
"We were waiting our turn," he said. "Tonight's our night
to stand guard while the other guys race."

Jeffrey tried to hand the blond boy the money, but he
refused again and began to climb back on his bike. The
others did the same.

"Start your car to make sure it works," the older one
told Jeffrey.

Jeffrey looked down at his new car. It was all but
demolished, its fender, doors, and hood caved in and bent,
with one headlight dangling down nearly to the fender.
He crawled back across the seat, managed a small contor-
tion to get himself across the gearshift, then turned on the
ignition. The tiny Honda engine gave a groan of protest,
but it started right up.

"Remember Pearl Harbor!" one of the boys yelled from
behind him as the other two laughed. The blond boy
helped Rachel into the car, then carefully closed the door,
latching it lightly so that she would be able to open it
again.

"You got far to go?" he asked them again.

"No, not far at all."

"Thank you," Rachel said to them. "Thank you very
much."

"Tell you what," Jeffrey said, trying still to impose
some small measure of order out of all that was going on.
"Why don't I drop back up here in a night or so and bring
the beer?"

"That's okay with us," said one of the boys—Jeffrey couldn't tell which one because they all had their helmets on now—"only don't bring your friends."

"Yeah. I don't want to know your friends," another said, his voice bouncing around in the hollow of his helmet.

"Neither do I," Rachel agreed.

Jeffrey turned the car around, headed back down Mulholland until Beverly Glen, then turned left and drove down the hill. At the corner of Ventura Boulevard, he pulled into a gas station. "I've got to use the phone," he said.

"Why here? Your place is just down the block," she protested.

"I'm not so sure it's any safer there than it was up on the hill," he said. "I want somebody to make sure for us."

"What do you mean? What is all of this?" She was somewhere between anger and desperation, and not sure which to express. "I think you owe me an explanation."

"Help is on the way. So is an explanation."

He was on the telephone several minutes, and she saw him twice pound his fist against the plastic cover of the phone, and once heard his voice rise but could not hear what he said.

"Let's go find an all-night coffee shop," he said when he came back. He seemed to have regained his composure. "We're to wait an hour before going back to my apartment." He stopped, waited a few seconds, and then went on. "And I want you to stay with me. For a little while anyway. I want to help you get over this."

He waited until they were seated in a booth at the back of a brightly lit Denny's open to provide coffee and light to the last of the night people before they left for home or work. It was not quite 2:00 A.M. They both ordered hot tea, and he waited until the waitress had served them and had walked away before starting to talk.

"You remember that inscribed Steinbeck you pulled off my shelf tonight?"

She nodded.

"It was the forged copy." He began the story there and worked his way back, stopping several times to make sure he was telling it right, and aware from time to time that Ketchum would probably have preferred he say as little as possible. But now she was in danger, too, and she was entitled to a share of Jeffrey's small amount of information and rapidly growing realization that he knew practically nothing at all.

"Who do you think it was tonight?" she finally asked.

"Zaki's people."

"Who else?"

"I wish I knew."

XI

"GOD DAMN YOU! You lying bastard!" Jeffrey yelled, his face red with rage, his anger so out of control he jumped from the barstool in his kitchen with such force that it clattered to the floor and he did not notice.

"I didn't lie," Ketchum corrected. "I just didn't tell you."

"Look. You mean to tell me the guy who shot at me Sunday morning was one of yours?"

"That's what I said."

"You sons of bitches have all the moral principles of vipers," he said, shaking his head in disbelief.

Rachel, still trying to grasp all that was going on, interrupted. "Why did you do that?" she asked Ketchum.

"When Jeffrey turned up the forged Steinbecks, one of my men was nearby keeping an eye on Zaki. When I discovered it was Jeffrey, it was an ideal situation. We had known one another before, had in fact worked together on occasion—"

"Shit," Jeffrey interrupted.

Ketchum went on as though he hadn't heard him. "And I knew if I asked him to help us smoke out Zaki, he'd refuse."

"Right," Jeffrey interrupted again.

Ketchum shrugged. He was wearing a sport coat that clashed violently with his trousers, and Rachel, who was not used to Ketchum's sartorial disasters and had not yet learned he used his own bad taste as a kind of camouflage, if indeed camouflage can be so glaring, looked at him with obvious curiosity.

"So one of my people went out and shot some blanks at Jeffrey to get him worried."

"I felt the goddamn bullets go by," Jeffrey insisted.

"You felt the paper wadding, that's all. And if it'd hit you, you'd have had a sting for about half an hour. No harm done."

"My ass! No harm? What in hell do you call this?" he asked, swinging his arm in a small arc to encompass himself and Rachel and, by inference, the battered Honda downstairs.

"A miscalculation on our part. I'm sorry."

"*Our?*" Jeffrey shouted, turning to Rachel to make his point. "Have you noticed that when big hero Ketchum does something, it is all in the first person singular, but if something goes wrong, the plural sets in? It's just like all those assholes in the CIA. They pass the buck."

"Look. Plain and simple," Ketchum said, his patience stretching to an infinite horizon, "we had no idea, no indication at all, what we were dealing with here. I had a routine request to track Zaki, to find out who his contacts are, to see if Qaddafi might have local agents. There is a lot of valuable—and secret—technology for sale here in California and we keep an eye on it. That's what we were worried about. Obviously there's a lot more going on."

"Obviously," Rachel agreed, her sarcasm unmistakable.

"I'll put a tail on you, Jeff. You'll be all right."

"What about her?" Jeffrey asked, nodding at Rachel.

"I'll put one on her, too. For a couple of days. I don't think they're interested in her. I doubt they've even seen her clearly enough. It was dark in the hills."

"You're full of it, Ketchum. When they came at us in the hills, they knew where to find us. That means they followed us to the restaurant. That means they saw us walking on Beverly Boulevard. That means they saw her."

Ketchum nodded.

"Jesus," Rachel said with such intensity both men looked up. "I don't believe this is happening."

"Well, it *is* happening," Jeffrey said to her. "Look, I want her protected. Lydia, too. I want them both out of it. Now. *Right* now."

"Lydia?" Rachel asked.

"My ex-wife. She had contact with Zaki through the library at UCLA."

"She did? How'd she do that?" Rachel was thoroughly confused. The simple addition of one more encounter and one more person was too much to comprehend just now.

"Zaki somehow got a recommendation to Lydia's boss at the library. She's a librarian there. He asked her to take Zaki along to Santa Barbara. That's when we found out Zaki didn't leave town when the thorough, efficient, loyal, and trusting Dave Ketchum here said he was going to leave."

"We knew he was ticketed, and we saw him go into the departure lounge."

"Yeah," Jeffrey shot back, "but *we* didn't see Zaki come

back out of the departure lounge and not leave the country, did *we?*"

"No, *we* did not."

"I said I want them both protected." Jeffrey was going to keep at Ketchum until he had all the protection he was after. His fists were clenched so tight his fingers were turning white.

"All right," Ketchum said.

"Not all right. I want your promise—though I imagine it's just as worthless as everything else you've been saying—that both women will be watched until Zaki leaves the country."

"Or until I'm sure they're not involved in any way."

"No, goddammit. I said until Zaki leaves the country."

Ketchum nodded. "I promise. We'll get the car repaired right away, too."

"No you won't. You'll total it out and get me a new one."

"I don't think they allow that."

"They'll allow it. You tell them to. You're the big cheese here, Ketchum. Tell them in the first person singular."

Ketchum nodded. Jeffrey's determination was too forceful to resist. That and he needed him. He was bait, now perfectly in place.

"What now?" Rachel asked.

"We wait. Those guys on Benedict were real. They'll probably come after you again. You absolutely certain you can't identify them?"

"Absolutely," they both said at once.

"Not even enough to see whether or not they're Arabs?"

"All we could see were helmets and leather," Rachel answered.

Ketchum stood up, stretched, rubbed his neck, and made to leave. It was nearly 7:00 A.M. A shaft of sunlight brightened the living room, reflecting off the framed poster of Picasso's large self-portrait from the Museum of Modern Art's 1980 Picasso exhibition. The sunlight intensified Picasso's stare, made him seem almost a fourth presence in the room.

"Coverage starts now," Jeffrey told him.

"They're downstairs waiting. I'll take care of it. I'll check with you later, Jeff," he said as he turned to leave. Jeffrey stood and walked back into the store to open the door for him. As he stepped into the hallway, Ketchum turned to Jeffrey. "Don't tell her you're getting paid." He spoke quietly, looking down. "It shouldn't get around."

"Rachel, step in here a minute," Jeffrey said, turning angrily away from Ketchum. She immediately appeared in the doorway, and the bright light from the apartment made her a silhouette whose expression was hidden in the shadows.

"I wouldn't . . ." Ketchum said.

"Rachel, there's one thing you should know. You know I've done favors—I guess that's what you call them—in the past. I thought all of that was long ago. At the time they offered me money and I made a big thing of refusing. This time when they forced me in, he"—Jeffrey jerked his head at Ketchum but did not look at him—"he offered me money. I accepted it. He has also said I'll get more if this goes on. I'm taking it. He just told me not to tell you."

"Why not?" she asked.

"I think he's looking to get your cooperation, too, because you'll think we're a couple of innocents in this together. I'm not so innocent. I'm taking the money. Before I couldn't. Now I can."

"Well then," she said, stepping into the room, "I think I should be paid for anything I might do, don't you?"

Jeffrey laughed, and when he sensed Ketchum's discomfort, he laughed even more. "You're something," he said to her.

"I begin to see the sort of people we're dealing with here," she said. "And I think it hasn't so much to do with patriotism, good for the democracy, that sort of thing. It's a bunch of grown men competing with one another to be the best spy. A game, that's all it is. Jeffrey, if I were you I'd get it from him in writing."

"I think that's a good idea."

"That's not possible and you know it," Ketchum said, the first hint of anger ruffling his steely, calm demeanor. "You know damn well it isn't."

"Well, I don't think he can take your word to the bank," Rachel said sharply. "I think they'd throw him out."

"Look. The two of you do as I say and you'll be taken care of. You can take it or leave it," he said, looking steadily at them, "and your only problem now is you can't leave it."

Neither Jeffrey nor Rachel said anything, and Ketchum let the silence settle for a minute before he continued.

"Jeffrey, I wonder if you know what was on those film cartridges you brought out of Cuba. Really know."

"You said defense plans, a couple of military installations."

"That," Ketchum said pointedly, "was just my way of saying it."

"What was on them?" Rachel asked.

"A detailed floor plan of the safe house where Castro was living at the time. Some Cuban exiles in Miami had definite plans for Castro and we were, I guess you might say, helping out."

"Christ," Jeffrey said as a chill began its descent down his spine.

"If you'd have gotten caught with those plans, you were dead. Anybody looking at the negatives could tell what they were for."

"You son of a bitch!" Jeffrey was about to explode again.

"At the time I believe you thought you were doing something patriotic."

"Yes, I thought that."

"Well, that's what you were doing then. That's what you are doing now."

"We'll see," Jeffrey told him, his anger dissipated by a thick, all-pervading fear.

"I'll check with you tomorrow," Ketchum said as he left.

"He may be an immoral, manipulative son of a bitch," Rachel said when he was gone, "but he's a very smart immoral, manipulative son of a bitch."

"He's that, all right," Jeffrey said, walking behind her into the kitchen. "We've got to outsmart him somehow. Use him. Look. I'm sorry about all this. Really sorry."

"I had no idea. I thought you were this nice bookdealer. I mean—spies, things like that. I never would have thought . . ." her voice trailed off and he could not tell if she was merely making a statement or if it was also a judgment.

"I don't think *spy* is the right word. *Courier* maybe, something like that. We all helped in our way. We had causes then. We don't now. At least I don't."

"I do," she said. "If Zaki works for Qaddafi, I want him

stopped. Qaddafi has made it very clear what he intends
to do with people like me."

"People like you?"

"You forget I'm a Jew."

"That isn't the sort of cause I was talking about. That is
a genuine cause and has always been one. It has to do with
the right of a people to exist. I'm talking about notions of
patriotism, fear of the Communist aggressor—that sort of
thing. It's like flogging people's paranoia. It's wrong."

"You're talking theory. I tend to think of it differently,
at least as it applies to me. It's personal. I'm the first generation of my family to live in this country, and most of
my family vanished before they got here. That's how it
happened in those days. Lena. My eccentric old aunt. My
God, if you knew what she went through to get here, what
she had to give up. And she came alone and waited two
years—it's a wait I can't even begin to imagine—to see if
her husband, my uncle, would survive and find her. It is a
miracle that he did. That's the exception, that's why it's
personal to me. No matter how your family tries to assimi-
late, to be just like everybody else, an essential difference
never leaves you. It just doesn't. I am only just beginning
to realize I share some of a . . ." She didn't know what to
call it and had to search for the correct word. "I guess you
might say commitment."

"I agree. But I don't go in for any silly notions of patriotism anymore. I've become your typical cynic. I just
don't believe. Qaddafi is a crazy man and I agree he
should be stopped at whatever price. But I don't want to
be involved. I'm an amateur. So are you. I want the stopping done by people whose profession it is to deal with
men like that. Hell, send in the army! But don't send in a
couple of people like us. I do not want to be some god-

damn pawn in their games, a lure on the end of some fishing pole being jerked by someone like Ketchum."

"Ketchum is one of those people whose job it is to stop the Qaddafis of the world."

"Right. But without me. And without you."

"I don't think I'd be any good at it anyway. You obviously have had some experience."

"Not all that much and, with one notable exception, not always by choice."

"You chose to help in Cuba? That's the exception?"

"Yeah," he said, holding his arms stiff, pressing his palms against his thighs. "And I just found out what it was I was doing. Precisely what I was doing. I can't believe it."

"I can't either."

"I wonder what he isn't telling us now? I'll bet there's plenty. Zaki's got some goons working for him, we know that now for sure."

"Well," she said, looking at her watch, "I hate to end this wonderful evening, but I've got a lecture to give at ten."

Jeffrey looked up at the kitchen clock; it was nearly 8:00 A.M. "What about that drink and the music?"

"There's a wonderful old Cole Porter song about that," she said, smiling at him.

"Oh, yeah? What's that?"

"It's called 'But in the Morning, No!' "

"Outsmart him. That's it."

"What?"

"Getting through this means I'll have to be one step ahead of Ketchum."

"And about ten ahead of Zaki," she added.

XII

"GUESS WHAT!" It was Ketchum, sounding jovial as a yahoo.

"The pope resigned to become a hairdresser," Jeffrey shot back.

"You're really quick for somebody who hasn't had much sleep," Ketchum said, issuing a great guffaw that was so loud Jeffrey held the phone away from his ear and consequently did not hear what Ketchum said next.

"What?"

"I said, 'Your friend Zaki drove to San Marino and paid a visit to Alfred Craventon today.' "

"So?"

"What do you suppose their connection is?"

"Books. Craventon has a big collection."

"I knew he had big bucks from the oil business."

"He spends a few of them for books and also art. For the good of the community, of course," Jeffrey told him.

"Of course. There was another man there. We're getting an ID on him."

"Tall? Kind of formal?"

"You mean overdressed?" Ketchum, who wouldn't know overdressed even if he were wearing it, asked.

"Yeah. In his sixties. Glasses. Kind of a large nose."

"That's him. My tail said he was an old queen of some sort."

"Victor Dreyfus is his name. He's sort of a curator. Does a lot of work for Craventon, runs his collection, is his corporate do-gooder."

"Dreyfus as in *J'Accuse*?"

"Yup." Jeffrey was in his office, at his desk, leaning back in his chair, his feet up, trying to stay awake.

"Shit! They were together three hours. I thought maybe we were on to something. I kept thinking of the oil connection."

"The oil connection?"

"Libya has a lot of oil, and Craventon imports oil."

"True. Well?"

"We'll check out Craventon and this Dreyfus guy. I'll bet it's books, though. Shit."

"Nice try, Dave." Jeffrey did not mean to sound solicitous, and had in fact intended slight sarcasm. That he failed was immediately apparent because Ketchum sounded assuaged.

"I'll keep on it, Jeff. Hey, my man reports Rachel went to her exercise class this afternoon."

"So?"

"Great figure, I hear."

"Swell, Dave. I really appreciate the information." As he spoke, Jeffrey heard the thunder of fast feet on the wooden steps and looked up as Michael, his book bag still on his back, bounded in the door, waved in greeting, and kept right on going to the refrigerator, where he pulled

out a Coca-Cola. Jeffrey watched as he tossed his homework out onto the cocktail table—sending Jeffrey's carefully ordered pile of magazines skidding off the edge onto
the floor in the process—reached over and turned on the
television, and settled back to do his homework.

"Just a minute, Dave. I'll be right back." Jeffrey put
down the telephone and strode into his apartment. With a
practiced motion—Michael had performed this small test
a number of times since he had been doing homework
under his father's supervision—Jeffrey punched off the
television. "And pick up the magazines. Small arms are
broken for less," Jeffrey said, going back to the telephone.

"Jeeze."

"Very articulate, Mike, very articulate."

"What? Who's articulate?" Ketchum asked as Jeffrey
picked up the phone.

"My son. My son is articulate. When he isn't trying to
watch television, that is."

Michael's look of feigned disgust made Jeffrey grin.
"Anything else you want to tell me?" he said into the
phone.

"That's it. Keep in touch."

"Don't worry, I will," he said, and hung up. "Now," he
continued, raising his voice and starting for the apartment, "we see how the homework is going."

"No we don't."

"Why not, Mike?"

"Because we don't, that's why."

"Okay then. I'll see it all when you're done."

"If you're lucky, dad, if you're lucky."

How is it done? he wondered, as he had wondered so
many times before. How is one child properly raised to be
equipped for the real world? Jeffrey hated the conflict of

parenting, the fierce desire to protect versus the instinct to let go, and he moved uneasily between the two extremes, never sure, always doubting his own logic. Neither he nor Lydia had particularly pleasant memories of their childhoods, and they were both constantly concerned about Michael's happiness. "I want him to know that we love him at all times," Lydia had said when they decided to divorce, and this vow they made in the midst of a dissolution had been kept at all times. He was quick, independent, a good student some of the time, anyway, and he wanted for nothing. But still . . . Jeffrey worried for him, wished for him, dreamed for him. He had never loved anyone as much, as intensely. As he stood and watched the boy doing his homework, his lips pressed in concentration as he computed columns of figures, Jeffrey suppressed the urge to walk across the room and kiss him on the top of his head. The notion failed, so he stepped quickly to him, kissed him, and went back into his office. Michael smiled up at him.

From the moment he found out he was to become a father, Jeffrey had made a commitment to open affection. His own father, driven by the demons of his own generation, a man who barely survived the depression and believed only in hard work, had been stern and undemonstrative. For many years Jeffrey had wondered if his father loved him, and it was not until he had his own son that he understood fathers love their children, some more than others, and few of them are capable of showing it.

Jeffrey's father had been ambitious for him, his mother even more so. His father, working his life away as a security officer for Paramount studios, felt he had spent his life guarding the treasures of others. Indeed he had, and it was perhaps because Jeffrey somehow sensed his father's attitude about the treasures of people he worked for that Jeffrey had very early on become—and remained—interested in the studio where his father worked. By the time he was in high school, Jeffrey was working in the mailroom of the studio during his summer vacations, the beginning of an enduring curiosity about movies and the people who made them.

Jeffrey used his knowledge of Hollywood well. One drizzly, overcast day shortly after he opened his store, Jeffrey was worrying about where his income that month would come from when in walked a secretary both he and his father had known for years and in her arms she carried a stack of scripts. He bought the lot and, with them, one small treasure. It was the script of *Viva Zapata,* the only original script John Steinbeck had ever written. Tucked inside it was a Xerox copy of Steinbeck's contract with Darryl Zanuck, and the script itself was liberally marked by Zanuck. The secretary had left Paramount briefly, worked at Fox, and taken the script with her when she went back to work at Paramount. Now she was retired, living on a fixed income, and delighted with the money Jeffrey paid her. She, as did many others, spread the word about Jeffrey's generosity, and before too long a major share of his business was comprised of scripts and letters. Jeffrey did well by the studio veterans, and in turn did very well for himself. The Steinbeck script, for instance, he put into a custom-made slipcase and sold for $3,000.

His father, he often thought, would be glad to see that some of those treasures had come to him finally, and that he had done well with them. Jeffrey wished his father had lived to see his only grandson, and was pleased his mother and Michael spent time together. She adored her grandchild and saw him often.

"Dad?"

"Huh?" Jeffrey was in another childhood.

"I'm done. Here."

"Good, Mike. That was fast."

"Not really. You kept falling asleep. It just seems fast."

"I was up late last night."

"Good book or good woman?" Michael asked, wrinkling his face into a conspiratorial grin.

"Neither, as a matter of fact," Jeffrey said, wishing he could finish the answer out loud, say that there was a woman but there had been an interruption. Mike did not appear sensitive to the notion of his father and other women, but Jeffrey was well aware that his son could cover up his own emotional rough spots quickly, and so he was careful about what he said. Instead, he went over the math columns and had caught just one error out of fifteen problems and was about to go on when Michael interrupted his corrections.

"You're counting on your fingers, dad."

"I know. 'Rote' is what they called it when I learned it."

"I do too," the boy giggled.

Then came the English homework, Jeffrey's least favorite of it all. He could always find the subject, not always the predicate. He could separate the adverbs from the adjectives. But he could not do it all, and it particularly embarrassed him because Michael had at one point taken some of Jeffrey's writing to school to show the teacher. She had been impressed and said so during parents night, by which time she had also learned about his business. Jeffrey was certain she also assumed he knew the mechanics of English cold, could diagram a sentence down to the last syllable perfectly. He could not. He had never been able to do it. His love of the language was for its romance, for the stories it could tell. He believed an intimate knowledge of the rules of the language would spoil its romance. In that assumption, at least for himself, he was correct.

"Good, Mike. Good."

"I'm going to ride up to the park and play now. See you later."

"Not too much later. I want you back before it gets dark. Your mother is coming by to get you."

This time the thunder of fast feet was down the stairs, away from him, and he could soon hear the clicking of bicycle gears as Mike unfastened the safety chain and rode away.

He wanted to nap, he felt he should work. He made several phone calls, filled a few orders, then latched the door to the shop and stepped through to his bedroom. It was white, like the rest of his apartment, but here the furniture was not contemporary. Two large, old oak cabinets with brass fittings he used as his closet, the drawers below them as his dresser. His bed was a queen-size (he had wanted a king-size, but the room was too small) and covered with a brown and tan striped comforter. He plumped a pillow and lay down. Within two minutes he was fast asleep.

The knock on the door awakened him nearly an hour later. It was Lydia, earlier than expected, and as soon as he saw her look around for their son, saw her look of relief when she did not find him, he knew she had something on her mind.

"I'm going away and I want you to take Mike," she said. Lydia was nothing if not direct.

"Off to some South Pacific isle with Mr. Right?"

"No. I've got a grant to go with a women's study group to India."

"What for? To find out how bad it really could have been for you?"

"No, Jeffrey. To participate in a study of the emerging
role of women in India. There are ten of us going and it's
serious. So don't make cracks."

"Serious? Like the nude encounter group in Mesopota-
mia last year?"

"Yugoslavia," she corrected him, "and no, that really
wasn't serious. Damn you, you know it wasn't."

"For how long?"

"Three weeks for the conference. Then I'm going to
Paris for a week."

"Oh?"

"I'm meeting someone."

"I see."

"Don't pretend hurt, Jeffrey."

He said nothing.

"I'm meeting Dave Grayson, not that it's of any great
importance to you."

"Oh, for Christ's sake, Lydia. I thought fucking the boss
was something people like you didn't do anymore. Didn't
have to do. Didn't believe in it as a way to get ahead."

"Fucking the boss to get ahead, as you so aptly put it,"
she said, speaking through clenched teeth, "was something I thought most men approved of as long as it wasn't
their wives who were doing it."

Jeffrey shook his head, then slumped down in the big
white armchair in his living room. "You know what I
wish, Lydia? Not just for you or for me, but for everyone
who is going—or will go—through what has happened to
us; I wish that in the process of changing their lot in life,
women would please learn from the mistakes of the men
who preceded them. One of the most often made mistakes
was fucking at the office. It works every way around, not
just fucking to get ahead. You don't get ahead, neither the

fucker nor the fuckee. I'm sorry that you can't see that."

"I happen to have genuine feelings for him," she countered, just at the edge of becoming uncomfortable with his logic.

"I'll bet. But I wonder, Lydia, I just wonder what would happen if you met Dave Grayson away from the office, in a completely different circumstance, what would happen between the two of you. I can guess."

"What?"

"Knowing how you tend to feel about men and knowing as I do—as everyone who knows him does—what an ambitious, self-centered asshole he is, I'll tell you what would happen. You'd be introduced, promptly forget one another's name, and walk off in different directions in two minutes."

"I see. You are aware, of course, that my friendship with him has helped you," she said, waving an arm to include his office. She was standing, her back against the kitchen counter. She was angry, but still in control of her emotions.

"I think of it differently. Or maybe it's that I'm the romantic here. I really don't know for sure."

"How, may I ask, do you think of it? Romantically."

"I think, and I have always thought, that your occasional attempts to throw business my way, to help me, are done out of a genuine sense of good feeling between us. We had a marriage that didn't work, and a child who is doing just fine. Out of that—that"—he wasn't sure he had the right word, but then he knew it was absolutely right—"failure in the marriage, a different sort of relationship evolved. We were both trying to be intelligent people, remember? *Modern,* I believe was the word you used a lot around then. There was, as a matter of fact, a spoken commitment to continuing our relationship. Different, but continuing. In return for that consideration on your part, I have been supportive of you and your work in the extreme. I am with Mike at least half of his waking life, which most fathers—divorced or not divorced—almost never are. I pay child support well in excess of the court ruling. I am, as a matter of fact, goddamn generous. You aren't the only one being generous."

She said nothing.

"Guess what, Lydia. I stay ahead without fucking to do it. And I would never throw it up to you that it was in part to help you get ahead. Whether I fucked somebody or not."

"I'm leaving in four weeks."

"Fine. But you know what I wish? I understand roles are changing and traditional attitudes are breaking down. Most of them deserve to be changed or thrown away. But I wish—goddamn how I wish—that men and women could like one another a little bit more. And I also wish that somehow, in the course of making all these changes in their lives, women would somehow avoid falling into the same traps the men before them fell into."

"I'll pick my own traps, thanks," Lydia said, staring at him coldly. "And the next time I turn up with somebody you don't particularly like, such as Narib Zaki, don't barge in and wreck my business with him. I don't care if he was some goddamn suspicious Arab. I was merely being his host at a library sale, and that was all."

"I will, plain and simple, warn you again about Zaki. He is a dangerous man."

"I am not seeing him again. He was *most* anxious to get away once you got through with him."

"Good."

"Well?"

"Well, what?"

"Will you take Mike?"

"Yes. I already said, 'Fine.' But it means I'll have to take him to New York with me for the Antiquarian Book Fair."

"So?"

"So, I'm going to take his trip out of your next child-support check."

"Your way of getting even, no doubt."

"No, my way of paying his plane fare. Anyhow, you'll be gone four weeks. That's a month, Lydia, so you won't need child support that month."

"Where's Mike?"

"He's at the park, should be back any minute now."

"Send him home when he gets here," Lydia said, picking up her purse and starting for the door.

"You know what?" Jeffrey asked.

"No, what?"

"You'll probably find the women in India barefoot, pregnant, and paranoid. As the expression goes."

"Well," she said, and it was clear that Jeffrey's attempt to end their conversation on a lighter note had fallen flat. "When I was married to you, I was paranoid most of the time. I also got pregnant."

"You know what, Lydia? One of these days, I think not too long from now, one of your colleagues at the library—a male colleague, that is—is going to pay you the supreme compliment of equality."

"What's that?"

"He's going to call you a prick."

She gave him a murderous look and then stormed out of his apartment, through his office and down the stairs. He remained in his chair, his energy drained by the argument. He wished he could sort emotion from logic in arguments such as these, especially with Lydia, but it wasn't possible. Never had been possible, not from her point of view either. It seemed to him they were destined to bear every small and large scar of their times, and he was sorry for that, wished it weren't so, and would have liked to make a small joke about it to her except that his humor had never helped her overcome her angry moments.

He was still sitting there, ruminating, depressed, when the phone rang.

"Me and the guys wondered if you'd like to come over to dinner." It was Rachel, her cheerfulness a sharp contrast to his mood.

"What guys?"

"My tail, as your friend Ketchum so indelicately put it."

"You mean it?"

There was the briefest pause before she continued. "You all right? You sound sore about something."

"No, no, I'm fine." Why, he wondered, didn't he come right out and say, "No, no, I'm not fine. I've just had an argument with my ex-wife. I hate arguing with her, I feel horrible, and I can't fake cheer right now"? But for Rachel he could fake it and he did.

"Well, what I mean is the guys will probably be outside in their car if you don't mind a little close supervision."

"I don't want any supervision at all. But, yes, I'll come. I could use some cheerful company."

"I had a nap."

"Me too." He laughed.

"Come early. I'll have dinner ready."

XIII

SHE LIVED IN one of the apartment-condominium complexes that lined the marina and beachfronts of Los Angeles by the thousands. Hers was nicely modern, with black birds of paradise fighting the banana trees for space, shading the lush ferns and begonias that grew profusely in their shade. Her apartment faced the water; comfortable but not lavish. It was clear at first look that she liked the California life-style, spacious and casual, and the contemporary furnishings were a sure clue that she had left her eastern past as far behind as possible. She showed him, with obvious pride, the extra bedroom she had converted into a study for her schoolwork and her book business. He looked closely at her poster collection, a group of seven large framed posters that took up much of the wall space in her living room and dining area.

"Russian avant-garde," Rachel explained.

"A special interest?"

"I guess you might say yes. I love the period, I've studied it, and I lecture on it from time to time. Mostly about the literature, not the art. My grandfather was part of the Russian avant-garde and when he fled in 1921—just before Stalin started murdering the avant-gardists or sending them away to Siberia—he brought a little bit of it with him."

"Wonderful stuff. Any of it original?"

"None of it. Nobody was allowed to bring anything out, though I found out not too long ago that quite a lot of it was smuggled out and is in this country. An exhibition is being organized—or so I hear." She was looking at him, concentrating on him as she spoke. "Say hello." She smiled at him.

He stepped to her and kissed her lightly on the lips. She was wearing a light green sleeveless crushed-cotton caftan that hung loosely about her. As she stepped to him to return the kiss, he could feel the warmth of her body beneath it, feel her breasts brush against the two layers of cotton separating their skin, and he gently put his arms around her, pulled her close to him. He could smell the moist sweetness of her skin, still lightly damp from the shower. He put his head down and kissed her shoulder, teased the edge of her collarbone with his tongue.

"I hope you like lamb," she whispered.

"I hate it."

"Not tonight you don't. I've made rack of lamb, and anyone allergic to garlic has to get within ten blocks' distance. You open the wine."

He could smell the garlic on the lamb, and wild rice steaming. They took their wine and stepped out onto her balcony.

"You can see the water if you lean out a little bit," she told him. He could see it was a balcony used often and tended well. A single chaise lay pointed in the direction of the low winter sun, and behind it a table and four chairs waited for summer. A lush fuchsia hung from a big basket, reaching nearly to the tile floor.

"You can grow things like that by the ocean," he said, "but not in the Valley. It gets too hot."

"These, too," she said, stooping down beside a clay strawberry pot filled with new earth. She poked around lightly, then unearthed the first new leaf of what would become a flowering tuberous begonia by summertime.

He leaned against the railing of the balcony, nodding in agreement, relaxed and feeling for the first time in a number of days peaceful and safe.

"What'd you do with your car?" she asked. "You didn't drive it here, did you?"

"No. Ketchum sent someone to take it away," he answered her. Even the recollection of that evening failed to disrupt his calm. "And I rented another."

"Send Ketchum the bill?"

"No, but I will."

"Do you suppose they can hear what we're saying?"

"It depends," he said.

"Depends on what?"

"On whether or not they want to hear it. If they want it, they'll get it."

She shivered at the prospect of eavesdroppers, turned, and went back into her apartment. He followed, locking the sliding glass door behind him. He poured more wine and watched as she bent over and opened the oven to check the lamb. He watched the side of her body outlined along the folds of her dress, stared with frank interest.

"Five minutes," she said. Unlike Jeffrey, she was a good cook. Like Jeffrey, she enjoyed the ritual around a meal, the preparation, the setting of the table, the tossing of the salad, the small challenge to make everything come together at the right moment. The table was set, everything was ready. There was even a package of matches next to the candles. As she tossed the salad, he carved the meat. It came together perfectly.

"Music?" she asked just before they sat down.

"Not necessarily, unless you want it."

They ate in silence; the sound of silver against china, the soft click of crystal raised in a toast, made the music to accompany the meal. There was a brief discussion about favorite restaurants in New York, but not much else, because the restaurants reminded them of eating and that in turn plunged them into the food before them.

"Wonderful," he said when he was done. "Wonderful."

"There's cheese and crackers and fruit."

"I'm too full. Here, I'll help," he said, rising as she began to clear off the table.

"No, you stay there."

"But you don't understand. I'm a great dish scraper. I give great scrape."

She smiled and shrugged. He followed her into the kitchen, scraped and rinsed the dishes as she handed them to him, then watched as she placed them in the dishwasher.

"Pots and pans next," he said.

"What are you, some sort of compulsive clean-kitchen type?"

"There have been rumors to that effect, yes."

"Well, not tonight." She was arranging crackers around a sliced apple and when she picked up the plate and another with several kinds of cheese, he stepped behind her and put his arms around her, nuzzling his lips along her neck, just behind her right ear. He felt her stiffen slightly, felt her skin tighten against his tongue, and knew in an instant a small secret for arousing her. She kept the plates before her, tilted her head lightly toward him, and did not move. He slid his hands up until he could feel the base of her breasts against her rib cage, then up again until he held them in his hands. She turned her head more and kissed him on the forehead. He was about to raise his index fingers and begin lightly stroking her nipples when she moved away from him and walked into the living room.

"Music," she said, only this time it wasn't a question. "You choose."

"No, you," he said, slipping off his loafers and settling into the big sofa.

"Got any Cole Porter?" he asked, remembering "But in the Morning, No!" and wondering if she'd remember, too.

She did and smiled at him. "I've got a lot of Cole Porter."

"Just kidding. It's evening."

She chose an album of Ella Fitzgerald singing Cole Porter, put it on, then settled in beside him on the sofa. To the sound of Ella's suggestive singing of "Anything Goes," she leaned forward and kissed him. It was a gentle kiss, yet full of promise for what was yet to come.

Jeffrey was unprepared for the intensity of his feelings, the extent of his desire. It had been a long time, and whatever tentativeness he felt was caused by a concern that it might all somehow end too soon. He began to realize that his aloofness, his distance, had really been a defense against loneliness, a fear of taking a chance. Opportunities had been plentiful, but mostly they were casual encounters made possible by the sharp change in sexual mores that had taken place just before Jeffrey was single again. When he had finally gone out on the prowl, he got as far as the bar of the restaurant downstairs from his store, and within two hours his bed was occupied by a manicurist from . . . he not only forgot where she was from, but her name, too. She was the first of a procession, a long line of casual encounters made possible by physical need. No more, no less, and for a long time it had been enough.

"Penny?" she said, looking at him, her finger tracing the edge of his lips.

He responded with a smile, then kissed her gently.

"How nice," she said. "Me, too." With that he stood, pulled her to him, held her against him, then followed as she led the way into the bedroom. He quickly returned to the living room, took a candle, and carried it into the bedroom. He watched as she slipped out of her dress, then reached his hands up past her breasts, grasping her neck lightly. He pulled her to him. She was wearing raspberry-colored silk bikini underpants, and he ran his hand across them before pulling them off. She placed her hand over her nakedness, and he gently removed it, bent down, and kissed the spot where her hand had been. Her hair was thick and sweet, and he lingered there. He had a sudden, thrilling sensation that it would last forever and that he wanted to do it all. She touched him with her hand, pulled at his pants. He stood and undressed, carefully placing his clothes on the chair beside the bed. He had taken off everything but his jockey shorts when she sat up on the edge of the bed, put out her hands to him, and pulled him close. As she kissed his stomach and ran her tongue along the hair on his belly, she pulled off his shorts. His erection gently bobbed against the soft skin under her chin. She did not move away, not for a few more seconds.

And when she did, it was to pull him gently back onto the bed with her.

He held her close and beginning with her ears, where he knew her response would be immediate, began kissing her everywhere. Her eyes seemed to shine in the candlelight, her body shimmered as though it were a mirage, except that when he reached out to touch it, it was there. He drifted close, then closer, and suddenly pulled away, looked down at her, and smiled. He saw her question and answered it.

"Not yet. I want it to last a while longer."

She took the initiative, began to tease him with her lips and her hands, gently at first, then her passion grew. Where her hands and her lips touched him, her hair fell and formed a halo around his body. Finally she sat astride him, holding him erect before her, caressing his testicles and his penis. She raised on her knees, held him and guided him into her. He reached up to her breasts, then her shoulders, and pulled her toward him. They moved in concert, slowly at first, until their rhythm was perfectly synchronized, and then they went from motion to frenzy. Her small gasps became moans as she moved against him and then, her back arched, her arms locked, her hands pressed hard against his chest, she came.

Fast inside her still, he rolled her over and began his movements again, wishing he could be so deep inside her that he could disappear completely in her passion. When he exploded, it was as though an electrical charge began in his fingertips and his toes, gathered momentum and force, and finally burst out of him. He expressed his ecstasy with every muscle of his body and with a deep and satisfying yell. When he was done, their bodies remained joined, and they glistened with sweat. He kissed her gently on the forehead, the cheeks, and then, finally, on the lips: soft, butterfly kisses, which she returned.

Finally he lay on his back, his right arm behind his head, and Rachel curled into his left shoulder, lying softly against him.

The record had ended, so Rachel padded silently into the living room. He could hear her latch the front door, turn off the stereo, and then make small noises in the kitchen. When she returned she had a tray, two glasses, and a bottle of white wine.

"Something from the dessert cart?" she asked.

"Yes, thanks. I'll have the cart itself," he said, reaching out to her.

She giggled. "You already did."

She poured and handed him a glass, then sat beside him on the edge of the bed. He lay on his side, propped up on an elbow, drinking thirstily.

"Would you like to spend the night?" she asked.

"I think I already heard you lock me in."

"Yes, you did. I didn't want to issue the invitation until I knew you had no choice but to accept." She leaned over and kissed him lightly on the forehead.

"I can't understand why somebody hasn't come along and snapped you right up," he said, looking directly into her eyes.

"Let's just say that I recently unsnapped myself and leave it at that."

He nodded.

"I have to warn you," she continued. "I injure easily. I'm not nearly as tough as I seem."

"I guessed as much," he said to her. "And I suppose I should warn you about myself."

"How so?"

"I've got kind of a sorry record at relationships. I guess I'm not really good at them."

"I don't believe that," she said.

"Then don't. Just remember I warned you."

"Hope springs eternal," she said.

He took her wineglass from her, then pulled her beside him, turned her onto her back. He took his wineglass and held it directly above her and traced a pattern with its base along her flat stomach, teasing a little circle around her navel. Then he tipped the glass slightly, pouring wine between her breasts. She squealed, tried to grab the glass from him, then relaxed as he began to lick the wine off her, following its narrow trickle down her stomach. When he reached the end of the wine he looked up at her and smiled, then put his head down again and kept right on going.

XIV

THAT SATURDAY AFTERNOON she met him at his apartment and they drove together to Alfred Craventon's in what Jeffrey had reconciled himself to thinking of as his "somewhat" new Honda. An agent had appeared early in the day with Jeffrey's old Prelude, repaired, repainted, made to look new, and had patiently explained that the government required three written confirmations before it would total out a car. Jeffrey's simply didn't qualify, even though a promise had been extracted from Ketchum. It was the nature of the bureaucratic beast, but it was nevertheless maddening, and it was also typical of Ketchum: Promise anything, then head for the door. As he drove, Jeffrey listened for telltale rattles or any sound he might use to form a complaint. Rachel, whose interest in mechanics was nonexistent, listened to his complaints and, when she realized the car and not she was receiving all of his attention, stared idly out at the other cars on the freeway.

"Really pisses me off," he muttered.

"You've said that three times already."

"The car will last a month and when it falls apart I'll be stuck with it."

"You said that, too."

The driveway leading up to Craventon's house seemed to Jeffrey to be even longer than before, the gardens more formal and sculptured than he remembered them from a week ago. An attendant took his car—Jeffrey listened and shook his head as the car was driven off—and they were soon lingering among three hundred or so guests of the UCLA Friends of the Library. The crowd was a mixture of upper-echelon faculty, wealthy alumni, bookdealers, and a few local literary glitterati.

Jeffrey, who tended to be ill at ease at large gatherings, noticed that several people looked up at him when he entered with Rachel on his arm. She was dressed in a simple black dress with a string of pearls around her neck and matching pearl earrings. She looked stunning. He, in turn, had worn the black pinstripe suit he saved for occasions such as this. "Parties and funerals," he said when she complimented him on his appearance. Because of her, he had actually been looking forward to the party, and in fact would have been happy anywhere as long as he was with her. He suspected he was taking the traditional fall of the lovestruck, but what he did not perceive was that she was encouraging him.

"Is Joan Didion here?" Rachel asked as they walked through the groups of people scattered about.

"I don't see her. But she's tiny and easy to miss."

"Keep an eye out. I want to see her. I think she is a sensational writer."

"Ever read her stuff from Hawaii? Her essays?"

Rachel nodded.

"If you know the place, know what it's really like and love it, then you see how perfectly she perceives it."

"You've been there?"

"Several times. Mostly to work, then for pleasure. I sometimes think that if I could go back to school, I'd go for a Ph.D. in Pacific culture or something like that."

"Really?"

"Really. Anyway, I don't think she's here. If I see her, I'll introduce her to you."

"You know her?"

"Yes, from long ago. When we were both working here as journalists."

"Of course. I'd forgotten. You know, you really do have an unfair advantage. Her books are collected a lot now and I suppose you have every one of them. Inscribed."

"Yup. Wanna buy some?"

"Not from you, I don't. I've seen your prices."

"Now what do you mean by that?" He was just about to maneuver the tease around to his advantage when he looked up and saw Lydia enter the room, every bit the dominant figure in the fresco formed by the people in the big rooms, her arm securely held by Dave Grayson, her boss and lover. He was a tall man, balding and given to wearing eccentric neckties. Long before Lydia had known him, Jeffrey had found him to be vain, ambitious, and shallow. He liked him even less now, though he told himself it had nothing to do with jealousy. That had ended long ago.

"I'll do you one better than Joan Didion," he whispered to Rachel. "I'll introduce you to my ex-wife."

"Terrific."

"She's actually rather nice. It's her ideas that are all screwed up."

"I've heard that before." Rachel turned and walked away, taking Jeffrey by the arm as she did so. She steered him across the library and out onto a big patio overlooking a yard—if you could call something that big a yard—that seemed to slope gently down an endless hill, broken by terraces. At the fourth level, a swimming pool and pool house interrupted the even terracing. There were tables and umbrellas scattered on the first two terraces, many of them occupied.

"This is what Mr. Craventon probably calls just a 'two-terrace party.' "

"Do you suppose so?" She laughed.

"Hell, I don't know. I can only get six people into my place. Don't you want to go back and have a look at the library?"

"Not right now. I'll wait—until there are fewer people in the room."

"Does Lydia's being here make you nervous?"

"I told you," she said emphatically, "I'm no good around wives."

"Ex-wife," he corrected her.

"Ex or otherwise. If you can believe me, I even tend to be sympathetic to ex-wives."

"Get to know Lydia before you say that," he said pointedly. "Oh, Christ. Him, too. I should have known." There, standing at one of the big doors leading from the library to the first terrace patio, were Lydia, Grayson, and, talking to them both, shooting his cuffs, a smarmy smile on his face, Narib Zaki.

"Did Ketchum say he was coming?" She tensed and turned away from the patio.

"No, and I spoke to him this morning. I told him we were coming here and he said nothing."

"You really are their bait, aren't you?"

"Shit." He turned with her, not out of fear but out of confusion. He needed time to decide what to do.

Waiters in black pants, short white coats, and bright blue and gold UCLA bow ties circulated throughout the crowd offering drinks and hors d'oeuvres. Jeffrey took a glass of wine, handed it to Rachel, then took another for himself. He directed her to one of the round white tables that dotted the lawn like scraps of paper from a three-hole punch, and they sat, their backs to the crowd.

"I wouldn't trust Ketchum as far as I could throw him," she said quietly. "And I couldn't even pick him up."

"I wouldn't try if I were you," Jeffrey answered. He was sitting straight up in his chair, his right hand holding his wineglass, the fingers of his left beating a steady, nervous tattoo on the tabletop. "He's the kind of guy who'd sew weights into his pockets if he thought there was a chance of losing."

Ketchum was letting him swim in the current of his own fear, she thought, and that struck her as both devious and disloyal. He was trying to use Zaki, too, but for what reason she couldn't decide. She was certain of one thing though: Jeffrey was just so much chum being carelessly tossed into the path of some hungry sharks. So, to a lesser degree, was she. It was Ketchum's job, she thought bitterly, to bring the shark to a frenzy.

Jeffrey looked around and saw one of the waiters offering champagne to a cluster of people he guessed from their appearance were well-to-do alumni. He idly watched the waiter cross to another group and then pass by and speak quietly with a second waiter. Then it hit him.

"Look," he said to Rachel. "Look at the waiter. That one."

She looked, then looked back at Jeffrey, puzzled. "What am I supposed to see?"

"Keep looking at the waiters. Look at as many as you can see."

She did, and on the fourth try, she got it, too.

"They're all over the place," she whispered. They watched together for five minutes, and when they were done they had counted twelve waiters, four of whom they recognized as the tails Ketchum had assigned to them.

"They're not here guarding us," Jeffrey said. "And if they are, it's just accidental."

"How do they get away with it?"

"Probably easier than anybody would think. Most of these waiters—especially at something big like this—are hired for scale out of the union hall. It'd be easy to stick in a couple ringers."

"But what for?"

"That's just it, I don't know."

A waiter approached offering wine, and Jeffrey took it. "Tell Ketchum we know you're here, he said as he took two glasses. The waiter pretended not to hear and walked away.

The fact that a party such as this—with all its academic pretense and scholarly attitudes, its mix of wealth and intelligence, its basically serious intent—should also be under surveillance by a government agency dealing in intrigue and spies seemed to Jeffrey to form a sharp contrast. He remembered what Ketchum had said about Zaki and Craventon, his speculation about some connection having to do with oil. But he also remembered Ketchum's sudden deflation when he had explained their common interest in book collecting. That, and the fact that Ketchum had said absolutely nothing when Jeffrey told him he and Rachel were going to the party at Craventon's.

"Jeffrey!" It was Lydia, brimming with conviviality, dragging Grayson and Zaki along with her. They had been circulating among the guests, greeting them, and when they came upon Jeffrey and Rachel, Lydia, feigning complete control, played through.

Jeffrey stood as Lydia, her gaze steady and its message unmistakable, reintroduced him to Zaki as though the encounter in Santa Barbara, and their subsequent conversation about the Arab, had never taken place.

Jeffrey nodded coolly at Zaki, shook Grayson's hand, and introduced them all to Rachel. When it came to saying her last name, he hesitated, then went ahead, figuring the omission would be too conspicuous and that if Zaki didn't already know her name, it would be easy enough to find anyway. Lydia greeted Rachel with a look of cool appraisal, careful calculation, and discreet curiosity. In the five years since they'd divorced, Rachel was the first woman she had seen with Jeffrey.

"I hear you've arranged for Lydia to go off to India," Jeffrey said to Grayson.

"Yes, good news, isn't it!" he answered. "We got her a grant at the last minute."

"Paris included?" Jeffrey asked, smiling innocently. Lydia shot him a withering glare; Grayson looked as if he were about to start sputtering in indignation and began to turn red from embarrassment. Zaki stood passively by, gazing off across the terraces, pointedly ignoring Jeffrey.

"Come along, David. Narib, you too. We've some people we want you to meet. From the Huntington," she said, naming a library certain to act as a lure to any bookdealer, Qaddafi agent or not. They quickly walked away.

"What was that all about?" Rachel asked. "I thought she would have liked to kill you."

"That's an understatement," Jeffrey said, sitting again.

He explained Lydia's trip to India, the stop in Paris, her involvement with Grayson, and finally their argument earlier in the week. He hoped his explanation seemed objective, but he doubted it. Rachel listened, and when he was done, she nodded, not really a nod of acceptance, but one of receipt for a particular bit of information. His thoughts were elsewhere now, on a new theme.

"Divorce has its own particular set of perils," she said. There was no hint of judgment, nor was there one of sympathy.

"C'mon. Let's go look at the library and leave them out here."

"First I have to make a stop. I'll be right back," she said, smiling at him.

He watched as she walked back into the house, and then he turned and looked out across the terraced lawn. To his right was a long table covered with a white tablecloth. In its center was a large crystal punch bowl with cups arranged neatly around it. Trays of hors d'oeuvres were staggered along the rest of the table, with stacks of small napkins beside them. Jeffrey stepped up, surveyed the food, and was reaching for a small slice of quiche when the sickening sweet smell of Canoe hit him. He turned and saw Zaki standing beside him.

"All this is so very lovely," Zaki said, his accent thicker than Jeffrey remembered it, his manner even more smarmy than before.

"This is all not so lovely as it looks," Jeffrey answered, turning slightly as he noticed a waiter approach. He was one of Ketchum's men, and he immediately began arranging glasses, all the while pretending to be unaware of Jeffrey and Zaki.

"That is perhaps so," Zaki said evenly.

There was a tense silence until Zaki took up the conversation again. "That is to say," Zaki explained elaborately, "that there are people here who are doing things they have no business doing."

"Such as?"

"I think you know very well."

"People don't always have a choice."

Zaki surveyed the quiche, then shifted his gaze to a platter of stuffed mushrooms. "I ate my first mushroom when I was at Cambridge. I learned a great deal when I was there, but I'll wager I was one of the few who learned to love mushrooms. Did you know, for instance"—he turned the mushroom carefully on its side and held it between his thumb and index finger—"that if there is a certain gradation in color on the side of the mushroom—a sort of light striping—when it is in its raw form, that it is poisonous? Death comes within eight hours."

"I'll keep an eye on the mushrooms I eat."

"You would do well to keep an eye on more than mushrooms. Death has many disguises."

"How poetic."

"The expression did not originate with me."

"Just what does originate with you?" Jeffrey turned and faced Zaki directly, and as he did he saw the waiter look quickly in their direction and take a step nearer them.

"Ah, very little. I do as I'm told."

"That is an excuse that has been used many times before."

"You might say it is a cliché as well as an excuse. My experience is that clichés become clichés because they have an element of truth to them." Zaki popped the mushroom into his mouth, chewed it carefully, swallowed, and then continued to speak, but this time his voice was low, almost a whisper, which only served to underscore what he said. "You have friends and they protect you. But I warn you, they can protect you no longer."

"From what?" Jeffrey could feel the sweat forming, felt the first of it run down his back.

"Don't be a fool," Zaki hissed between his teeth. Suddenly he looked up, smiled a big smile that was a masterpiece of hypocrisy, and said, as though nothing had happened, "Aha! Here is your lovely lady."

Jeffrey turned quickly just as Rachel stepped to his side. "Mr. Zaki," he said before she could speak, "was just telling me about poison mushrooms."

"Oh?"

"You will excuse me, please. I must be going," Zaki said, turning away. "It was good to speak to you again, Mr. Dean."

"That was about getting out of the way," Jeffrey said.

"I see." She sensed it was more than that, but it was obvious Jeffrey wasn't ready to say just how much more.

"Or else," Jeffrey added. She looked up at him, fear showing in her eyes, the set of her mouth. "C'mon," he said, abruptly changing the subject, "have a look at the books the Craventon millions are buying."

For the next fifteen minutes Rachel, with Jeffrey standing beside her, inspected Craventon's elaborate collection, neither really seeing, both thinking their private thoughts, dealing with their particular fears. She concentrated her attention on the modern first editions, asked Jeffrey an occasional question, but was otherwise silent. Jeffrey looked up and saw that the signed Ross Macdonald he had delivered the week before was already in place with other books by the writer. He pointed it out to her.

"I gather UCLA gets the library when Craventon

dies?" she asked as they looked down at a glass case containing Somerset Maugham's handwritten manuscript of *Mrs. Craddock*.

"That seems to be what Craventon is promising, although Lydia says they haven't got it in writing yet. The Huntington has also come courting, but Craventon is a UCLA alumnus and it looks as though they get it all."

She whistled softly. UCLA was both a fine and a rich library, and Craventon's bequest would be the largest of its sort the university had ever received. "I'd sure like to get my hands on some of it," she said quietly.

"According to Craventon, several people already have," he said to her. "Speaking of which," he said, looking across the room. There, in dark suit and sporting his best-for-the-community-spirit grin, was Alfred Craventon, shaking hands with some recent arrivals. Beside him, similarly attired and with a red carnation in his buttonhole, was Victor Dreyfus, his eyes darting around the room from one visitor to the next. When his glance settled on Jeffrey, he stopped, and—so it seemed to Jeffrey—flinched slightly, before nodding in recognition. Jeffrey walked toward them with Rachel.

"Ah, Jeffrey. How good to see you," Alfred Craventon said when he saw him. "A few more people here than the last time we spoke, eh?"

"There sure are," Jeffrey said. He introduced Rachel to Craventon, and again to Dreyfus, though he had met her before at the book fair.

"Oh, yes, yes, of course," Dreyfus said when Jeffrey reminded him, but Jeffrey had the distinct sense that Dreyfus didn't remember at all. He was the sort of man who used good manners to disguise his lack of interest. And at this moment—for most of his moments, Jeffrey supposed—Dreyfus's only interest was Alfred Craventon.

"How are you doing at finding my Steinbecks?" Craventon asked him.

"I've found *Sweet Thursday* but not *Cannery Row*," Jeffrey told him. "But soon, probably early next week." Jeffrey noticed Rachel tense at the mention of the two titles. "They were stolen some time ago from Mr. Craventon's collection," he said to her, "and he's asked me to replace them."

"Mr. Craventon often loses books because of the large number of charity events he and Mrs. Craventon allow here," Dreyfus intoned, almost as though he were referring to a shrine and not a home. A shrine to avarice, Jeffrey thought.

"I'm sorry to hear that," Rachel said politely.

"And my Chandlers?" Craventon asked Jeffrey.

"No luck yet. They're quite scarce. There's an auction in San Francisco. I'll be there when they come up."

"Good. I want them."

Jeffrey shifted his weight from one foot to the other, and as he did he looked up at Victor Dreyfus, who remained standing to the side and just slightly behind Alfred Craventon.

"Nice talking to you again, Jeffrey," Craventon said, extending his hand. As Jeffrey took it, he saw that Craventon's nails were manicured, and that there was an ornate gold ring on his index finger. His handshake was more perfunctory than it was friendly.

"Good to meet you, Miss Sabin," he said to Rachel, and then he turned and walked off.

Victor Dreyfus looked right through Rachel as though he didn't see her, then looked up at Jeffrey. He was, Jeffrey sensed, suddenly agitated beyond his normal high level of agitation. It seemed to Jeffrey that only his hands remained relaxed. He rubbed them lightly together, his eyes darted around the room.

"Jeffrey. A word with you in private, please. You'll excuse us, Miss . . ." Dreyfus said.

"Of course," Rachel said. "I'll be waiting near the front door."

Dreyfus's eyes were magnified by the thickness of his eyeglasses, and his bifocals added a further distortion. When he spoke, it was quietly and furtively.

"Listen very carefully, because I cannot repeat this." He stepped closer to Jeffrey but did not look at him. "You must go away for a while. For your safety." Dreyfus pointed to a bookcase. "Look in the direction I point. Pretend to be interested."

"I am interested," Jeffrey said, "but not in the books."

"I say this only because you have been kind to me over the years. I know people say things about me, and you have not. Now listen carefully. It will all be over in a week, then you'll be safe. Right now you're expendable and if you keep nosing around they'll get rid of you." Dreyfus's arm swung in the opposite direction, and for a second Jeffrey forgot to look.

"They've already tried."

"I'm not surprised. This is a serious thing and a dangerous thing. Who sent you to do this?"

Jeffrey ignored the question by asking one himself. "It's a hell of a lot more than a couple of forged books, isn't it?"

"Yes. But I can't tell you more. You accidentally stumbled onto something, but it is not what it seems. Not at all. Now go and stay away. For your own safety."

"What about yours?"

"I'm very much needed right now. I'm not expendable. Not yet."

"You saw Zaki talk to me?"

Dreyfus nodded.

"Is Craventon involved?"

"No questions. The less you know, the better. Now go, go quickly."

Any other time and in any other circumstance, Jeffrey would have thought Victor Dreyfus was enjoying the drama of the moment, but he knew from the way the older man spoke, from his manner, he meant what he was saying. Zaki's thinly veiled threat and the agents disguised as waiters were proof enough.

Jeffrey repeated the conversations with Zaki and Dreyfus to Rachel as they sped down the Pasadena Freeway. They both tried but could not figure out what it was Ketchum wanted or what Dreyfus and Zaki had warned Jeffrey about. They fell silent as Jeffrey turned off the Pasadena Freeway and onto the Hollywood Freeway. Suddenly he reached behind his seat and handed her the thick *Thomas Guide* to the streets of Los Angeles.

"Look up Redfern Drive. The twenty-four-hundred block. Somewhere in Hollywood."

She thumbed the pages quickly. "Off North Vine Street in the hills. Not far from the Hollywood sign. Why?"

"Instinct. I once interviewed a man who was supposed to be the great new thing for working out psychological problems. It involved all sorts of things, and when I read his work and met him, my instinct told me he was a fake. But I couldn't prove it, so I didn't write anything. A few weeks later I was at a brunch and I found myself talking to a very well-known analyst. He, it turned out, was writing a review of this man's book for a psychiatric journal, and he asked me what I thought of him. I said I thought he was a fraud, and the analyst was very surprised. He told me I was right, and that people who did what I did—if they're lucky—arrive by instinct at conclusions people like him spend years reaching scientifically. The man was a fake and the analyst had finally found this out."

"What is your instinct this time?"

"It is that if we look around carefully we might find out what it is that makes Victor Dreyfus so very much needed right now. 'Not yet expendable,' as he puts it. I'm going to make a stop and I want you to stand guard. Look at it this way: There are two kinds of bait—live and dead."

She looked at him, her question unstated but unmistakable.

"Live bait," Jeffrey answered, "if it swims fast, just might survive. I intend to swim very fast for a while."

He was thinking fast, too, speculating. Zaki. A warning from Dreyfus. There is a process of thought, known to those who study it as marginal thought: concepts and ideas that skim by just on the edge of consciousness and usually escape without capture. Jeffrey was midway through an involved marginal thought of which he was not at all conscious—he was too busy planning what he was about to do at Dreyfus's house. But one word, swimming alone in a turbulent ocean of thought, popped to the surface.

"Oil," he said.

"What?"

"Do you suppose? . . . My God." He couldn't believe what he was thinking, couldn't grasp the implication of it all. If it was true. If.

"What? For the last time." She sensed his excitement.

"Oil. Craventon. Qaddafi. One has it, the other wants it. Something . . . some deal . . . I don't know what. No wonder the place is crawling with government agents."

If it was so—and there was every possibility it was—a lot of questions were not being answered as they drove into the hills. But the biggest questions remained unanswered, and unattainable. Maybe, maybe there would be a clue at Dreyfus's house. Speculation filled their minds, unspoken, unbidden except for that one word which had escaped into Jeffrey's consciousness.

"Could be," she said after a short silence. "Craventon. Hard to imagine."

Darkness was settling on the Hollywood Hills as Jeffrey turned off at Gower Street and headed up North Vine Street. Several sharp, hilly twists later, he pulled up at 2414 Redfern Drive, an address he had memorized because of the many books he had mailed there. Victor Dreyfus's house was an old Hollywood bungalow, perfectly maintained. Even the grass that grew down the center of his short driveway was manicured. The house was dark. Jeffrey parked, then rummaged around in his glove compartment for the flashlight he kept there.

"I won't be long. If anybody comes, I'll come right out. Stay low so you won't be easily seen."

She watched as he walked quickly around to the back of the house, then she looked at the other houses on the street. It was dinner hour and the street was empty.

XV

THERE WAS A small garden covered with white lattice between the garage and the house and it was filled with meticulously tended begonias and cymbidium orchids. Jeffrey paused as he passed through it, deliberating once more whether or not to go on. He saw there was a small workshop built off the end of the garage, and from where he stood he could look in the dining room window into the house, where one light shone in the living room. He didn't have the slightest idea how to break into a house.

He walked the few steps into the backyard and found on his immediate left a step leading to the back door. Just past that, above a newly planted garden of tomatoes, were the three kitchen windows, two of them louvered. Jeffrey tried the door, then walked across the patio and tried the door there. They were both locked. He lifted several flowerpots, thinking he might find a spare key stashed for emergencies, but he found nothing.

Once again his misgivings stopped him. He was weigh-

ing what it was he was about to do when a memory jolted
him into action. He saw Rachel screaming as the motorcyclist tried to force them off the side of the canyon, and
when this image came into focus, it obliterated any misgivings. He stepped up to the louvered window closest to
the driveway, pushed gently on the screen, and when he
saw the hook move loosely in its eye, he pushed and
pushed again, slapping it with the palm of his hand, until
it popped open. It took him less than a minute to remove
six of the twelve louvers and crawl through the window.
Easy. He was surprised at how easy it was.

The kitchen counter was directly below the window
and as he came through he sent the coffeepot clattering to
the floor, startling him into an awkward push-up as he
tried to pull the rest of his body through the window
without falling off the counter or making any more noise.
As he crawled in, a large black cat jumped up onto the
sink and meowed a greeting, sending his pulse soaring. He
quickly unlocked the back door and then returned to the
kitchen to replace the coffeepot, the louvers, and the
screen.

If ever a house was a perfect reflection of its owner, this
was it; overdone. He hastily surveyed the cluttered collection of Victorian chairs, tables, lamps, and mirrors that
crowded the living room and dining room. There was a
plush love seat covered in maroon velvet and an old floor-
model Philco radio in one corner. There were few signs of
human habitation; the house seemed to be a museum display with Jeffrey an interloper from another time. He
turned instinctively to the bookshelves that went from
floor to ceiling along one side of the room, then stopped
himself. He wasn't there to look over Victor Dreyfus's
book collection—not yet, anyway.

A desk, banded in chrome and made of highly polished mahogany, was positioned more for display than for work. Jeffrey looked quickly through its drawers but found little. The center drawer contained Dreyfus's checkbook and a collection of bills, nothing worth noting except perhaps that the checkbook register indicated Dreyfus had sent Jeffrey a check that same day for $235, the balance of his overdue account. Most bookdealers carried a number of overdue accounts, and Jeffrey was no different: It was a gentlemen's business conducted as tradition dictated, and that tradition did not include interest charges except in rare cases.

He found very little of interest in the bedroom, either. Dreyfus's bed was an elaborate affair with a white satin headboard and matching covers that seemed to Jeffrey to be better suited to Mae West. The dresser top was covered with the paraphernalia of a vain and particular man: a silver brush and mirror; cut-crystal bottles of cologne; a photograph of Dreyfus, taken in his late twenties or early thirties, in which he resembled a young Noel Coward but with more hair. It was as though time had stood still for Victor Dreyfus, and his conscious decision to live in the past meticulously enforced.

Jeffrey opened the dresser drawers one by one and slid his hand under the pile of neatly ordered socks. Nothing. He did the same to the stack of carefully folded underwear and found an eight-by-ten manila envelope, well worn. He opened it and out slid a series of photographs of naked young men, all with erections, several of them in the midst of ejaculation. Jeffrey's immediate reaction to the photographs was acute embarrassment at violating the most intimate recesses of Dreyfus's life. He had broken into his house for one reason: to find out what was going on, and how Dreyfus was involved. That was one thing. This was another. On the infrequent occasions he had given it any thought at all, he had decided Dreyfus was either asexual or homosexual, but it hadn't provoked any response in him. He was not the sort to be threatened by such things, nor was he in the least judgmental. His emotion as he slid the envelope back into its hiding place was one of sadness for Dreyfus, for his lonely life and for the fact that the world was such that Dreyfus felt he had to conceal his sexual preference.

Were they blackmailing him? Could be. Jeffrey remembered his conversation with Dreyfus just an hour or so earlier in which he had said he was not expendable. Not yet. For the first time, replaying the remark in his memory, Jeffrey caught the tone of desperate cynicism in Dreyfus's voice and his curiosity became even more insistent. He walked down the short hall, looked in the bathroom quickly, then walked up to the closed door of what he assumed was the second bedroom in the small house, and opened it slowly.

It was the second bedroom all right, but it wasn't used as a bedroom. It was a workroom. Jeffrey's flashlight beam was too small for him to determine what sort of workroom it was; it struck only fragments without the whole, so Jeffrey eased the door nearly shut and turned on the overhead light switch by the door. Even then it was several seconds before he realized the room's purpose. The first thing to catch his attention was a big worktable, a solid wood slab held in place by two sawhorses, and beside it a wooden drafting table whose angle was adjusted so that Jeffrey's eyes fell on the paper in place waiting to be used.

Across the small room from the desk was a bookshelf that held several small bottles. He bent to inspect them, and when he saw their labels, he knew. They were bottles of casein, the coloring chemical used in ink. He picked up the two well-thumbed books that sat at the edge of the worktable, and turned them to see their spines: *Collecting Autographs and Manuscripts* and *Great Forgers and Famous Fakes,* both by Charles Hamilton, a man who had made a career out of exposing forgeries and determining the authenticity of documents and signatures. The very same man whose works Zaki had sarcastically recommended to Jeffrey when he had tried to purchase the forged Steinbecks at the book fair. He flipped through *Collecting Autographs,* a reference book he himself often used except that now he was seeing it quite differently. Its title page announced that it contained more than eight hundred famous signatures. On a hunch, he turned to the index and looked for "Steinbeck." Not there. But it was not hard to find a sample of Steinbeck's signature. The world of instant copying made it easy to keep, too.

"Jesus Christ," Jeffrey muttered. Dreyfus was a forger. He had little doubt that it was Dreyfus's handiwork in the Steinbeck books. Did Craventon know? He doubted it. Four cigar boxes lined the edge of the desk and one by one he opened them. They were filled with every kind of pen imaginable, including a set of six quills. Dreyfus obviously moved back and forth through history with ease as business demanded. He looked around but could find no signature in progress, no indication of what he was working on. Obviously Dreyfus took care to leave nothing in the open.

He was closing the lid on the last cigar box when it slid out of position. As he pushed it back, he saw the edge of a small white envelope under it. He reached for the envelope and his hand suddenly stopped as though halted by an invisible barrier. With a sudden rush of tension, he realized his fingerprints were all over the house. He began to take care not to leave any more, as though making no new fingerprints would erase those already left. He pushed the base of his palm against the edge of the cigar box to expose the rest of the envelope, positioned his index finger against the sharp edge of the envelope, and flicked it open with the nail of his other index finger. He used the same finger to nudge the contents of the envelope onto the desk. Four small photographs fell out. In the uneven light, Jeffrey at first thought they were all of the same person; but as he looked more closely, he discovered each was of a different person. The extreme similarity was caused by the fact that they were all dark-haired and bearded, with dark eyes forming a sharp contrast to the blue background in each of the photographs. Arabs, he guessed, but of what use to Dreyfus? Had they anything to do with Zaki?

The pictures themselves provided no answers, just clues, and the rush of speculation spurred Jeffrey into action: Using the tip of both index fingers, he slid the photographs off the table and back into the envelope and placed it back in its hiding place, carefully lining the cigar boxes up exactly as he had found them.

He looked in the wastebasket and found it empty. He inspected the top of the desk again and found nothing new. There was a big magnifying glass at one corner of the desk and an architect's lamp at the other. The room, like the rest of the house, was perfectly ordered. The only difference was that this room, unlike the others, was all business. He was about to leave when his gaze fell again on the bookshelf with the bottles of casein. On the top shelf was a row of bottles, all but three of which were empty. Ink bottles. One was black, another an off-white, and the third green, not dark but rather the color of a lawn that has been seared by the summer sun, bleached but without the brown burn. He stared at them for a second before turning off the light and closing the door.

He went to the bookshelf in the living room to see if any of Dreyfus's collection had inscriptions, inscriptions that might be by Dreyfus. He saw a Mark Twain, pulled it from the shelf, and found no signature in it. Then he saw a Steinbeck and reached out to it. A pair of headlights briefly illuminated the room. Dreyfus was home. Jeffrey bolted for the back door. He locked the first lock but could not work the drop lock without a key. He hoped Dreyfus wouldn't notice—and that if he did, he'd think he himself had forgotten to lock it.

He was just about to start through the small garden when he heard the car door slam and realized he wasn't going to make it. In a moment he'd be face-to-face with Victor Dreyfus. Jeffrey turned and headed back into the yard, staying on the lawn so as not to make noise. He saw the workshop and walked to it—it was only three steps away in the tiny yard—then squatted down behind a giant hydrangea.

He heard the rattle of keys and what he assumed was the rustle of a paper bag, and as the sounds approached his heart seemed to beat louder and louder until he thought its pounding would give him away. He watched with mounting desperation as Dreyfus walked to the workshop door, turned a key in the lock, then in a second lock. As he opened the door, his hand flicked on a light switch that sent a shaft of light through the hydrangea. Jeffrey ducked the light coming through the bush, crouched closer to the ground, and took the position of a sprinter waiting for the starting gun.

He heard, and could almost see, Dreyfus moving around the room. There was a thunk as the paper bag was left on a table, followed by the hum of a machine starting and then abruptly stopping. A brief silence followed and as Jeffrey peered through the big flowers he could see Dreyfus bend over and connect a grounded plug leading to a small machine on a pedestal. Dreyfus stood for a minute, his hands on his hips, then reached into the paper bag and pulled out a piece of metal about four inches square and inspected it carefully. He studied it for a minute or two—it could not have been much longer, but it seemed to Jeffrey a small eternity—before reaching out and placing his hand on the small machine he had just connected. He touched it lightly, then felt it again, and by his motion Jeffrey could tell he was waiting for the machine to warm up.

Dreyfus abruptly turned and walked out of the workshop, passing within a foot of Jeffrey, his keys dangling in his hand. Jeffrey held his breath as Dreyfus unlocked the back door, turning the bolt lock twice without—or so it seemed—realizing it had been left open. Jeffrey watched as Dreyfus switched on the kitchen light and set to making a large pot of coffee. It was obviously going to be a late night and there was work to be done. When Dreyfus left the kitchen and the bedroom light went on, Jeffrey guessed he had gone to change his clothes before going to work. He was about to run for the car when he paused, guessed he had time while Dreyfus changed and made his coffee. He went into the workshop.

It was a small, narrow room that smelled of ink, sweat, dust, and dishonesty. He recognized the machine Dreyfus had just plugged in as a laminator, not all that different from the kind that could be found outside supermarkets from time to time, except that on this one there was no protective cover and a short roll of plastic was behind it on a spool almost like toilet paper. The other machine in the room, the largest one there, was an offset press, an old model Multilith 1250 according to the label on it, one that had obviously seen better days but, Jeffrey assumed, still worked well enough. Standing in the corner of the room was a big roll of paper, the sort fashion photographers use for backgrounds. It was blue, the same color as the photographs of the four Arabs in the extra bedroom.

The small metal block he had seen Dreyfus inspecting sat on a table beside the press. Jeffrey picked it up and looked at it, puzzled over it a second before he realized it was a numbering head, the sort used to place numbers on documents.

Staying in a crouch so that he could pass by the dining-room window without being seen, Jeffrey ran down the driveway to the curb, and quickly to the car.

"What took so long? He's been home fifteen minutes," Rachel said to him as he jumped in and she started the car.

"Don't turn on the headlights until you're past the house," he told her.

She drove slowly for about twenty yards until she was past the house and they had seen shadows of movement through the blinds in the main bedroom. Then she switched on the lights and sped up.

"What'd you find?"

"All the tools of the trade of a master forger. Dreyfus is not what we all thought he was, and he's in this—this whatever it is—all the way. He's not expendable, Dreyfus said, not yet. That means he's doing something for them—Zaki probably—and hasn't finished his work yet."

"I have a hunch it's something more than a Steinbeck signature," she said as she accelerated and turned onto the freeway.

"You bet. With that equipment he can forge some kind of official government document."

"Such as?"

"A passport, probably," he said, thinking of the pictures and realizing by their size that was probably their purpose.

"Who for?"

"Those four guys under the cigar box." He explained what he had found.

"But why?"

"My guess is that Zaki is probably sneaking agents into the country for whatever purpose he's been told to do it."

"And that's where Ketchum and his people come in."

"Right."

"And Craventon?"

"Somewhere. I'm not sure where."

"Do you suppose Ketchum knows Dreyfus is a forger and is stringing us along about that, too?"

"Possibly. But I'll bet he didn't know who he was the day before yesterday, and maybe, just maybe, he hasn't gotten his information on him yet from Washington or wherever they store lists of people like Dreyfus. If he's known to them, that is. He might not have a record."

"While you were in the house, I noticed something, speaking of Ketchum."

"What?"

"Our tail. Nobody followed us. Our protection has disappeared."

"Because I lied to them. After I talked to Dreyfus and just as we were about to leave the party, I looked at my watch and saw it was five-thirty, just half an hour until the guard would change. Two teams were about to drive to San Marino, one for me and one for you, and I figured it was a waste of time. Also, I wanted to stop by Dreyfus's and look around without Ketchum knowing."

"So what did you do?"

"I found a familiar-looking waiter, took some champagne, and told him not to send reinforcements in, that we were going directly to my apartment and you'd be spending the night there. I told him we'd check to make sure somebody was there when we arrived."

XVI

HE COULD SEE her standing in the kitchen, still in her elegant party dress but now wearing a big white apron. She stood at the stove, seasoning the canned corned beef hash and frying the eggs for dinner.

"Over easy, please," he said, cupping his hand over the mouthpiece of the phone. He was waiting for Ketchum to come on the line.

"My eggs are never dependable, especially at a strange stove."

"David?" Ketchum sounded far away; there was a light sound of static and an echo. "Are you here in town?"

"Orange County. I live in Orange County," came the immediate response, the slight hint of irritation. Jeffrey caught it and decided against any apology for interrupting Ketchum's Saturday night.

"Victor Dreyfus. The man you saw at Alfred Craventon's house with Zaki. Have you gotten anything on him?"

"No, nothing. Is that what you're calling about?"

"You'd better check again." He saw Rachel stop stirring and look in his direction, her smile a reflection of his moment of small triumph. "Victor Dreyfus is a forger. A very good one, probably, and I don't just mean a forger of books."

It took several minutes to tell Ketchum what he had found, to describe the equipment in as much detail as he could remember: the offset press, the numbering head, the laminator, the workroom, and—he was about to begin his first mental check when he remembered—the four passport-size photographs under the cigar box full of pens.

He was about to tell Ketchum about the nude photographs in the pile of underwear, too, but once again he felt he was invading the very private life of another human being, and he knew all too well that the only reason for telling Ketchum would be so that he could move in and blackmail if it looked as though that were the most effective way of getting the information. He deliberately omitted the photographs.

"Anything else?"

"Nope."

"Good work, Jeff. Good work."

"Self-preservation, David. I've never quite been sure who my friends are on this."

"We'll have someone on Dreyfus right away. Soon as we can get in and take a look, we'll decide whether to let him go and see what we get or bring him down." Jeffrey's sarcasm about friends was, as usual when Ketchum was doing business, pointedly ignored. But not for long this time. "I am your friend on this one, Jeff. Just be careful not to get too far ahead of us. That was a clever trick you pulled on my men at the party today, and I gave them holy hell for it. It seems they thought since you were a paid participant, you were telling the truth."

"I was, David. Don't blame them. We were coming straight back here and I knew the shift was about to change. I figured I'd save them some time and effort, that's all. I got the idea of going to Dreyfus's place while we were on the freeway. I was telling Rachel something he'd said, and that made me think of going to his house."

"What did he say?"

"He told me I'd accidentally stumbled onto something and that it wasn't at all what it seemed. He said to go away for my own safety. When I asked him if he was in any danger, he said to me, 'I'm very much needed right now. I'm not expendable. Not yet.' "

"Is Dreyfus going to that book auction in San Francisco tomorrow? The one you're flying up for?"

"How the hell did you find that out?"

"You bought two round-trip tickets—one for a plane leaving at noon tomorrow, the other for a plane leaving at four P.M. Monday. The first ticket is in your name, the second is for Rachel Sabin. You have a confirmed reservation at the Huntington Hotel. You did all of this through the travel agent across the patio from your office."

Jeffrey turned so that his back was to Rachel, who was now opening a bottle of wine. "Yes, I'm going. I don't know about her—I haven't asked yet. And I haven't any idea about Dreyfus at all. My guess is that he would very likely go to it. It's a big auction, probably the biggest of its kind, so I would imagine he'd be there for some of it."

"Jeff, I've been trying in the most direct damn way I know how to let you know that this isn't just some ordinary intrigue."

"I am well aware. I've been aware of that from the start.

What I can't seem to get out of you is just what is at stake here. I am not some fucking chess piece. Neither is Rachel."

"We know that. We've been with you all the way, helping whenever we can."

"But not saying a hell of a lot, right? Like what this is all about?"

"We're trying to find that out, too."

"I don't for one minute believe that. You know—you know a hell of a lot more than we do." The sound of activity in the kitchen, the constant motion of a dinner being prepared, suddenly stopped. He turned and saw Rachel staring at him, concern showing on her face and in her posture.

"Zaki is scheduled to go back to London tomorrow afternoon. He went and got his ticket today."

"Jesus Christ, will your people follow him onto the plane this time just to make sure he gets the hell out of here? And, I repeat, when are you going to tell me what is going on here?"

"Soon. I promise you. It's a very—very—delicate thing."

"Delicate, my ass!" He was tempted to bring up his speculation about Craventon, but the cutting edge of his own sense of survival cut the temptation off instantly, did not even give him time to form the sentence in his mind.

"Take it easy, Jeff. I'm trying to level with you. We don't know it was Zaki. Not at all. I will tell it all to you as soon as I'm allowed. Now is the time to be careful. Don't start anything without checking with me. It might be very dangerous."

"Just how dangerous? Tell me that."

"Those guys trying to run you off the road weren't kidding. You play it passive right now. Keep going about your business. If they come to you, we're ready. If you stir things up, you're dead."

Jeffrey's grip on the telephone had tightened so that his hand hurt.

"Her, too," Ketchum added.

"Will you be tailing us in San Francisco?"

"Yes. Of course."

For the first time Jeffrey felt a small sense of relief. Whatever else Ketchum wanted, however it was he was using Jeffrey and, now, Rachel, those unmarked cars with two men in them meant safety, and he welcomed them.

"How dangerous?" she asked when he hung up.

He repeated the conversation word for word.

"Is the 'us' in San Francisco you and me?"

"By way of ruining a small surprise I was saving until later this evening, yes, it is."

"Well, then. I have just one clue." She had taken a deep breath and turned back to the stove, determined to get the evening back on course. "The rest will be saved until later this evening as planned."

"You know, you really are a very considerate lady."

"What's considerate? I like surprises, and I like antici-pating them. And as they've been going lately"—she flipped an egg and looked directly into his eyes—"it's about time for a good one. Wouldn't you say?"

He put an album of Joshua Rifkin playing Scott Joplin on the stereo, set the table for dinner, and turned himself to the pleasures of the evening—anything to put his break-in at Victor Dreyfus's and his conversation with David Ketchum behind him, if just for a little while. He had planned that they go out, but his desire to call Ket-chum, and Rachel's insistence that she cook whatever she

found in the kitchen, had changed his plans. Rachel's idea
to stay in was exactly right. They ate in silence, listening
to the music, drinking their wine and eating. His egg was
perfect. For all his independence, and for all the pleasure
he took in being single, he was at heart a thoroughly do-
mestic man. His apartment, though masculine and somewhat spare, needed only closer inspection to reveal his
domesticity. Everything was orderly and clean, and it was
obvious he took pride in that.

When they had finished eating, he stood up and began
clearing away the plates. She interrupted his ritual, insisted she complete it. "Go. Sit. Have some more wine.
Listen to some more music."

He poured another glass, then settled on a Cleo Laine
album. He put it on the turntable, and as he hit the play
switch, he caught the scent of his sweat, the light, sour
smell of fear and anxiety, and he wanted to wash it away.

"I think what I'm going to do is go take a shower.
Breaking and entering makes me sweat a lot."

"Oh?" She put down the plates she was stacking and
walked to him, putting her arms around his waist. "It took
me a long time to realize I like the smell of men."

"Uhmm," he said, nuzzling his lips against her ear,
darting his tongue in and out.

"Feral."

"I didn't know you were kinky."

"Just a little. We all are, aren't we?"

"Yeah."

"Well, you go shower, and then why don't you slip into
something comfortable?"

"Isn't that what *I'm* supposed to say?"

"Yes, but this is your place, not mine."

He shaved, and as he stepped into the shower he heard

her flip the Cleo Laine record, humming the music. He stood in the hot water a minute, letting it pound out the fatigue and relax him. He grabbed a washcloth and soap and covered himself with lather. He was standing beneath the shower, his face full of soap, his head bent back so the water could hit his chest, when he felt her hand on his shoulder, felt her rub lightly across to his neck, then down his spine, stopping just in the crease of his buttocks, then starting around to the front of his body. He dipped his head and washed the soap from his face and looked at her. She was naked; a light tan line lightened her hips and breasts, and as he looked at her he could see the blue veins beneath her nearly translucent breasts. He reached out to them.

"No, no," she said softly, stepping behind him. "You can't touch me. Not yet."

"This another one of your kinks?"

"Where do you want me to touch you? Wash you?"

"Guess."

She took the soap and began rubbing it on his chest, scrubbing hard. She kneaded the muscles in his neck as she washed him. Her hands were strong and insistent. His erection was immediate, but she seemed not to notice, or if she did, she chose to ignore what was an obvious request for her attentions. She brushed it lightly with her hip, and once again he reached out to her.

"No . . . no . . . not yet."

"Please?"

"Say it again." She was standing on her toes, her lips nearly touching his, her body bent to escape his protruding penis.

"Please," he said, at last finding no resistance when he put his arms around her and pulled her to him. They washed each other, some places much more thoroughly than others, and when he turned off the water she looked up and smiled. "This is a new extreme of squeaky clean."

Their lovemaking continued as they dried one another off and went directly into the bedroom. As Jeffrey pulled back the big comforter, she reached between his legs from behind and touched him lightly. And when she got into bed beside him, she slid under the blanket and he gasped with pleasure as he felt her lips on him. Finally he could stand it no longer. He pulled her up beside him and began kissing her, slowly at first and then quickly and intensely, as though afraid some part of her might escape his passion.

Whereas the last time they made love she had seemed steady and growing in her excitement, this time he noticed she experienced little freshets of passion, in between which she lay back and smiled, her eyes closed. Her passion began closing in on her as the sweat of their bodies mixed. He went so far as to summon the image of David Ketchum to prolong the moment, but even Ketchum was not enough to forestall the explosion that was growing inside him. She followed seconds later, just as he was beginning to wonder if he could last any longer.

"There's something about you I don't understand," she whispered, her lips touching his ear. "I don't understand what it is that makes me act as I do. I want to be sexual with you. I want to do things to you and have you do things to me. I'm not usually like that."

He smiled, but said nothing.

"I'm not," she insisted. "I'm really not. I guess somehow I sense my sexuality isn't a threat to you. That it won't scare you off."

"Wear me out, maybe," he suggested.

"I'm being serious. This is important. These are strange times in the history of relationships between men and women. I want to understand something."

"I know they're strange times. God knows, I know that. I think maybe it's very simple. We met, something clicked, and we're right now at the point in our relationship— God, I dislike that word—where we physically can't get enough of each other."

"Yes. I feel that."

"I noticed." He laughed and she slapped him, not hard, but it smarted pleasurably.

"You into that, too?"

"Sorry. No pain. Not intentionally, anyway."

"Look, I'm just like any other guy. You're no sexual threat to me, right? I've got news. You're no threat until the first time I can't get it up. Then I'll get upset. I always do. Everybody does when it happens to them."

"It happens to women, too. Nobody ever seems to understand it correctly. For us it's 'Not tonight, I've got a headache.' My mother used to tell me that that was nature's rejection, not mine."

"Some mother."

"Now. San Francisco."

"The big Goldman auction is Monday and Tuesday. Probably the biggest collection of mystery and detective fiction to ever come on the market."

"I've read about it."

"I assumed you weren't going."

"Right."

"Well then. I propose a lesson in book buying for you."

He lifted back the covers slightly, began tracing an idle design between her breasts with his index finger. "I'm going up tomorrow to look the books over. My research

shows that you finish with classes at two P.M. Monday. I
have a ticket for you on the PSA flight at four. That way
you'll get there in time to watch the end of the first day's
auction. Then we'll go up to the Huntington Hotel, clean
up, and go out to dinner." He smiled, pleased with his
plan and delighted by the fantasies it brought to him.

"And then?"

"And then on Tuesday we'll go to the auction, and we'll
be back in Los Angeles early in the evening."

"There's one problem."

"I know. I figured you'd get somebody to do it for you."

"I will. It's a written midterm for both Tuesday classes.
The exam is ready. I'll have the teaching assistants give
it."

"Then you accept?"

"One condition. I choose the restaurant and I buy the
dinner."

"Agreed."

She was fast asleep beside him several hours later when
he awoke. He listened to her steady deep breathing for a
minute before he slid out of bed and padded quietly
across the bedroom carpet into the bathroom. He was
starting back to bed when he suddenly paused, then
stepped to the bedroom window. It looked directly down
on the parking lot and the alley behind the store. He saw a
car glide quietly into the lot, its lights off. He watched as
the car door opened, its interior light emitting a dull glow.
The driver walked to another car in the parking lot, exchanged a few words with its driver, then returned to his
car. The other car started and drove away. Jeffrey looked
at his watch. It was 2:00 A.M. exactly. Changing of the
guard, he thought to himself, except they're guarding me

from what they're hoping will come after me. He was struggling against an undertow, and he wondered just how far he would be made to swim. He knew the answer: until he'd swum too far.

It was some time before he fell asleep again, and when he did, it was a restless, dreamless, disturbed sleep.

XVII

THE DEALERS GATHERED in a run-down storefront in a derelict section of Golden Gate Avenue, took their places on uncomfortable metal folding chairs, and settled in for three days of bidding on the largest collection of mystery and detective fiction ever to go on the auction block. They came from as far away as London, and all of the well-known New York dealers were on hand, as well as all the others from around the country whose interest was in this specialized area of book collecting.

They were a diverse and unusual group of people, predominantly men, whose casual manner of dress and behavior belied their strong bond of common interest. Jeffrey, however, wore a tie, a brown herringbone jacket, and slacks—partly because he wanted to use the auction to create a businesslike impression and partly because Rachel was meeting him. Jeffrey knew many of the dealers and during the long Sunday afternoon before the auction he had socialized with them as they all sorted through the dusty lots of books tied with yellow string. The musty air was dense with excitement, and Jeffrey forced himself to concentrate on the books he had marked in the catalog, those he intended to bid on for himself, and those he had agreed to bid on for others. Next to the ones for his own business, he had marked his top prices in blue, but he could exceed these prices if he wanted. Next to those books he was going to bid on for various customers, he had marked the top prices in black. Each price was carefully noted, and on a separate sheet he had written down the name and phone number for the client. Now, as the auction was about to begin, he held a red pen in his hand to mark down the actual prices.

The 7,000 volumes—in 3,236 lots—had once reposed on the shelves of the library of Wendell Goldman, a wealthy San Francisco manufacturer whose consuming passion was books. Speculation about the fate of the collection had begun immediately upon the old man's death two years before. The collector—then well into his eighties and still carrying his battered briefcase full of lists of the books he wanted everywhere he went—had stepped out of his Nob Hill mansion and seen a car about to roll down one of the precipitous hills that had made San Francisco both famous and hazardous. He tried to stop the car, which had just begun to move. The car rolled right over the frail old man and killed him. His death was ruled accidental, but it lent a certain magic to his collection. After all, how many famous book collectors are killed in an accident that sounds as though it came right out of one of the pulps the victim so loved?

Wendell Goldman, it turned out, went for quantity as opposed to quality, and a great many of his books were not in the best of condition. Still, there were treasures aplenty and one in particular that Jeffrey wanted, wanted for himself. He knew a number of the other dealers would be after it, too, and he was ready for what would no doubt be an expensive contest.

It was lot 48, and it went on sale in the first hour of the auction: a single copy of *The Mask of Dimitrios,* published in 1939 in London, Eric Ambler's third and most famous book. Its title had been changed to *A Coffin for Dimitrios* when it was published in the United States later that same year, and a copy of the American edition was also on sale. The American edition, though relatively rare, was nowhere near as scarce as the British first edition, and for an intriguingly Amblerian reason: The warehouse where the books were stored between being bound and distributed to bookstores was bombed by the Germans during the blitz of London and very few copies survived. It was a book the auction house in a moment of vast underestimation, had valued at between $50 and $75.

The auctioneer, a florid man in a three-piece suit who looked at his catalog through Benjamin Franklin glasses and spoke to the assembled audience with a humor inadequate to any occasion—particularly one as suspenseful as this—opened the bidding for *The Mask of Dimitrios* at $50. Jeffrey sat on the edge of his chair, his right elbow resting on his right thigh, his right hand holding a four-by-seven index card on which was printed the number 24. It was his account number for the auction and he did not raise it until the bidding had passed $200 and moved from $5 to $10 increments.

He made his first bid at $230, turning several heads in his direction. In less than a minute, the bidding went over $350, and where there had been seven bidders, there were now only three. One, a dealer from Santa Barbara, Steve

Grant, was a friend of Jeffrey's. Jeffrey and Steve, who had had dinner together the evening before, did not exchange glances during the bidding. Each had known the other was after the book, and each was careful not to let the other know his top bid, making sure their friendship would be unharmed by their competition. The third hopeful buyer still in the bidding was a London dealer, whose desire for the book was understandable, but Jeffrey figured that like most British dealers he was unable to pay the sums American dealers now paid. He was right—the man dropped out at $400.

Only Jeffrey and Steve remained, and by now the air in the room was thick with excitement. The first big book had come up and the first big price was being established. It would be more than the price for one single book, it would be a price that would set the tone for much that was to follow.

"Four twenty-five. Do I hear four twenty-five?"

Jeffrey held his card up, flicked it with his wrist instead of nodding at the auctioneer.

"I have four twenty-five. Do I hear four fifty? Four twenty-five—going . . . going . . ." There was a deliberate pause as the auctioneer gave Jeffrey's competition time to reconsider. It was a masterful pause because it worked perfectly.

"Four fifty. I now have four fifty. Do I hear four seventy-five? Four seventy-five?"

Jeffrey raised his card and flicked it again without hesitation.

"I have four seventy-five. Do I hear five hundred? I'm at five hundred. Going . . . going . . . Five twenty-five!" Even the auctioneer seemed surprised at that price, as well he might have, for he was the person who had estimated the book's value for the catalog and had been far under its potential. "I have five twenty-five. Five twenty-five—going"—the man was looking directly at Jeffrey, peering over his Ben Franklin glasses and putting out a direct challenge—"going . . ."

It was more than Jeffrey had intended to spend. But it was also a book he had sought ever since he'd begun collecting, and his competitive nature would not permit him to lose this book. So be it. He gave one short flick of his card, wondering if he was going to have to go even higher.

"Five fifty. I have five fifty. Do I hear five seventy-five? Five seventy-five? Going . . . going . . ." The auctioneer was a man whose flair for the dramatic somewhat exceeded his capacities as an actor, but even under the circumstances his calculated pause was effective. It had been Jeffrey's intention to one day forcefully establish his presence, even among the bookdealers who already knew him, and this day was it. "Five fifty. Going . . . going . . . gone! Sold to number . . . number?"

Jeffrey was so astonished he'd lowered his card and had to hold it up once again.

"Sold to number twenty-four for five hundred and fifty dollars."

There was a burst of applause, and Jeffrey felt a flush of pleasure. He tried to mask his excitement by carefully marking down the price in red in his catalog, this time circling the number as well. The circle meant he had bought it. The tingling in his spine and the sweat forming in his armpits were a part of the excitement, and he was oblivious to everything but the auction.

The retitled American edition was the next book up, and this time, seeing Steve was after it as well—there was a questioning look from Jeffrey and an answering nod from Steve—Jeffrey dropped out of the bidding early. There was more applause when his friend got the book, but the price this time was less than a quarter of what the much scarcer English edition had sold for.

Jeffrey did not bid again until lot 304 came up several hours later, a first edition of John Buchan's classic *Thirty-nine Steps,* which had later been made into a film by Alfred Hitchcock, a film that contained a brief airplane chase after the hero, a sort of filmic foretelling of what Hitchcock would work into a fine dramatic frenzy in *North by Northwest.* Jeffrey had been ordered to go no further than $175 by the television producer who had asked him to bid on it. Jeffrey thought he had a very good chance, but there were others willing to pay more and the book went to one of the Santa Barbara dealers for $200.

The Santa Barbara group was something of a phenomenon among bookmen, a small nucleus of dealers who had two reasons for settling into one of the most agreeable cities in the country. First of all, the Black Sparrow Press, one of the best small presses in the country, was located in the city and its books were sought after by many collectors. Second, the climate and living conditions in Santa Barbara were ideal for a group of businessmen who did the vast majority of their business by telephone and mail. They were also a force in the business because they would, especially on rare occasions such as this, choose bidding partners, increasing their spending power by sharing the cost of the books. Steve was Jeff's partner in several of the books in the auction, books they agreed to purchase because they were reasonably certain they would find collectors—either individuals or institutions—who would spend the extra money for them.

One of the authors they had agreed on was W. R. Burnett, who had over the years written a number of books that became successful films, most famously *Little Caesar, High Sierra,* and *The Asphalt Jungle.* Jeffrey and Steve had agreed to bid jointly on these three books, and when they came on the block Jeffrey sat silently as Steve, one row ahead and two seats to the left, ran up the bidding. They had decided the evening before that if Jeffrey wanted to go higher, he was to lightly tap Steve on the shoulder.

The bidding on *Little Caesar,* which had been estimated at \$40 to \$70—they thought it low for a book and dust jacket in fine condition printed in 1929—was over almost before it began. Jeffrey and Steve had agreed to go to \$500 for it and were delighted when they knocked it down to \$150. They got *High Sierra* for \$140, again less than they had agreed to spend, but their luck ran out on *The Asphalt Jungle.* They had a ceiling of \$100, and when that number was surpassed, Jeffrey leaned across and tapped Steve on the shoulder. "We made it up on the other two," he whispered. Steve nodded and then bought the book for \$150.

The two friends now owned the books jointly, and the plan they had concocted several months earlier was about to become a reality. It had begun when Steve appeared with several scripts by W. R. Burnett, offering to sell them to Jeffrey. Jeffrey hadn't bought them, but they had made him think of the writer himself, who was now beginning to be collected. Signed or inscribed copies of his books were extremely rare, and both Jeffrey and Steve had wondered if he was still alive. Jeffrey began checking his sources in the studios, calling old-time agents, and following any leads he found. It was a casual search, conducted on the off-chance some information would eventually turn up. It did in the form of W. R. Burnett himself, who was in his eighties, living in a condominium in Marina del Rey, and still writing despite fading health. Jeffrey telephoned and, as was usually the case, the old writer was delighted by the attention. When Jeffrey arrived a week later to take Burnett and his wife out to dinner, he had with him seven copies of books Burnett had written, and when the dinner was over, they were all either signed or inscribed.

With Steve's help, Jeffrey bought whatever Burnett books he could find, and some of the finest were at the auction. In addition to the writer's three most famous titles, the partners also bought six lesser-known books. They would soon all be signed by Burnett and, because of the signatures, would bring prices far in excess of what they had been bought for originally. Jeffrey had explained to the inquisitive old man exactly what he was doing, and Burnett's participation had been enthusiastic from the start. It was, he told Jeffrey, his only hold on immortality and he was at an age when immortality was a comforting thought indeed.

When the last of the Burnett books came on the block—a lot of two novels written in the late 1950s, both of which Jeffrey and Steve had several copies of already signed—the auctioneer looked directly at Steve, expecting him to bid. Instead, he found Steve's back and Steve shaking the hand of the man he had fought so hard to outbid on the Ambler novel.

"We celebrate over dinner," Steve whispered.

"Can't. I've got a date. Next week? In L.A.?"

"Okay," Steve said with a big smile, "but you pay."

"Why me?"

"You got my Ambler."

"You're on."

Jeffrey lost out on the two James Cain novels he wanted. *The Postman Always Rings Twice* and *Mildred Pierce* were snapped up by a Santa Barbara dealer Jeffrey was certain was bidding with a silent partner.

It was an engrossing and demanding experience, and from the time he bought the Ambler book, Jeffrey succumbed to it. He did not particularly notice the passage of time and was startled to hear the auctioneer apologize for the late break for lunch.

Jeffrey's bidding had been noticed and he was establishing himself as an ambitious dealer, an image he wanted to promote. He also wanted to appear smart, and so he let it be known that he did in fact have a customer for the Ambler novel, one who would probably pay more than the auction price. He told himself this was only a small lie: He was his customer and had been willing to pay more to get the book. If he had been candid, had told acquaintances at the auction that he had bought the book because he simply had to have it for his own, they would have understood this also. But to have a customer was far better. He knew, too, that when all the Burnett books from the Goldman collection—several of which contained Goldman's bookplate—reappeared in Jeffrey's and Steve's respective catalogs a few months hence, signed and priced accordingly, his stature would increase still more, and would attract other dealers as customers and new collectors. The Goldman auction was critically important to Jeffrey's plans for the future and he had calculated his bids accordingly.

It was late in the afternoon, and the true denizens of Golden Gate Avenue, the bums and winos who had stared blankly through the window from time to time during the day, were beginning to appear. It was exactly 5:30—though Jeffrey was far too preoccupied to notice the time—when Goldman's collection of books by Raymond

Chandler went on sale. Two of them—*The Big Sleep,* Chandler's first book; and *The Long Goodbye,* his next-to-last—Jeffrey was determined to purchase for the collection of Alfred Craventon. When the Chandlers came up for sale, Jeffrey quickly looked around to find Victor Dreyfus, for it had been Dreyfus who had okayed the purchase and who, Jeffrey was certain, would be attending the auction. He did not see him and turned instead to begin the bidding on *The Big Sleep.*

It was a copy in fine condition, and Jeffrey expected to pay dearly for it. He did.

In another short, dramatic auction, followed by the third round of applause of the day, Jeffrey bought the book for $1,900, establishing a record for a Chandler book. Jeffrey smiled to himself; he knew Craventon would immediately pay $3,000 for it.

He wondered again why Craventon had asked him to bid on the Chandlers and why he hadn't asked Victor Dreyfus to do it for him. Jeffrey was certain Dreyfus did all of Craventon's bidding—in more than one sense, too. And why wasn't Dreyfus at the auction? He had been at Craventon's side at the party when Jeffrey was instructed to do the bidding. Still. There was something slightly off about what was—or wasn't—going on. Jeffrey could give no fact or reason for his feeling. He sensed something was wrong, and it made him uncomfortable if only because he could not explain what it was.

"You're a real big spender."

He turned and found Rachel sitting directly behind him.

"You were here for all of that?"

"I came in right at the start. I didn't want to disturb you," she said as he moved a chair aside and she stepped through and sat down beside him. She was wearing a tailored black and white tweed suit. Class, he thought as he looked at her. Real class.

"It's for Alfred Craventon. He'll pay three thousand for it and there's one other coming up that he wants."

"Nice profit," she said, nudging him lightly in the ribs.

"You still buy dinner."

"I don't welsh. Ever."

He looked at her and smiled, his eyes revealing his thoughts, and her reaction acknowledging them.

"Good to see you, too," she said simply.

"Did our friends come up with you?"

"No. One watched me onto the plane and another picked me up at the airport. And he graciously offered me a ride down here. He said this wasn't exactly a swell neighborhood."

"No, not exactly. Unless you like to drink Thunderbird and sleep in doorways."

His attention shifted back to the auction and he began bidding on *Farewell, My Lovely,* but soon dropped out with a shrug.

"Too bad. Why didn't you stay in?" she asked.

"It wasn't a very good copy and the dust jacket was torn in several places. Hard to resell at a high price. I don't like to spend that much unless I've got a customer."

When the bidding ended at $1,400, he watched as she turned and looked to see who had bought it, then noticed—was he imagining it?—a look of respect when Rachel looked at him. This had been an exciting and special day for him, and now it was even more so. He felt like an experienced angler showing the stream to a new fisherman, and the fact that it was Rachel and that she had both a professional and personal interest in him made it all the better.

"Here we go," he said, pointing to his catalog, underscoring *The Long Goodbye* with his finger. "There are two of them on sale," he whispered to her, "and the second is the better of the two copies. I hope they don't all already know that."

Jeffrey stayed briefly in the bidding before dropping out at $125, and together they watched as the bidding went to $180.

"I think I'm up shit creek," he whispered. One eighty was the high figure on the auctioneer's printed estimate, and Jeffrey assumed that the other bidders knew the second copy to go on sale was a good bit better than the first.

He could barely hide his excitement when he bought the second, better volume of *The Long Goodbye* for $140.

"I don't think I'd want to be up against you on any of this," she said to him.

"How about just plain up against me?"

"Tend to your business and we'll see."

"I'll tend to it up and through Charles Dickens, but not a minute more."

"Very well then," she said, suddenly sounding very professorial. "It is common knowledge that Dickens is considered a precursor of what we know as contemporary mystery novels. His last book was *The Mystery of Edwin Drood*, and it was Dickens's attempt to become a part of the Victorians' growing interest in thrillers and mysteries. He wrote it in 1870, and never completed it."

"Thank you, Professor Sabin."

"Dr. Sabin," she corrected him, "as soon as I complete my thesis."

"There's just one Dickens I'm interested in today. Not to buy, because it isn't in very good condition." He flipped through his catalog and found the listing for *Bleak House*, which was on sale as originally printed, advertisements and all. The estimate was for $400 to $700. "I have this desire to one day buy a set of the complete works of Dickens. I loved his books when I was growing up."

"Me too. *Tale of Two Cities* in particular," she whispered.

He nodded in agreement.

For the next half-hour they watched the bidding, and between bids he pointed out various dealers and told her about them. A few she knew already, but most were new to her. She also listened attentively as he described the fine points of the auction and described the other books he planned to buy.

The auctioneer was introducing the first of six lots of the novels of Len Deighton when Jeffrey felt a newspaper tap him gently on the shoulder and turned to find the newspaper was held by David Ketchum. Rachel turned and saw him, too, and they all distinctly heard—and understood—Jeffrey's greeting.

"Shit."

Ketchum motioned them to an unoccupied corner at the rear of the room.

"Victor Dreyfus is dead. His throat was slit."

Rachel gasped, her hand instinctively reaching for her mouth, two fingers crossing her lips to silence herself.

"Jesus." Jeffrey felt his stomach knot and had to swallow hard several times before he could say more.

Ketchum filled the silence immediately. "You said those photographs were under one of the cigar boxes in his extra bedroom?"

"Yeah. The last one on the left as you faced the desk."

"Gone. So is the numbering head."

Ketchum waited while what he'd said had its intended impact on Jeffrey and Rachel. Then, spreading the newspaper on a glass display case set against the wall, he tapped a stubby finger against the lead story in what turned out to be the latest edition of the *San Francisco Chronicle.* "Have you seen this?"

They hadn't, and as they leaned close to read, Jeffrey couldn't help but notice that the first shelf of the display case contained the pièce de résistance of the entire auction, a slim, fragile paperback volume that in 1888 sold for one shilling—Jeffrey had earlier calculated the original value at fifteen cents—and was the first appearance of Sir Arthur Conan Doyle's Sherlock Holmes. Jeffrey had heard there were already sealed bids on the book for up to $13,000. He looked at it briefly before shifting his gaze to the newspaper, willing himself out of his pleasure in the day's progress and into the harsh reality of Dreyfus's death and the newspaper Ketchum had placed before them. It was a story that made the daring adventures of Sherlock Holmes seem mild by comparison.

Washington—U.S. security agencies have bolstered their bodyguard forces and tightened border controls after being warned that Libyan or other Arab hit teams are out to assassinate President Reagan and other top American officials.

A State Department spokesman confirmed today that "reliable" sources in the Middle East had warned U.S. officials last week that an assassination squad was about to infiltrate the United States, possibly from Canada. The report included the names of six alleged killers, the spokesman said.

As a result, the Secret Service, the FBI, and other government security agencies have intensified measures to prevent harm to the president, the vice president, or cabinet officers.

> Another State Department official, speaking off the record, suggested that the assassination team was operating under direct orders from Muammar el-Qaddafi, the radical leader of Libya and a sworn opponent of the U.S. and Israel.

The story went on to detail the measures being taken to protect the president, vice president, and cabinet officers. Jeffrey stopped reading. He felt his knees weaken and his head grow light as he realized what was now about to begin. He noticed that Rachel was still reading intensely, that what had occurred to him had not yet occurred to her. To keep himself steady, he placed his hands, palms down, on the edges of the glass case and went back to the story. It reported that U.S. security agencies knew who most of the assassins were and planned to intercept them when they entered the country. When he finished reading the piece, Jeffrey looked up at Ketchum, an unmistakable challenge to tell the rest of the story.

"There's just one problem with this story," Ketchum said, tapping the newspaper.

"What's that?" Rachel asked. Jeffrey already knew.

"We don't know who they are."

"You what?" Rachel's look was pure astonishment.

"We don't know who they are."

"But it says you do," she protested, angrily tapping her right index finger on the newspaper. "Right here."

"That's what we want them to suspect. What it is," Ketchum said without expression and without looking at Jeffrey, "is managing the news a bit to our advantage. Jeff, those four pictures under the cigar box—"

"I think I can identify them," Jeffrey told him.

"They might be our men and then again they might not. The chances are they're it. Zaki went through customs at Heathrow four hours before we found Dreyfus's body. I had the house staked out right after we spoke to you, but Dreyfus's car was in the driveway, and my stake-out saw Dreyfus go from his shop into the house at just after midnight."

"But somebody saw you watching and went in another way."

"Yup. By the time we got on to it, Zaki was safely out of the country and Dreyfus was dead."

"What about Craventon?" Jeffrey asked.

"Vanished," Ketchum said, turning his palms up in a gesture of conspiratorial frustration.

"He *is* in on this somehow, isn't he?" Rachel interrupted.

"Yeah, but we don't know where or how. My best sources inform me that if he's involved at all, it's that he's being used somehow."

There was a pause while Rachel digested the information and Jeffrey questioned the facts he had and tried to incorporate them into what he was certain was a far more complicated story than Ketchum was telling them. Ketchum, his hands thrust into his coat pockets, stood watching, as though waiting to see if they would believe, would continue to cooperate.

"You were right about Dreyfus," Ketchum finally said, turning slightly as a well-dressed woman walked toward the cabinet then turned away when she saw them talking among themselves. "He is a master forger, but with no ar-rests or convictions since 1942, and then it was for tam-pering with draft files. His own, in fact. What he's done since, we don't know for sure, but what he did for Zaki— that is, we have to suppose it was for Zaki—was forge four green cards."

Jeffrey shook his head in disbelief.

"I imagine he did a very good job on them. Those four men—Qaddafi's assassins, their entry into the country arranged by Zaki—are going to be on their way pretty soon. If the cards work—and I imagine they will—they'll pass right through customs as resident aliens. Safe and sound."

"Well?" Rachel asked.

"Unless we stop them," Ketchum continued. "And we begin by getting back to L.A. and looking at some pictures they're sending by Telex right now."

"I'll need a minute," Jeffrey said. He went to the cashier and wrote a check for the books he'd bought. While he waited for the messenger to go and pull them from the shelves, he sought out Steve, deciding what to say to him as he said it.

"Look, there's an emergency. I've got to leave." For emphasis, he handed his two remaining catalogs to him. "I'm sorry to impose on you, but I wonder if you'd do my bidding for me. My customers' books are circled in black, my own are in blue."

"You all right?" Steve asked.

"Yeah, yeah. Fine. It isn't me. It's a friend. I'm sorry. Don't bid on mine when you're after the same ones. Just put an *X* through the listing. Really. No problem at all." Jeffrey was whispering.

"You want me to find somebody else to do them?"

"No. That'd be silly. Hurt your chances. There's a couple of Hammetts I want. If you can get any of them . . ." Even his whisper was attracting attention from the dealers sitting close-by. In one day he had become conspicuous and discovered the consequences of being known. The other dealers no doubt thought a plot was hatching and they strained to hear.

"You sure you're all right?" Steve asked. "Can I do anything else?"

"No, I'm fine. Just try to get the books. If I'm not back by tomorrow noon, go on without me. I'm sure I'll be back."

"See you tomorrow, then," Steve said.

Jeffrey looked up and heard the auctioneer announce lot 893: Dickens's *Bleak House.* Jeffrey walked quickly to the back of the room where Rachel, her suitcase beside her, and Ketchum, pacing impatiently, waited. He picked up his package of books and they left.

Rachel was already in the back seat and the driver had started the engine as Jeffrey and Ketchum walked around to the other side of the car.

"One more thing about Dreyfus," Ketchum said quietly.

"Yes?"

"His penis and testicles had been cut off and stuffed in his mouth. That's what some Arabs do to traitors."

"Good God."

"Did Dreyfus tell you anything that might lead you to suspect who it was he was really working for?"

"No. I told you everything. He just warned me."

"That may have been enough. It could be they'll really come after you now. They may think you know much more than you do."

"Shit. Everybody thinks that. Except me."

Ketchum said nothing. The car was speeding down the freeway for San Francisco International Airport before it occurred to Jeffrey that his clothes and everything else— including the bouquet of flowers he had bought for Rachel—were in his room at the Huntington Hotel.

"It's been taken care of," Ketchum said. "It'll be on the next plane and you'll have it right away."

XVIII

FOR FOUR HOURS, in an impersonal room equipped with what he thought of as federal functional furniture, Jeffrey sat and looked at photographs with David Ketchum. He was in an office on the fourteenth floor of the Federal Building on Wilshire Boulevard. Below him he could see the busy streets of Westwood and the white and red lights of southbound and northbound traffic on the San Diego Freeway. The red lights trailed off into the Santa Monica Mountains and he wished his car were among them, heading home. The coffee they drank had a flat, machine-brewed taste to it, a taste the cheap styrofoam cups made even worse.

Despite its marble facade and spacious lobby, the Federal Building was just another cold, indifferent, institutional government building no more adapted to its particular environment than any other government building in any other city. It was, every inch of it, government issue. Jeffrey wondered how many thousands of gallons of beige paint were needed for the walls, how many

215

thousands of gray metal desks and gray metal chairs were needed to effectively depersonalize a building this big. The main lobby and the reception area of the fourteenth floor—and, Jeffrey assumed, the reception area of every other floor—had a photograph disguised as a painting of President Reagan. Even he looked institutional, his gaze artificially sincere, his countenance feigning interest. Nothing welcomed, everything imposed.

Rachel had insisted on accompanying him, and while he and Ketchum sorted through photographs—carried by the armloads in and out of the office by one of the agents who had been guarding Jeffrey—she sat quietly, reading Jeffrey's copy of *The Mask of Dimitrios*. Jeffrey looked up at her once, only to be struck by the irony that she was reading a spy classic, caught up in a spy fiction, to ease her anxiety about a similar reality.

"You sure you can recognize them?" Ketchum asked after two hours of sorting through photographs.

"Yes. I think so. One or two of them at least," Jeffrey said, rubbing his eyes and staring back at the faces before him. They were all, Ketchum had said, Arab underground leaders of one sort or another, some of them already in the United States.

"Any four could be our men," he patiently explained time and again.

"They're beginning to look like a room full of Chinese waiters," Jeffrey apologized. He sensed the pressure, wanted to help, but was unable to find a familiar face.

Rachel looked up and smiled. Ketchum shoved another stack of pictures in front of Jeffrey.

When it happened, it seemed to Jeffrey as though the picture made eye contact with him, not he with it.

"Him!" he announced triumphantly. Almost the same picture.

Ketchum grabbed the photograph, picked up a telephone, and read the number on the back of the picture into it. Within a minute an agent walked into the room and handed Ketchum a computer printout.

"Zamel, Nafir," Ketchum read. "Libyan revolutionary and Marxist, educated in Russia and trained by the KGB. He's believed to have headed the attack on the El Al plane in Rome. He's our man all right."

Jeffrey looked at the picture again, studied it, hoping it would reveal something more about Zamel, Nafir, trained assassin. Rachel, too, put down the Ambler book and looked at the picture.

"He's not in this country now," Ketchum added. "At least not under his own identity."

"How do you know that?" Rachel asked.

"Every immigration agent at every port of entry has immediate access to a computer in San Diego. Every passport, every green card, every temporary visitor goes into that computer."

"That's impressive," Rachel answered.

"Also valuable," Ketchum added. It was the first time she had seen him smile genuinely. "Within five minutes from now, every immigration agent will have the name of Nafir Zamel and all of the necessary information. Within an hour, they'll have his photograph."

"Maybe," Jeffrey added hopefully, "they'll even have Nafir Zamel."

The phone rang and Ketchum answered it, omitting a greeting and simply stating his name. Jeffrey and Rachel listened intently to half of what seemed to them both an almost abstract conversation.

"Full documentation, yes. Credit cards, the works."

Ketchum listened.

"No. Too dangerous."

He listened again.

"What if they don't take it?"

Ketchum listened more, pausing once to look at Jeffrey and Rachel, and then turned away from them, making it obvious that what was being discussed involved them.

"All right. You'll let the cousins know?"

Ketchum listened some more. Finally, he turned again to look at Rachel and Jeffrey. "Mr. and Mrs.," he said into the phone, "will do."

Rachel's cheeks colored slightly and she folded her hands primly in her lap. Jeffrey looked up, glared briefly at Ketchum, then went back to sorting through the last pile of photographs.

"Not here," he said to Ketchum when he hung up. "If any of the others are here, I didn't recognize them."

"Uhmmm," Ketchum said, obviously thinking about something else.

"Well? What was the conversation about?" Jeffrey nodded at the telephone.

Ketchum paused, then took the plunge. "We want you—both of you—to go to London. Tomorrow." Ketchum quickly looked at his watch. It was just after 1:00 A.M. "Today. The link between Narib Zaki and"—he looked down at the printout he still held in his hand—"Nafir Zamel is not certain but very likely. We want Zaki to see you."

"I think I know why," Jeffrey said evenly. "But why Rachel?"

"Double the bait, double the catch."

"All right. Count me in," Rachel answered immediately.

"No," Jeffrey said, his anger rising. "Look, this is no time for lectures, no time for poses of loyalty or patriotism. That stuff doesn't count, at least not here and not now. In some other place, maybe, but not here. We are dealing with the most cynical, the most devious people there are. That's our side I'm talking about. The other side simply defies explanation. No—no, they don't. You want to know what they did with Victor Dreyfus when they killed him?"

He could see Ketchum wince, and he could see that doubt was beginning to blur Rachel's determination. She shrugged indecisively. He told her.

"Why do they think he's a traitor?"

"No one is saying for sure, but it seems Victor Dreyfus made the serious mistake of warning me. That, apparently, was enough."

"You forget something," Ketchum interrupted. "He had done his work—they were through with him. Maybe they figured what they did—the way they did it, that is— would keep you and me farther away from this whole thing."

"There is—in a way—a right and a wrong here," she said, choosing her words carefully. "After all, some Arab fanatic has no right sending someone in to assassinate the president. We do rather well at getting rid of our own anyway. It's wrong. It should be stopped. They've seen me, they've already tried to kill me, and obviously they figure I'm involved. Well, I am."

"You can be disinvolved," Jeffrey said to her.

"How? If I don't go to London, who's to say I'll be safe here? And wouldn't it be better if there were two of us in London instead of one? For all I know, they may think I'm one of his"—she nodded in Ketchum's direction but did not use his name, could not think of it at that moment— "people. An agent or whatever it is you guys call yourselves. I'm going, Jeffrey. I've got nothing to lose and something to gain."

He looked at her, watched her without blinking as she

spoke, and he knew the force of her determination, understood her reasoning. He wanted her with him.

"All right, then, Dave," Jeffrey said quickly, hurrying to get the words out before they lost the peculiar logic they acquired as they formed in his mind. "It's a new deal. The trip to London will cost twenty grand."

"Sure."

"Ten for me, ten for her."

"Real patriotism, I'll say that," Ketchum said sarcastically.

"Let's call it 'practical patriotism,' if you'd like. I don't really care what you think of it. You've used us and used us again. We're entitled to something for that. Anyway, that is the deal. Payment is in advance. We see deposit slips at our banks or we don't get on the plane."

"Now wait a minute—"

"No. You wait. It just might be that if you have an investment in us, you'll take better care of us."

"I see." Ketchum was about to make a counteroffer, or at least that's what Jeffrey sensed was about to come, but the bargaining was interrupted by an agent walking into the small room carrying two manila envelopes.

"All right. Write your account numbers and your bank addresses before you leave here and we'll get you the deposit receipts this afternoon. Now, your cover." He dumped the contents of the envelopes onto the table.

"Amazing," Rachel said as she looked them over. There were three credit cards, two driver's licenses and passports—all with photographs of Jeffrey and Rachel on them—in the names of Mr. and Mrs. Roger Thomas.

"Mr. and Mrs.," Rachel said, not addressing anyone in particular.

"Easier that way. We already know you're—ah—

friendly—so we thought you wouldn't mind." Ketchum paused briefly, then continued. "The plane leaves at five-thirty this afternoon. TWA. Your drivers will have the tickets when they pick you up."

"And you?" Jeffrey asked.

"I'm coming. And there will be others, too."

"British?"

"Probably not. We're letting them know, but we're asking to handle it ourselves. Better for you, too. One tends to take better care of one's own, if you get what I mean."

"Why all this stuff"—Rachel waved at the passports, credit cards, and driver's licenses—"if Zaki knows who we are already?"

"When you walk into Zaki's store, you'll go in as yourselves. But at your hotel—and everywhere else—you'll be Mr. and Mrs. Roger Thomas. A precaution for your safety."

"Fucking incredible, isn't it?" Jeffrey said to her.

"Is this real?" she asked holding up a gold American Express card made out to Mrs. Roger Thomas.

"You mean, if you use it will it work?" Ketchum asked.

"Yes. Will it?"

"Yeah, it works. Use it to pay your hotel bill when you leave."

"Who gets the bill?" Jeffrey interrupted.

"It comes directly to us. Okay. Go home, get some sleep. Don't tell anyone where you're going. Rachel, you're to call in sick with appendicitis tomorrow. We'll have a hospital and a cover all arranged. Jeffrey, you just close up shop and leave your message machine on. Tell anyone who asks you're going to the desert for a few days in the sun." Ketchum sounded like the coach of an underprepared but determined high-school football team.

They walked out of the office and into the small waiting room. There on the floor beside the door was Jeffrey's suitcase. His raincoat was thrown over the chair beside it, and on the adjoining chair were the roses he had bought to give to Rachel. When he had last seen them, they were sitting in a glass, full of water, propped up against the mirror over the bathroom sink. Now they were nearly dead. Rachel looked up at Jeffrey and smiled her thanks.

Within two hours, Jeffrey had had a long, hot shower, most of a bottle of wine, and had tumbled into bed exhausted. He quickly fell asleep, and then just as quickly blinked awake, his eyes wide, his heartbeat accelerated. He tossed, he sweated. He got up twice to go to the bathroom and get a drink of water. Finally, he decided to go for a run. But it was still dark—it was just 4:00 A.M.—and there were two men sitting in a car outside his apartment who would stop him from running. He pulled on a robe, then padded quietly into his bookshop, turned on the light, and proceeded to look through his mail.

He began by methodically cutting each envelope with a letter opener, then spilling its contents onto his desk. There was the usual assortment of advertisements, a couple of bills—one for $300 from Mike's orthodontist, which caused Jeffrey to grimace—several catalogs from bookdealers, and an even dozen mail orders for books from his latest catalog. Also five checks from customers. Good. At the bottom of the pile was an envelope addressed to Jeffrey by a formal, trained hand. He turned it over and instantly recognized the elegantly engraved return address. He slit the envelope open, took out the carefully folded matching letter paper, opened it, and withdrew Victor Dreyfus's check for $235, sent, Jeffrey figured, just hours before he was murdered.

Jeffrey took his bank-deposit stamp from the center drawer, turned each check over, stamped it, added them on his calculator, filled out a deposit slip, and put them in a postage-paid envelope addressed to his bank. He'd mail them first thing the next morning and they'd be credited to his account by the time he reached London.

He knew if he waited until he returned, Dreyfus's check would be useless and he'd have to go through all the logistics of petitioning his estate and dealing with lawyers, and by the time he got his money—if he did get it—it would have been hardly worth the effort. He paused and thought of Dreyfus. No doubt he'd thought of his murderer as a friend and felt no fear: Ketchum had said there had been no sign of a struggle.

To escape thoughts of Dreyfus, and to escape speculation about what lay ahead for himself, Jeffrey took his new prize into his hands.

The book jacket on *The Mask of Dimitrios* contained the title and Eric Ambler's name, the title at the top, the author at the bottom of a dark blue cover turning a lighter blue at the edges. In the center of the cover, on a sea of dark blue, so dark it looked almost black, was Dimitrios's mask, a white death mask, unmoving, uncaring, its eyes closed, its lips closed, almost pursed. He stared at it several minutes, then turned the book over in his hands, caressed it, and remembered how excited he'd been when he first read it. How long ago was that? Long, long ago. He'd been in his teens. Sixteen, probably. He had longed to be a Latimer, longed to share in his adventure, to solve the riddle of Dimitrios.

He could not have imagined then, any more than he could actually understand now, that life would deal him his own Dimitrios; that by solving the mystery of a minor forgery, he would uncover an even greater mystery. Victor

Dreyfus was dead, his genitals stuffed into his mouth. He had warned Jeffrey. The realization brought sweat to his brow. Narib Zaki. Nafir Zamel. Names as exotic as Dimitrios Makropoulos and Colonel Haki. And finally, Alfred Craventon. He didn't remember anyone ever sweating in *The Mask of Dimitrios.*

He looked up and saw the first rays of sun begin to filter through the big pepper tree outside his window.

XIX

"STICK CLOSE," Ketchum had said as they went to their rooms. The long polar flight, and a wait to go through immigration, had taken its toll. Even though it was early afternoon in London, it was still long before dawn in Los Angeles, so the weary travelers decided on a nap.

"Wouldn't you know," Jeffrey said as he and Rachel trailed behind a bellboy carrying their luggage, "that in a city full of famous hotels, Ketchum would choose the Hilton—complete with Trader Vic's?"

"Somehow it doesn't come as a great surprise," she whispered back to him. It was ridiculous feeling this way, but there it was. She felt she was sneaking into the hotel—Mrs. Thomas indeed—for a tryst, and that what might be acceptable in modern America was simply not done in traditional London. She had been to London several times before, had been there less than a year ago, in fact, but this was the first time she had ever checked into a hotel with a man and with both using assumed names.

Yes, they had reason and, yes, there was something more important involved. But, yes, she felt guilty, too.

She explained all of this to Jeffrey when they were inside their hotel room. He had immediately started pulling clothes out of his suitcase, full of nervous energy, and he kept on going while she talked.

"I see," he said when she was done. "Staying in hotels makes you horny. That it?"

"That isn't the word I'd use," she said to him, turning slightly so that he wouldn't see her smile. He had used exactly the right word. When she looked back, she saw he was pulling off his clothes with such speed he was left standing in his underwear in a matter of seconds.

"You too?" she said.

"First things first," he said, rummaging around in his suitcase. He pulled out a pair of dirty running shoes, shorts, and a T-shirt. "I'm going running. I have a friend who's a doctor and he told me that if you travel, the first thing to do when you arrive is get some exercise, then take a short nap—no more than two hours—and force your body onto local time. That way you have less jet lag."

"I wonder what they called it before jets?"

"No idea, no idea at all. That was before my time." He went into the bathroom and emerged minutes later in his running clothes as she hung the last of her clothing in the closet.

"You look cute in shorts," she said to him.

"I'll bet you do too."

The lobby of the Hilton was indistinguishable from other Hiltons in other cities except for the large map of London in a glass case near the entrance. Jeffrey traced his finger through the famous sections of London: Covent Garden, Mayfair, Picadilly—all names that for him had a

special resonance. Then he found he was across the street
from Hyde Park. He plotted a route through the park,
tried to memorize the turns. He crossed into the park
through an underground passage, and started his run.
Within minutes he was off his course, but he kept on
going. He figured he could always stop and ask someone
to point him in the direction of the Hilton.

He made it all the way through the park, and then, as
he came to Hyde Park Corner and saw the traffic, he
turned and ran back in. Finally, his sense of direction
failed him and he had to stop and ask directions. It was
good that he did, for had he followed his instinct, he
would have run in the wrong direction. He took care at
intersections because he still did not trust himself to look
the correct way to catch oncoming traffic, and he noticed
several places where English-language signs had Arabic
translations beside them, indications of England's
newest—and wealthiest—visitors.

Jeffrey was not familiar with London, and had not been
there in almost fifteen years, but he was nevertheless a
confirmed Anglophile. He had succumbed early when he
read his first Dickens novel and he had remained happily
caught up in the magic of English writing ever since, an
affection that soon included England, and London in particular, as well. No series on "Masterpiece Theatre"
escaped his notice; no biography of some famous, accomplished—and usually eccentric —British figure escaped his
eye. He had come to London on extremely short notice
and for reasons he never would have imagined, but they
were not enough to impair his fantasies. He needed no
time to think of all the places he wanted to go in the city;
he knew them all already, had known them for years.

She was asleep when he let himself into the room, and

did not stir. Nor did she stir after his shower when he slipped into bed beside her. The warmth of her body, the smell of her perfume engulfed him, and as he closed his eyes the rest of his body awoke. He turned and moved toward her, reaching out to caress her arm, then to move the lock of hair that had drifted across her forehead. Then he pulled the covers aside and looked at her, sensed the rhythm of her deep sleep and saw her nipples pressing against her nightgown. He reached for her breast as she awoke and smiled at him.

"Still horny?" he asked.

She turned away from him in mock protest. She wanted to say yes, and she wanted to reach out and grab him, but she also wanted him to beg a little. He moved against her and she could feel his erection pressing against her buttocks.

"Well, I notice *you* are."

"I was wondering if you'd notice."

"How could I miss?" she said, sliding a hand across her body and taking him gently in her hand, then sliding her hand down to his testicles, stroking him lightly until he moaned quietly.

This time their lovemaking was uninhibited and abandoned, her moves against him insistent and demanding, her desire for him obvious. Several times he tensed, then pulled quickly away from her, and when she looked at him and her eyes asked him why, he would murmur, "Not yet, not yet." He postponed it until she was in a frenzy of desire, and when she had her orgasm, it was with such force that she let out a small yelp of pleasure. He withdrew, turned her over, and began tracing her spine first with his tongue and then with his penis. When he reached its base, he continued on, forcing her legs apart and taking his pleasure every way he wanted it. Finally he urged her up on her knees, then reached for her hand and let her guide him into her. They were both moist with perspiration and their bodies so full of their mixed juices that it seemed to him he was sealing himself to her, and the thought of it made him want her even more, made him want to become a permanent part of her. When he came, it was with a force that caused his back to arch and his calves to flex with quick, small cramps of pleasure.

Afterward she lay on her back and he on his side and they looked at one another, touching lightly. His passion was spent, but his penis remained slightly distended, and when she touched it lightly he could feel a response stirring in his groin. He moved toward her and she quickly guided him into her. This time, though, as if by mutual consent, there was no motion, no movement whatever. He lay upon her easily, supporting himself on his arms, and she kissed him lightly on the forehead. They remained this way for some time, until his blood began to course through him again and his penis retreated.

She smiled at him and traced an imaginary pattern through the hair on his chest. "I guess that's what Ketchum meant when he said we should stick together."

"I doubt it."

"Hotel rooms do something to me."

"I noticed," he said.

It seemed to him that every cell, every pore of him was alive and tingling with anticipation. He had no thought now of what was ahead, nor of what had brought them to London. The contrast was sharp, the danger real. But at this second it did not matter. He forgot all that for a few short hours. When he tried to sleep, his eyes refused to close, his mind would not slow.

"I'm hungry," he said a short while later. She was dozing again, but he knew her well enough now to know she was a sunny waker, full of cheer, while he tended to be slow to wake and not very alert. He bounded out of bed, opened a few drawers, and finally found the room-service menu.

"I've got a better idea. What time is it?"

"Four-thirty," he answered.

"Let's go shopping," she said, scrambling out of bed.

"What?"

"Harrods. We'll walk around a bit, then go to the food halls, buy everything we want, and bring it back here and have a picnic."

They entered the great department store looking like American tourists and left two hours later looking like a cross between tourists and natives: They had gone on a spree with the American Express cards Ketchum had given them. Jeffrey's two pairs of pants would not be out of the alteration department for another two days, but the pleated wool skirt and the sweater she chose fit perfectly, and the loose-fitting pea coat he bought did too. They hadn't been bargains, but they were fine British goods and Jeffrey thought he and Rachel both looked terrific. They also carried two shopping bags, with their old clothing and their bounty from the food halls inside. The food halls had astounded Jeffrey with their incredible range of merchandise, from dozens of kinds of tea biscuits to fresh-killed pheasant and a selection of wines and cheeses that nearly caused him to sink into a fit of indecision, so afraid was he that he'd miss something good. In the end they'd bought four bottles of wine, five different cheeses, bread, crackers, and samples of various pâtés. They also bought mustard, a small packet of plates, utensils, napkins, and, finally, a corkscrew.

"That ought to do it," Jeffrey said as they piled their purchases on the check-out counter.

"For at least three days," Rachel agreed.

Ketchum was pacing the lobby, waiting, when they walked into the hotel.

"Look. After this, whenever either one of you goes somewhere, you check with me first. I've been looking for you for over an hour. I don't want the two of you wandering off." Ketchum paused, but only briefly. "We start first thing in the morning. We believe Zaki is here, but we haven't seen him yet. Smithson—the guy who works in the store for him—is there. We've arranged a stakeout in the loft of the building across the street from the bookstore, and beginning first thing in the morning we're going to be watching for the men who belong to the faces on those passport photos."

Ketchum's tone had hardened, and his manner had become tense and businesslike. He no longer made statements, he issued orders. Both Jeffrey and Rachel were struck by the change, his suddenly narrowed focus, the sharp absence of his usually gregarious manner.

"Thanks for the clothes," Jeffrey said.

"And the food," Rachel added.

Ketchum glanced at the big Harrods shopping bags, but ignored their remarks.

"If they turn up, the embassy will get the British to help us and we can all go home. If they don't turn up, *you* go in. And this time you're going to let them know you know what they're doing."

"I hope they show up before that happens," Rachel said.

"Jesus," Jeffrey murmured under his breath.

"Meanwhile, if you go out, there will be someone in the lobby to tail you. Probably nothing will happen, but it's a precaution worth taking."

The change in Ketchum had dispelled the carefree mood they'd been in.

Nonetheless, they tried to recapture it. They set out their bounty, uncorked their wine, and began their small celebration. The encounter with Ketchum had abruptly ended their brief period of ignoring—if not forgetting— what it was that brought them to London. Jeffrey turned on BBC radio and they ate in silence, listening to the London Symphony performing two Liszt concerti, music that otherwise might have been the perfect thing for such an intimate and romantic setting, but that even two confirmed music lovers had trouble concentrating on. Jeffrey drank a bottle and a half of wine before he was done, and after he had helped her clear up the dinner, he went to bed and slept soundly. Rachel listened to the rest of the symphony broadcast as she sat in bed reading a guidebook to the British Museum. She hoped she would have time to go, but it didn't seem likely. She wondered why she even considered the possibility.

XX

THEY GOT THEIR first look at Serendip Books early the next morning. Led by Ketchum, they strolled down Long Acre in Covent Garden, past Hamish Hamilton Ltd., the British publishers Jeffrey admired most. The copy of Raymond Chandler's *The Long Goodbye* he had bought just a few days before had been published here. Hamish Hamilton occupied a small, unremarkable building just two stories high, with a small display of their newest books in their window. Chandler must have stood here dozens of times. Jeffrey was unprepared for the lack of pretension, the simplicity of such a famous publisher. Had such a company been in New York, it would have occupied any number of floors of some East Side highrise and would have presented an entirely different impression. He liked the British style better.

They walked past one antiquarian bookstore and then another before coming upon Serendip Books, which occupied a building Jeffrey guessed had been built sometime before World War I.

"Go have a look," Ketchum told them. "There's no one around this early."

It had a sedate wood and glass front supported by cement pillars reaching up to an iron balcony on its second floor. The door handles were polished brass, and when the three of them peered into the store itself, they could see polished walnut cases on either side of the narrow room and two glass-topped display cases in the center. Jeffrey wondered what was displayed in the cases and half hoped he would have the opportunity to go into the store and browse. Several of the bookshelves were open; others were behind glass doors with shiny brass locks on them. The carpet was a dark maroon, and just inside the door stood a brass hat-and-coat rack and a big umbrella stand.

"Very classy," Jeffrey commented.

"Just what you'd expect," Rachel agreed.

"The perfect front," Ketchum reminded them.

They followed Ketchum across the street and into an empty storefront with a "To Let" sign in the window. He fumbled with his keys and then unlocked the door. This, too, was a narrow building and it smelled of must and moisture. The only leavings of the previous inhabitants were two old, broken glass display cases and a roll of badly worn carpet. Ketchum motioned them to the back of the store and up a flight of stairs to a loft, every inch of which was crowded with wooden packing crates covered with Chinese markings.

"The loft's rented to some Chinese store owner who imports junk from China," Ketchum told them as they threaded their way through the stacks of boxes. "Lots of snuff bottles and plates and teacups and cute little statues of Buddha. I tell you, I don't know who the hell buys that crap, but they sure export a lot of it."

They had come to a small clearing between the two windows, which looked directly down and across Long Acre into Serendip Books. The shades of the lookout windows were partially drawn; the shade on the left window folded slightly so that the lens of a Polaroid camera had a clear view across the street. The camera itself was on a tripod, and its shutter was connected by a long cord to a chair beside the other window, just out of sight of the street. Between the two windows were a long, narrow table and three more chairs. Jeffrey and Rachel did not see the man step out from beside the tallest pile of packing crates and did not know of his presence until he spoke.

"Morning, Dave," he said to Ketchum. "Nothing so far. These our friends from Los Angeles?"

"Jeffrey Dean, Rachel Sabin, meet Roy Carver. Roy is a public-information officer at the American Embassy and he helps us out from time to time."

Roy grinned innocently, and slipped the gun that was in his hand back into the holster inside his leather jacket.

"Aren't those illegal in England?" Rachel asked.

"Yes," Carver answered directly. He was a short, balding man who looked older than his age, which was thirty-eight, and gave the impression of being in bad physical shape. In fact, he had been a champion wrestler in college and was still in fine trim. His height and bulk made him appear overweight, which indeed he was, but it was mostly muscle. As soon as he saw the man's thick neck, Jeffrey adjusted his initial impression. They shook hands, and then Carver turned to Rachel.

"You won't be staying long today, Miss Sabin." She looked from Carver to Jeffrey, then back to Carver. "No need, really. We wanted you to see the place, then you're free to go out for the day. We'll have somebody tailing you, but there's no reason you have to spend all day here.

"For you," Carver said, turning to Jeffrey, "we have a large carton of photographs to go through. Everybody who's been in and out of Serendip Books for the four days we've had it staked out. If you identify them, we'll be moving on to the next phase of the operation."

"Which is?"

"It's a need-to-know situation," Ketchum shot back, "which is our polite way of saying it's none of your business until it suits our purposes to make it your business."

"That's Dave's way of saying it is also safer for you not to know everything," Carver added diplomatically.

"Roy, here, is in charge now," Ketchum added, his disapproval of the arrangement obvious. "You're working for him. You, too, Rachel."

For a moment Jeffrey considered responding to Ketchum in kind, but then quickly decided the most effective rejoinder was no rejoinder at all. He ignored him and spoke instead to Carver. "Then why are you the man on duty so early in the morning?"

"I wanted to be here to meet you."

Carver's simple explanation of why he was there, the very directness of the way he spoke, inspired trust. The man seemed to have none of the manipulative guile of Ketchum, and this, under the circumstances, was a welcome change. "I hope I can help," Jeffrey replied.

"You can. Start through the pictures. There's coffee and rolls just around that big crate there. Help yourself. You, too, Miss Sabin. Dave."

"Rachel," she corrected him.

"All right, Rachel. That's much better. Have some coffee. Then you'll have to leave. I want you off the street an hour before the store opens, just in case Smithson shows up early and recognizes you."

"Is he part of this?" Rachel asked.

"We don't think so. We've learned that when Zaki took over the business three years ago, Smithson was already there. Had been there, in fact, for fifteen years. He runs the business—at least that's the word among bookdealers here. Zaki comes in for the big decisions and things like that."

"Has Zaki been around?" Jeffrey asked.

"We haven't seen him."

"Have you had anybody in the shop?"

"Yes, twice."

"Dave, you check out the two agents who went in as soon as you leave here."

Carver had issued his order politely, yet it was clear Ketchum did not like receiving it. He nodded. "C'mon, Rachel. Let's get going."

She fixed Jeffrey with a look that mixed pleading with an apology and asked Carver when Jeffrey would be back at the hotel.

"Probably after five. Whenever the shop closes. We'll be out about fifteen minutes after that."

For the next hour—Serendip didn't open until 11:00 A.M. and Carver had discovered it was Smithson's custom to arrive promptly ten minutes before opening time—Carver and Jeffrey drank coffee and sorted through the pile of photographs. His first impression was that it seemed an unusually large number of people came in and out of the store in the course of four days, but it was an impression formed without consideration for the realities of business in London. Tradesmen, salesmen, and others went into the store, and there was a large drop-in trade, too. Long Acre was a busy street in the midst of a very busy section of the city.

He had inspected just ten pictures when he identified his first customer.

"Lipton. Renfield Lipton. He's a bookdealer. In London." Carver looked disappointed. Five pictures later Jeffrey found Lipton again, this time leaving with a package under his arm. Jeffrey noticed that Serendip didn't put books into plain paper bags or even the more modern plastic ones so many stores now used. Serendip wrapped customers' purchases in brown packing paper and tied them with colored string, as good, old-school dealers had done for years. It was a practice now limited to a special few: those who preferred the traditional way of conducting business. Jeffrey wondered if it was Smithson who carried on the tradition and if Zaki even understood it.

At exactly ten minutes before eleven, Smithson appeared, withdrew a set of keys from a long gold chain in his pocket, and unlocked the two locks on the heavy walnut-and-glass front door. Jeffrey watched as he removed his hat and raincoat, hung them on the hat rack, then stepped into the darkness of the store. Soon lights turned on and Serendip Books was on view, from one end of the shop to the other.

"Is there an upstairs?" Jeffrey asked.

"Yes. Directly above the stairway at the back of the store is a small shipping room. Then there's a storeroom. Well filled, too. And Zaki's office. An elegant little place where I imagine he entertains special customers and does his other business. When he's here, of course."

Jeffrey said nothing, but he must have looked slightly impressed.

"I must say I'm glad I've got company," Carver said, grinning. "You can refill the coffee cups. I can't get away from the window very easily, and until I've got you working the camera, you can do it for me. Damn. It's clouding up. Going to rain, probably. When the clouds come on, it gets dark and the Polaroid pictures aren't as clear as I'd like them."

The complaint was so plaintive, so unexpected, that it made Jeffrey smile. "I thought you guys had the very latest equipment. I mean, Christ, if you can overthrow governments, you ought to be able to take pictures from across the street."

"The one is easier than it sounds," Carver shot back with a grin, "and the other is not so easy when your employer is a cheapskate. Ah, here comes customer number one."

Jeffrey jumped up to look out the window, but Carver waved him back. "You throw a shadow during certain times of the day and by the time you get to the window all you see is the person's back as they're going in. I try to get them going in, I always get them coming out. I'm pretty good at this."

"I'll bet you are."

The picture popped out of the camera and Carver dropped it into a carton at the base of the easel. Jeffrey continued on through the photographs on the table.

"Here's another. A New York dealer. Specializes in detective fiction." He inspected the photograph more closely, then laughed. "And that pretty blonde he's with isn't his wife."

"What's his name?" Carver asked, reaching for the picture.

"Will Stanton."

Carver took a pen out of his shirt pocket, scribbled the man's name on the picture, and placed it in a small manila folder next to him on the small table beside the windowsill.

"I seriously doubt Will Stanton would have anything—"

"You never know. You wouldn't believe the amount of information that gets passed back and forth because of some sexual blackmail or involvement. Most people keep it pretty much confined to their imaginations, but others don't. And, by God, one thing you learn in this business is that people have the most incredible goddamn sexual habits."

Jeffrey kept on going through the stack of pictures, pausing only when the first customer left Serendip Books and his picture emerged from the camera. It was nobody he recognized, so he carefully replaced the picture.

"You say this Stanton runs a business of selling detective books?"

"Yes. Detective and mystery fiction. A bigger area than it sounds. And he's one of the most successful."

"Spy novels, too?"

"Yes. Of course."

"I never read that stuff. It always makes me feel like I've got the most boring goddamn job in the world."

"What do you read?"

"Biographies. I love biographies. Political biographies, especially. Tell me about this business of yours. About what books are especially valuable. And I want to hear all about those faked Steinbeck signatures and Alfred Craventon and Victor Dreyfus. The works."

Jeffrey paused, not sure where to begin, not sure how much Carver already knew.

"From the beginning. And say what you want about Ketchum. This is just between us."

He did just that, beginning with the Los Angeles Antiquarian Book Fair less than two weeks ago, when he walked down the aisle—he could see the carpeting and the

bookstalls as clearly as if he were there at that moment—
and into the Serendip Books Ltd. booth.

When he was done, he asked the questions he had held
as fair barter for all that he told Carter. "Where does Craventon fit into all of this?"

"We're not sure. What you're asking isn't just one question, it's several dozen—and we've got nothing to go on
but speculation. It isn't often somebody like him even
comes near something like this. We can guess—if he is involved—what his stake is—"

"Oil," Jeffrey interrupted.

"Billions of dollars' worth. But getting involved in the
assassination of the president, even for billions, isn't typical of a man like Craventon." Carver paused while Jeffrey
waited for more. There wasn't much. "We don't know
where he is right now, but we'll probably be on to him
within the next twenty-four hours."

"Jesus, I hope so."

A gentle rain began to fall, and the loft suddenly grew
cold. Jeffrey was glad he had worn his pea coat. He continued sorting through the photographs, all the while telling Carver everything he could remember. Carver, in
turn, frequently interrupted with questions, or to announce the coming and going of still another customer,
the latter announcement followed within seconds by the
click of the camera's shutter, then the whir of its ma-
chinery as it ejected the photograph. The sound, though it
had no rhythm of its own, its frequency dictated by people
whose appearance they had no control over, nevertheless
gave them a certain motion: Carver would look at the picture and hand it to Jeffrey, who would look at it and
dump it into the box.

The day passed quickly. Carver was a curious and interesting man, full of questions and easy to talk to. Jeffrey, who tended to be somewhat reticent and was not comfortable with long, sustained conversations, found Carver an agreeable companion.

Once, after a long series of questions from Carver— mostly about Ketchum's appearances during Jeffrey's time in Central America, and about the trip in and out of Cuba—Jeffrey, who had not asked many questions because he knew from his experiences with Ketchum they probably would not be answered, asked Carver to explain his work. Carver responded with a short discussion on the work of a public-information officer in a major American embassy. When he reached the end of his short spiel, he looked up at Jeffrey and grinned. "That, at any rate, is the official line. I'm a spy. You know that and there's no danger in my saying it to you. But more might not be good for you to know, and anyway I'm not allowed to say much."

"Can you tell me why the British aren't working on this?"

"We use them to deliver information. There's a whole complicated relationship—there always is when you're dealing with fanatic governments and terrorism."

"Do the British know this is all going on?"

"They know the most important part. We'll tell them the rest if we have to bring them in. But I don't want to unless we have to."

"Do you think Zaki is the agent trying to get Qaddafi assassins into the U.S.?"

"Didn't Ketchum tell you?"

"No. He told us he suspected Zaki. That's all."

"David thinks information withheld is power. I suppose in a sense it is. But you're entitled to know on this one. Do you think our penny-pinching government would fly the three of you all the way to London and put you up in an expensive hotel on a mere suspicion?" Carver smiled at the notion. "We know it's Zaki. What we don't know is if he's in town now. And if he's about to make his move. That's where you come in."

"Tell me exactly where I come in."

"Both of you. Tomorrow. We make our move. Time is running out."

"How?"

"Zaki was in London two days ago. He came here from Los Angeles. We know that. Tonight we'll know if he's still here. And if he is, you're going to lure him out of hiding."

"How will you know if he's here?"

"Let's say we have a friend inside the Libyan Embassy and leave it at that. Zaki's orders are to check in with the embassy every fourth day."

"Tomorrow?"

"Tomorrow."

"Then?"

"If he checks in, you and Miss Sabin are going to take a walk down Long Acre and drop into Serendip Books."

"And?"

"If Zaki isn't there, we'll give you enough to say to Smithson to get him going. We'll scare him into getting in touch with Zaki for us."

"Then we wait?"

"And then we wait. It won't be long."

At the end of the day, Carver and Jeffrey watched as Smithson closed up the store, put on his raincoat and hat, picked up his umbrella, locked the two locks with the keys on the long key chain, and walked off down the street. It seemed to Jeffrey he was watching Smithson's arrival played backward on a projector, revealing the same details but in the exact reverse of how they happened—and what had happened was nothing.

Fifteen minutes later, Carver and Jeffrey stepped out of the empty storefront, locked the door, and walked in the opposite direction down Long Acre to the corner of Drury Lane, where they hailed a taxi.

"How about dinner? You and Rachel. On me," Carver said as the taxi pulled into the driveway in front of the Hilton a few minutes later.

Jeffrey hesitated.

"I'll understand completely if you decline. I'll have time to get to know Rachel a little bit tomorrow. She'll be coming with you."

"Thanks anyway. I know I sat on a chair all day and did nothing, but I'm whipped."

"Jet lag. I'll see you tomorrow then. Ten sharp. I'll have Dave bring you two on down."

Walking into the hotel lobby, Jeffrey was struck by the ordinariness of their conversation, the casual invitation as though they were a couple of insurance salesmen in town for a convention.

She was in the room waiting, all showered and fresh, a bottle of wine on ice in the bucket she had ordered up from room service.

"What'd you do today?"

"I spent the whole afternoon at the British Museum. Walked and looked until I couldn't keep going. Then I got you this." She pushed a package across the bed and he recognized the wrapping immediately: Harrods. He opened the gift box and found inside the beige V-neck cashmere sweater he had admired but refused to buy for himself the day before. She had noticed he liked it and she had protested mildly when he had said it was too expensive. He kissed her now and pulled her to him.

But the sense of foreboding would not leave, would not be dispelled in the shelter of her arms.

"Tomorrow the bait goes on the hook."

"I know. Ketchum explained."

"He did?"

"Yes. He told me you had agreed to everything."

"I see. They told us separately so that neither of us could back out. And you agreed, too?"

"Yes. Yes, I did."

XXI

SHORTLY AFTER 1:00 P.M., Roy Carver turned to them and said simply, "Okay, you're going across the street."

They had been tucked into their small corner of the loft across Long Acre from Serendip Books since ten that morning, and there had been no sign of Zaki or any of the others Jeffrey was supposed to be able to recognize. He had seen so many Arabs in London, looked questioningly into so many faces, that he no longer thought he could recognize the four faces from the passport photographs. Certainly they were not among the large pile of Polaroids that now formed five neat stacks—one for each day of surveillance—on the table between the loft windows. There wasn't an Arab among them.

He looked across at Rachel, who was sitting at the opposite end of the table, waiting for Carver's last-minute instructions. If she was nervous, she did not show it. In fact she seemed the essence of calm. He was wrong, of course; she was just a better actress than he gave her credit

for. He himself was anxious to the point of nearly shaking.
He could feel the moisture in his armpits and could smell
the sour sweat of fear. He stood up and pulled on his coat
and at the same time reached across to hand Rachel hers.

"A couple of things first," Carver said to them, turning
slightly in his chair so that he could see both the bookstore
and Jeffrey and Rachel. "The important thing is to press
Smithson to find out where Zaki is. Threaten him a little
if you have to, but don't let on about the terrorists. Just
tell him that you are looking for Zaki, that you want to
talk to him about his work for Qaddafi. Make it sound
very serious, but don't give the facts. We want Zaki to
think you're curious and snooping around, and that you
know something. We don't want Smithson to know too
much or he might get scared off."

Jeffrey nodded. "And if he puts us in touch with Zaki
immediately?"

"Tell Zaki this: that you know everything—you know
what he's doing for Qaddafi, you know who he's sending
in—and that for a price he can buy your silence. Tell him
you both know, then make your offer." Carver paused,
considered what he was going to say next, then went
directly to the point. "I say 'both' because he already
knows Rachel is somehow involved in this, or at least he's
relatively certain of it. And Sabin is a name sure to arouse
his anger."

Rachel tensed.

"To call him an anti-Semite is to make a vast understatement. We think he was part of the group that
planned the Palestinians' murder of the Israeli athletes at
the '72 Munich Olympics."

"Good God!" Rachel stammered. "I knew there were
people like him, but I never expected I'd . . ." Her sen-

tence trailed off, while Carver and Jeffrey listened without comment. Finally, Carver spoke.

"Don't worry. We've got you covered. We'll have somebody right behind you from now on, very close behind. Ready? And when you're through, wander on down the street that way"—he pointed in the direction opposite the oncoming one-way traffic—"so we can give you better cover. It's just a precaution. Zaki's probably sitting by a telephone miles from here. Good luck."

They walked out of the storefront and strolled several doors down the street before crossing Long Acre. Once across, they walked slowly toward Serendip Books, pausing once to look at a display of books in a used-book store on the street, using the occasion to turn quickly and look up to see if they could spot Carver. They couldn't, but they knew he could see them, and that was a form of assurance they both needed.

The inside of Serendip Books was even more elegant than it had seemed from peering through the window the day before. There were Oriental rugs, and every wood surface in the place was polished. Everything was perfectly appointed. As they entered, Smithson was hanging up the telephone and pushing the leather-bound telephone book back into its proper corner of the large desk from which he watched over the store. He stood and nodded at Jeffrey and Rachel, nodded in such a way that they both guessed he did not recognize them, and then turned and began talking with a customer.

They pretended to browse. The two glass-topped display cases in the center of the store contained prints of the shipbuilder's design for the *Mary Rose*, the flagship of the English armada. The ship was now—over four hundred years after the battle in which it was sunk—being explored by divers in the cold, treacherous currents off Portsmouth. A neatly mounted cutting from the *Times* told the whole story, listed some of the recovered treasures, and detailed the raising of the remains of the ship's hull from the ocean floor.

"These designs are suddenly worth a fortune, I'll bet," Jeffrey muttered to Rachel.

She nodded, and when they both looked up, they saw Smithson staring at them, his pale complexion paler, his stare steady. He had recognized them after all; it had just taken him a few minutes. He said nothing.

"I believe we met at the Los Angeles Antiquarian Book Fair," Jeffrey said politely. "This is Miss Sabin. I'm Jeffrey Dean."

"How do you do," Smithson said, not offering his hand or volunteering his name.

"Smithson, isn't it? Thomas Smithson?" Jeffrey asked.

"Yes. It is. What can I do for you?"

"I'd like to get a message to Mr. Zaki."

"Oh?"

"Yes, it's rather complicated. Would you like to write it down?"

"That won't be necessary. If you'll wait fifteen minutes, you can tell him yourself."

Rachel stiffened and Jeffrey saw her hands, which were grasping the edge of the display cabinet, tense and her knuckles turn white. He felt his heart skip a beat and had to take a deep breath before he could speak.

"We'll wait," he said.

"Mr. Zaki is a very busy man," Smithson said coldly, "and he's been away. He won't have much time to speak to you."

"He will when he hears what I have to say."

Smithson said nothing, just turned and walked back to his desk, pausing on his way to adjust a couple of books. Jeffrey, fighting down his anticipation, trying hard to keep control, set about browsing with a grim determination. Rachel followed, but did not browse with the same intensity.

He came to a glass-encased shelf of Dickens books, glanced at their titles, and couldn't resist.

"I'd like to look at these, if you don't mind," he said across the store to Smithson, who turned quickly and started for the bookcase without comment. His hands were shaking as he opened the cabinet. He did not stand by as Jeffrey looked through the books, but returned quickly to his desk.

Only three of the books were in good condition, and those three were treasures: a first edition of *Dombey and Son;* a first of *The Personal History of David Copperfield;* and a handsomely boxed proof copy, unbound, of the privately circulated *Life of Our Lord,* a small book Dickens wrote for his children and which had been kept a family secret for many years. Jeffrey inspected each book carefully, then figured out the prices in American dollars. The proofs were only $200, a price he thought low. *Dombey* was $950, and the *Copperfield* $2,000.

"I also have a *Nicholas Nickleby* coming in tomorrow, in very fine condition and inscribed," Smithson said from his desk.

Jeffrey, startled that the man would even communicate with him about business after his cold greeting, spoke without turning. "A first?"

"Yes. The inscription is short, and I'll have authentication with it."

The word *authentication* caused Jeffrey to turn and face

Smithson. Was there some communication being issued, some special clue? Had he known the Steinbecks they were selling in Los Angeles were fakes? There were many questions, but just now there could be no answers.

"That would be good. How much is it?"

"About . . ." Smithson paused as he translated pounds into dollars. "About nine thousand American dollars."

Jeffrey loved Dickens's books, but Dickens was not his specialty and was far too expensive for him. He simply didn't have the money. Yet. *Nicholas Nickleby* and *David Copperfield* were books hard to resist. Then something occurred to him, and it made him ask another question.

"What time tomorrow?"

"My customer is bringing it in just after eleven A.M."

"Let me think about it. I might be interested. In both the *Nickleby* and the *Copperfield*," Jeffrey said, smiling for the first time since he'd come into the store. Rachel shot him a glance that implied she wondered about his sanity, but she said nothing.

Just then the door opened and in walked Zaki. He was wearing a tailor-made three-piece gray suit, but his swarthy complexion made him clearly non-English. He stopped immediately when he saw Jeffrey and Rachel, and there was no mistaking the malevolence in the look with which he ackowledged them.

"I thought, Mr. Dean, that we had an understanding."

"You mistook a conversation for an understanding. Or should I say you seem to be unable to differentiate between a threat and a conversation?"

"I see. What is it you want now?"

"A brief conversation. In your office. Perhaps this time we can reach an agreement."

"What about her?" Zaki nodded at Rachel.

"She will participate in the conversation, too."

"With much pleasure," she said, the hatred in her voice sending a chill down Jeffrey's spine.

"Very well. Follow me."

They climbed the stairs, walked past the wrapping room and through the storage space—it was exactly as Carver had described it—and into what he had said was "Zaki's elegant little office." It was both. Nothing in the room, not even the decanter full of liquor or the letter opener on the elaborately carved and inlaid desk, belonged to this century. Only the electric lights, and they, too, seemed somehow to look old enough to be acceptable.

Zaki made no gesture of welcome, offered no invitation to sit down on the leather sofa facing the small marble fireplace.

"Well, what is it? I warned you. I thought you understood."

"Oh, I understand, Mr. Zaki. The one who did not understand was you."

"How?"

"I have an offer for you. A very generous one under the circumstances." Jeffrey surprised himself with his clarity, his control. He even thought to sit down and to nod at Rachel to do the same. Zaki remained standing, suddenly a visitor in his own office.

"I know much more than forged Steinbecks, Mr. Zaki. For instance, I know about certain things that went into the planning for the 1972 Olympics." Zaki flinched slightly, but did not move. His gaze shifted suddenly to Rachel, and she stared defiantly back at him. "I don't think it's necessary to go into details. I also know about your association with Mr. Qaddafi, and your work for him."

"I don't know what you're talking about."

"Very well, then. I also know what Victor Dreyfus was doing for you. About the—shall we call them 'documents'?—he was preparing for you."

"I'm afraid these things that Victor Dreyfus told you are all the imaginings of a disturbed, devious mind. He is a troubled man."

"Was, Mr. Zaki. *Was* a troubled man. You know English too well to use the wrong tense. I also know what you plan to do with the documents and when you plan to do it."

"I had not known about Mr. Dreyfus. A pity."

Zaki stood, did not move. The smell of Canoe began to fill the small room. His left hand stroked his beard, an attempt to appear casual that did not work. He remained silent for less than a minute before he spoke.

"You could get yourself into very serious trouble, Mr. Dean. These are dangerous rumors."

"Facts, Mr. Zaki. Here's my offer. You meet me here tomorrow morning at eleven-thirty. I will come alone. Miss Sabin will be waiting somewhere else, and will be making some telephone calls if I do not return within the hour. I'm sure you can guess whom she will be calling."

"Go on."

"You will give me one million pounds, in cash, in a suitcase. A very good suitcase, if you don't mind. In return for that, we will keep your secret. Forever."

"You are making wild guesses. Victor Dreyfus did not know half of the information you claim to know. He could not have told you. You lie."

"Oh?" Jeffrey's heart skipped two beats this time. So. Zaki thought what information there was had died with Victor Dreyfus. He must still think the government didn't know or that Ketchum and his people hadn't moved in.

Could it be? Jeffrey decided to toss out his clincher and see how Zaki took it.

"Either you accept my offer or tomorrow the British and American governments will be given the information that Nafir Zamel is one of the four men—and they'll get the other names along with his"—Jeffrey prayed his lie wasn't obvious to Zaki—"being sent into the United States on forged green cards to assassinate the president."

It suddenly occurred to Jeffrey, and at the same time to Rachel, that there was a hole in the scheme, one that had to be filled rapidly. Rachel thought how to do it first.

"And if you try to get them in before you give the money to Jeffrey tomorrow"—Rachel spoke harshly, in a tone he never would have imagined her using—"we'll know about it as soon as they leave. The telephone numbers I have are answered all night, too."

"You work for the Israelis?" Zaki interrupted.

"No. I'm in business for myself. So is he," she said, nodding in Jeffrey's direction. "But I'm a Jew, and I know all about people like you."

"What is your hotel? I will meet you there tomorrow morning. This isn't a good place." Zaki's collapse came out sounding like a command, but it was a command that rang hollow.

"This," Jeffrey answered quickly, "is a perfect place. I will be here at eleven-thirty exactly. And I will leave here at eleven-forty exactly. My taxi will be waiting. And you will be, too."

With that Jeffrey stood and started for the door. Rachel was right behind him. Zaki remained where he had stood for the entire conversation.

"How do I know you aren't working for the Americans?"

"How do you know?" Jeffrey said. "You don't. But

American agents—even double agents or whatever the hell it is they're called—don't walk out of stores with one million pounds in cash. It's very embarrassing to get caught by your employers doing such a thing. I'm an independent," he added, "just like her."

"How did you"—Zaki didn't want to admit anything, but he did want to ask his question—"discover these things you claim? Certainly not with those two Steinbeck books."

"And why not? They were poor forgeries. And you were an interesting man. We just went to work and started checking things out. That's how people like us work. We're not unalike, you know, you and me. We all love rare books, don't we? I don't know about you, but we expect to be buying quite a few of them."

They left and closed the door behind them, and as they walked through the store, Jeffrey paused and spoke to Smithson. "I'll see you tomorrow morning. I can only stay a few minutes, so please have the books ready. I may indeed buy them."

"Very well. I will see you then." Smithson was warming. He was a true bookman and he was on the trail of a big sale. Jeffrey smiled at him and Smithson actually smiled back.

Once out on the street, they did exactly as Carver had told them: They walked against the traffic. They saw a man look up from a store window across the street as they left the store, then saw him hurry across behind them. When Jeffrey looked at him, the man nodded. Their cover was sticking close and making sure both Jeffrey and Rachel knew it. At the corner was a black Jaguar sedan, and at the wheel, Roy Carver.

"Well, how'd it go?" he asked as they got in.

Jeffrey could not hide his elation. It had gone perfectly. He repeated the entire conversation with Zaki.

"Jesus, I can't believe it. After all the time we've spent looking for him, he just shows up when you're there. There is a God. Go on."

Jeffrey did. So did Rachel.

"I'm sorry to spoil your afternoon," Carver, obviously pleased by everything that had transpired, told them finally, "but what I want is for neither of you to go out in public, especially not in crowds. I can't let them find you. You can go to dinner tonight, but you've got to let me know now where you're going so we can secure the place. But that's all."

"Langan's," Jeffrey said quickly. "At eight."

"I'll have a driver pick you up at seven-thirty."

They drove on a few minutes more before Carver asked another question. "Do you think Zaki believed you?"

"What? That we knew what was going on?" Rachel asked.

"No. Did he believe you were working on your own?"

"Yes, I think he did. Do you?" she said, turning to Jeffrey.

"Yeah."

"Good. That means he's going to move heaven, earth, and every hotel register in London to find you and get rid of you before tomorrow morning. You know too much to live. Both of you."

"Terrific," Jeffrey said quietly, his elation evaporating in an instant. Rachel slumped down in the seat, suddenly very tired and very frightened.

XXII

LANGAN'S WAS EVERYTHING she'd told him. It was old, with cream walls lined with an eclectic collection of art, its main floor busy, nearly all of the white, elegantly set tables full. The waiters, too, were just as she had described them: old, cross, and very good. He and Rachel were shown to a table looking directly onto two David Hockney prints. Jeffrey let out a low whistle of admiration.

"You like Hockney?" Rachel asked.

"A lot. I've been thinking of buying one."

They were waiting for the wine list when she leaned over and said, "Did you know that Langan's spinach soufflé, its most famous dish, is not served on the second floor?"

"Why not?"

"I don't know for sure." She smiled. "But I imagine, given the nature of soufflés, that they probably fall on the way upstairs."

"I always wondered." He grinned.

The lighting in the restaurant had been carefully planned to be flattering at all angles and, it seemed to them both, gave the evening its own special aura. They drank wine before and after dinner, and anyone who looked at them—and a number of customers did—saw a good-looking, well-dressed couple clearly enjoying their dinner. No one would have known that they were forcing themselves to relax and that there was a man sitting in a black Jaguar sedan—the same one Carver had picked them up in earlier that day—guarding them, sending a report from his car radio every half-hour, giving their whereabouts to a clerk at the American Embassy several blocks away, who in turn passed the information on to Roy Carver and David Ketchum, both of whom were living temporarily in the imposing building on Grosvenor Square.

"We're here. It's happening. And right now, this is the good part," he said quickly as he saw her glance nervously out across the street to the waiting car.

"You're the good part."

"Then let's go back to the hotel and get down to the good part."

"We've got all evening."

"You like to tease."

"Me? Tease? You haven't seen anything yet."

"I want to see more. Lots more."

She paused, a light hesitation settling on her.

"I mean it," he insisted gently.

"I know that. It's just that so much has happened. We might just get back to Los Angeles, settle into our respective lives, and find we bore the hell out of each other."

"I want to make something work, something important. I want to try. Do you?"

She thought for a moment, folded her napkin carefully, then placed it back in her lap.

"Yes," she said finally. "Yes, I do."

So simple, so direct. She understood such an approach now, could even accept it under the circumstances in which it was offered. He was asking her to look away from everything else that was happening, to look only at the possibility of the two of them together. Nothing calculated, no false security, just a simple offer. He, on the other hand, knew he was taking a chance, but he wanted to try once more. Finally. He wondered if he would ever have such feelings again. He hid—but not quite—a small smile at the whole idea. She saw it and understood. Just then, and only for a matter of seconds, not even a minute, they were just another couple, in love, resting in the hazy glow of food and wine, anticipating what was yet to come. The world around them, the peculiar nature of their presence in this restaurant in this city at this time, was not part of what they were feeling. They were alone in a world of their making and, for them, it was perfect.

He signaled the waiter for their check, pretended to have no reaction when he saw they'd spent $115 for a dinner for two, paid the bill, and took her by the arm as they walked out of the restaurant. They stepped outside and headed for their car. They could see the back of their driver's head. He was sitting behind the wheel, his arm resting across the top of the seat beside him.

"We'll go back to the hotel now, thanks," Jeffrey said as he opened the door for Rachel. She got in and he closed the door after her, walked around to the other side of the car and got in and closed his door. As it shut, he turned to look at Rachel; and as he did, he saw her mouth fly open and heard her sharp intake of breath. His head flew around and he saw, facing them from the passenger seat,

one of the four men whose photographs he had seen on
Victor Dreyfus's desk. There was no mistaking it. And he
was pointing a gun at them.

"Your driver is dead. If you don't do as I say, you will
be, too." He gave the agent, whose arm had not moved, a
shove and he slumped over the wheel. "You will help me
get him into the seat where I am now. We will pretend he
is drunk. Quickly."

"No," Rachel almost whispered.

"Don't be a fool," the man hissed. "I am not alone. Do
not try anything." He reached closer to her and put the
muzzle of the gun against her heart, pushed it against her
breast. She moved quickly to get out of the car. Jeffrey
did, too. As they did, the Arab jumped out ahead of them,
the gun sticking out against the wool of his coat.

"Both of you. Hurry. We must appear as though nothing has happened."

Jeffrey began pulling the dead man out from behind
the wheel. There was a bullet wound in his chest that the
Arab had attempted to cover by buttoning the man's coat.
It was nighttime, the street lighting was inadequate, and
there were few people on the tiny street, so it worked well
enough. As they dragged him around the car, Jeffrey
looked up to see who else was watching. He could see at
least two men standing idly half a block away who he
thought could be Arabs, and he imagined there were
probably more.

He and Rachel had put the dead driver's arm across
their shoulders and were dragging him to the door as the
Arab held it open. Jeffrey sagged slightly, attempting to
maneuver himself between the Arab, the dead man, and
the car door. He didn't quite make it. So, as he undraped
the arm from his shoulder, he braced his other hand into
the body's armpit and gave a gigantic shove.

"Run!" he screamed as the body fell against the Arab and knocked him over, landing on top of him in the middle of Stratton Street. Rachel turned, instinctively starting out against the flow of one-way traffic. He ran after her. Stratton is a short street, not even fifty yards long, and by the time they reached the corner and started around it, two shots had been fired at them. The first missed, but Jeffrey felt a light sting when he heard the second shot. They were halfway down Mayfair Place, still going against the traffic, when he realized the sting he'd felt was the bullet striking his arm just below the shoulder. He looked down and saw the first small flow of blood begin to slide out from under his shirt cuff. He said nothing. When they reached the corner on Berkeley, they stopped, unsure which way to turn.

"This way," she said, motioning to her left. "The embassy is about five blocks away. I'm pretty sure I remember where it is." She started off, then turned around when she realized he wasn't with her. He was just behind her, but he was holding his right arm to his side with his left hand.

"You all right?"

"I think so. There's blood, but not much pain."

"Oh, my God! They shot you!"

He turned and could see two men running toward them along Mayfair Place. "Run! I'll be right behind you."

Within a minute they arrived on Berkeley Square, where it seemed every light was on and the park was full of people—couples on the benches, others walking their dogs. At the corner was a red telephone booth.

"Wait. They won't shoot here. Too many people. How much is the pay phone?"

"Twenty pence."

He grabbed the phone book, flipped through it, and

found the number of the embassy. He dropped in the coin and started to dial the number.

"No. No. Not that way," she said.

"What?" The coin fell out.

"Dial the number first."

He did.

"Then, when they answer, drop in your coin. They can't hear you until the coin goes through."

"Hello? Hello? You hear me?" He waited a beat and then spoke. "This is Jeffrey Dean. Get me Roy Carver. This is an emergency."

Carver came on the line immediately.

"They got the driver. They're after us."

She stood beside him, shielding him and looking over her shoulder. The two men chasing them were about half a block away. "Hurry, they're coming."

"We're in a phone booth at Berkeley Square. . . . Where?" Jeffrey looked through the windowpane of the phone booth. "Yeah. I see it. Okay."

He jumped out of the booth and they started running. "Roy will meet us at the corner of Davids and Grosvenor. He'll have help with him."

"Now I remember. You turn left on Grosvenor to get to the embassy. We're very close. Three blocks maybe."

They took off across the square, past the Al Saudi Bank. She was exactly right. In three blocks they arrived at the corner of Grosvenor and could see the lights of the square a block away. They could also see a man running toward them. Carver.

"He said he was bringing help," Jeffrey said as they saw the figure draw closer. It wasn't Carver. He ran under a streetlight and they saw the unmistakable plaid suit. It was Ketchum. He reached them, stopped, and without greeting them, spoke.

"Well, well. I thought you'd never make it," Ketchum said.

"Well, we did. Now let's get going. I've been hit."

"You sure have," Ketchum said without emotion. "Now just wait right here."

"Hell, no. They're right behind us."

"They're here already," Ketchum said evenly, taking a pistol out of his coat pocket and showing it quickly. "Just hold still. They're paying me a lot of money to get you two. More than you asked Zaki for. Much more."

"I—I—" Jeffrey was dumbstruck. Ketchum. Working for the Arabs. He couldn't believe it. Neither could Rachel.

It was a revelation nothing had prepared them for and, in fact, everything had indicated simply could not be. Ketchum, the perfect government functionary, manipulative, tightfisted, and immune to every insult. No wonder; he was getting away with more than anyone could have imagined. It is at moments such as this that lifelong cynics are created, and had it not been for the fact that both Jeffrey and Rachel had lives far away from this sort of thing, lives that nourished them both, they might never have recovered. As it was, Ketchum's admission, his cold disinterest in their plight except for its inconvenience to him, stunned them both.

"Where's Carver?"

"Probably dead by now. You weren't supposed to call. I told Zaki where to find you and that was to be it."

"You and your goddamn lecture about patriotism."

"Yes. And you listened. Too well, I'm afraid."

Rachel had taken Jeffrey by his good arm and he could feel her trembling. She was standing half behind him, using him as a shelter against what she couldn't understand and didn't want to see. He gently took her hand off his arm and then reached for his wound. The blood was now coming through the dark wool of his suit jacket. He clutched the arm and moved slightly, staring at Rachel as he did, hoping she could somehow read his mind, could interpret his imagined signals. As he drew alongside Ketchum, he pretended to grow faint and slipped to his hands and knees. As he did, he looked up and tried to wink at Rachel, but in the poor light of the corner he was not sure she saw him. Ketchum reached to pull him up.

"Get up, I don't want you attracting attention."

Jeffrey could see the two Arabs. They were less than twenty yards away now. He let his weight go dead when Ketchum reached down to pull him up.

As he did, Rachel literally ran right into Ketchum, stopping as soon as she had him off-balance. It was an old, old trick, but it worked. Ketchum fell backward across Jeffrey, his head striking the cement wall of the building, knocking him momentarily senseless. Jeffrey reached down, grabbed the gun out of Ketchum's hand, and they turned to run.

It was too late. The two Arabs were too close now, so Jeffrey, remembering how he had seen it done in the movies, stiffened his two arms—the pain from his wound caused him to wince—aimed the gun, and pulled the trigger. The first Arab went down immediately. The other ducked down behind Ketchum's ample body.

"Run!" Rachel yelled from behind him. He turned and could see she had started out ahead of him. They raced all the way to Grosvenor Square. Across its green lawns they could see the Roosevelt Memorial and, almost straight ahead, the white marble facade of the American Embassy. Its lights were on, and as they drew close they could see several groups of men fanning out across the front of the embassy and an ambulance, its lights flashing, parking directly in front of the building.

Two of the groups of men were running directly toward them, and when Rachel began waving, they ran even harder.

"You all right?" the first man asked.

"He's shot. I'm all right," Rachel said.

They were escorted back across the edge of the square and onto the embassy grounds. The other men raced for the Arabs and Ketchum. As they came to the entrance, the big doors opened and two orderlies came out bearing a stretcher. A third carried two intravenous bottles, one with blood and the other with a clear liquid, draining into Roy Carver.

"I'm sorry," he said to them when they came up to him. "Very sorry."

"Are you all right?" Jeffrey ignored the apology.

"They tell me I will be, yes. But it'll take a few days."

"Good. But what the hell happened?"

"That's why I'm saying I'm sorry." Carver grinned, his face pale and the blood nearly gone from his lips. "We used you."

"I'm aware of that. We knew that all along."

"But you didn't know how."

Rachel was catching on quicker than Jeffrey. Understanding appeared in her eyes, and her questions stopped.

"The whole thing was just as it was explained to you. Except for one major difference. We were after one other person. Someone on our side who was selling information to Qaddafi's people through Zaki. We just found out who."

"Dave Ketchum."

"That's why it was me who answered the phone, Dave who got to you first. In between he tried to kill me."

"And nearly succeeded," a well dressed, gray-haired
man with a small black case in his hand interrupted. Neither Jeffrey nor Rachel had noticed him come out of the
embassy. "No more talk. I want to get you to the hospital.
You can explain the rest tomorrow."

"There isn't any more."

"What about the assassins?" Jeffrey asked.

"We had two of them tracked down hours after you left
Zaki and the two we missed were the ones they sent out to
get you. The ones Zaki dispatched, that is."

"Jesus Christ. I think I just shot one of them."

"Good. I knew if we could find Zaki, he'd lead us to all
the other people we wanted—including our own. Zaki is a
very smart man, but he has one flaw."

"What's that?" Rachel asked.

"He has the hubris of the genuinely arrogant. He
thought he could get away with anything," Carver said as
he was carried off to the ambulance.

The man with the gray hair and the black case turned
to Jeffrey and gestured toward the ambulance. "You, too,
please, Mr. Dean. I imagine you won't even have to spend
the night."

Jeffrey looked quickly to Rachel.

"She'll be looked after," the man said. "We'll have her
back to the hotel long before you get back. We'll all talk
tomorrow."

They were in the ambulance, racing through London,
and the doctor was bent over Carver, watching him carefully. An orderly had ripped Jeffrey's shirt off his shoulder
and was wrapping his wound. Jeffrey watched, and when
Carver looked up and gave him a dazed smile, he asked
his question.

"Craventon?"

"Innocent victim. Claims he was used."

Jeffrey's cynicism could not be hidden, and Carver looked at him steadily, as if to find the answers to the same questions he was asking himself. "You don't think so?"

"Oh, I think he was used, all right. But only because he couldn't work it all around to his own best advantage. He isn't the sort of person who will be used. At least not without getting even."

"It will interest you to know that our people in Langley believe that Craventon's fingerprints on the Steinbeck books postdate their forgery. It's a small but very telling point—nothing we can use on him in any way. Just thought you'd like to know."

"Where is he now?"

"Back home in his mansion, making a big donation to UCLA to try to cover up the bad odor."

"That's a lot to cover."

"He's got a lot to cover it with."

XXIII

"IMAGINE THAT," Rachel said, buckling her seat belt. "Telling us the ambassador would like to thank us personally but couldn't because he could not acknowledge that anything took place at all. Especially not that."

"Is that what got you?"

"Yes. In a funny kind of way."

"You know what got me?"

"What?"

"Ketchum, double-dealing for millions of dollars and all the time refusing to pay us what we asked. Goddamn penny pincher—and it wasn't even his money."

They were in the first-class cabin of a TWA 747, sipping champagne as the huge jet taxied out for takeoff on the nonstop flight back to Los Angeles. They had met early that morning with the embassy people and been thoroughly debriefed. The one Arab they hadn't caught the night before had been intercepted trying to get out of the country with his Libyan passport. The Libyan Embassy was enraged and had lodged an official protest with the

271

British, blaming—quite rightly—the Americans. The British responded by sending the man packing, but not before taking away his forged American green card.

Zaki had raced for refuge in the Libyan Embassy but was intercepted by the British, who whisked him off to one of their special interrogation centers. He would not emerge for some months, but when he did he would be of no use to Qaddafi: His cover, his value, would be worthless. He would be neutralized.

Ketchum was already on his way back to the United States, accompanied by one of his former colleagues, his fate to be decided in court. Jeffrey and Rachel no longer thought of him as manipulative; he was a devious, dangerous man who had used them and then planned their deaths. His payment was to have been two million, and it came with a guaranty of political asylum in Libya, where he was to go into business with two other CIA agents who had, it was stated carefully by Carver, "gone free-lance."

Earlier that afternoon Rachel and Jeffrey had gone to the hospital to visit Carver. Rachel brought him a big bouquet of flowers. Jeffrey brought him a set of the writings of Churchill, whom Carver had told Jeffrey he admired greatly. He was recovering rapidly and had been informed he would be home within three days.

Jeffrey and Rachel decided to stay on two more days, days they planned to spend sightseeing, and Jeffrey had even begun to sketch out an itinerary, planned carefully because it hurt to use his right hand. The meeting that morning at the embassy ended that plan. They were told to leave London immediately; reaction in the form of revenge was still a possibility. They were given tickets made out to their assumed names, and told to use their false passports. The passports and all their credit cards would be picked up when they were met in Los Angeles.

"Ah, well," Jeffrey had said, trying to sound philosophical about missing out on his dreamed-of days in London. "I had promised to go on a Cub Scout camping trip, and Michael's going to be staying with me for a month."

"Somehow I can't see a sandy sleeping bag taking the place of a hotel room," she said after the plane took off.

"Neither can I. But when you meet him, you'll probably find he's worth the effort."

"If that's an invitation, I accept."

"It was an invitation," he said, leaning across and kissing her lightly on the cheek. "Now," he said, starting to stand and reach for the latch on the overhead rack. Instead, halfway up, he winced in pain.

"I'll get it. What do you want?"

"My carry-on bag. I want to show you something."

"What?"

"Get it and I'll show you."

She stood up, opened the latch, and lifted down the bag. It was heavy. "What have you got in there?"

He took the bag, put it on his lap, and opened it. There were two carefully wrapped packages tied with colored string in the suitcase. He handed them to her. "One is for you, one is for me."

"What are they?" She was smiling, tearing at the paper. "Easy, easy."

When she saw what it was, she looked up and burst out laughing. "So that's where you went this morning!"

"Right. Good old Smithson and I did some business. He's really a nice chap." Jeffrey picked up the copy of *The Personal History of David Copperfield*, held it briefly, then raised it up and sniffed it. He did the same with *The Life and Adventures of Nicholas Nickleby*.

"How much did they cost you?"

"Me? Nothing. Why do you ask?"

She smiled.

"I'm telling you they cost me nothing. They cost Mr. Roger Thomas eleven thousand dollars."

She put her head back and laughed. "He bought them with his American Express gold card, I presume?"

"How did you guess?"

"Don't leave home without it."

"Dave Ketchum," he said, speaking quietly, "gave us that advice. And the credit cards."

"You know," she said, taking a sip of her champagne, "I never quite thought of it this way before, but it would seem that one nice thing about revenge—at least this sort of revenge—is that it works."

"Right."

They settled back for the long flight to Los Angeles.